THE MARCABOTH WOMEN

VIÑA DELMAR

THE

MARCABOTH

WOMEN

HARCOURT, BRACE AND COMPANY
NEW YORK

For Rowena

—THE FOLKS-IN-LAW

THE MARCABOTH WOMEN

A DIAMOND bracelet made a very nice birthday present. It adequately met all the demands that might be placed upon a birthday present. To begin with, it was something that a girl wouldn't buy for herself. Secondly, it was a gift that created no problem by its bulk, fitting nicely into any drawer or box, and it didn't have to be fed or combed or taken out for a run in the park. It was a thoroughly practical gift, something to give the woman who has everything.

When, all wrapped in its white tissue paper, it was handed to an excited lady, it produced just the proper amount of suspense. The white kid box within the tissue was unmistakably a jeweler's box, and delight and excitement were heightened by the sight of it. Then when the lid was raised and upon its satin bed the bracelet was discovered with all the jewels sending forth a small, heavenly blaze, then indeed a man knew that he had made no error in choosing this. It was the only gift. There was no other.

Later, when the birthday had gone, the bracelet still glittered upon the lady's arm, and for weeks, for months, even perhaps for the entire year she would say, "Oh, yes, it was my birthday present." And she would smile again as she had smiled when she had first opened the white kid box.

But it was true that there was a certain short stretch of hours in which a diamond bracelet failed a man. These were the hours that immediately followed the dying down of the first ecstasy. During those hours the bracelet became something that had been wonderful and would be wonderful again, but right now you couldn't ride in it, you couldn't listen to it, or you couldn't learn to fly it. The bracelet is certainly gorgeous, darling, but what shall we do this evening? What plans did you make? After all, it is my birthday. Are we just going to sit here and look at each other? Where are you going to take me?

These questions had troubled Simon Marcaboth all morning. What to do with Ruby on her birthday? Where to take her? There were the obvious places of course: Ciro's; Mocambo. But he and Ruby would certainly just sit and look at each other there. His mind momentarily raced off to examine another question that had been tormenting him for weeks. Would a man of fifty be a fool to take dancing lessons? Or would a man of fifty who was married to a girl thirty years younger be a fool not to take dancing lessons? Or was a man of fifty a fool in the first place to have—?

He caught himself up sternly. This was not solving the immediate problem. What to do with Ruby on her birthday? They didn't have to go to Ciro's or Mocambo alone of course. It was fun to go to those places with a bunch. They could take a bunch with them. A bunch of what? Daffodils? It would have to be daffodils. They didn't know any people. Maybe it would be fun to take a box of old snapshots and look those over while the orchestra played. Or maybe they could take a BB gun and— Simon sighed. People. You should know people. There were times when you needed them—certainly not in the sentimental, slobbering way that you read about on greeting cards or heard in a throbbing baritone's song. You had to have a hole in your head to want a friend so good and true that he was willing to share everything you had. Those kind of friends a man could do without. When a man is sick he can hire a nurse to take care of him. She does it a little better than an old pal, and she never comes back later to remind you of how good she was to you. But people you should have. They dress a party when you want to go somewhere. So who could he get tonight to take to Mocambo? He thought of the people he knew. They wouldn't do. He and Hannah had known them together. They were his age or older. Just the thing for Ruby's birthday, he thought sardonically.

They would ignore Ruby and talk about Hannah. Or maybe they would look at Ruby and shake their heads.

He thought about the people Ruby knew. They wouldn't do either. Here in the privacy of his own mind it was safe to play for a moment with the idea of himself facing an evening with Ruby's former acquaintances. So what would be so terrible about that? Were they dirty? Did they have contagious diseases? Were they vicious? He stared down at the gleaming surface of his desk. He was too smart not to know what was wrong with Ruby's friends. He was too smart not to know what was wrong with himself.

I don't want to know such people. Such people I only take for my second wife.

He sighed again, and then abruptly got to his feet. For the first time he became aware of his secretary. She was watching him expectantly.

"You wanted to dictate, Mr. Marcaboth?"

"In a minute. I have to see my brother. I'll be right back."

He stepped out of his office thinking how he had forgotten having buzzed for his secretary. Ruby was a full-time job. Once a man got thinking about Ruby, he was sunk. You couldn't think about anything else if you had Ruby on your mind. Funny how he had never thought about Hannah during business hours. With Hannah you could live like a normal human being. She was there and you were here so it was a simple thing. You could forget her. God rest her soul, poor Hannah.

He crossed the hall and walked into his brother's office. Wolfe did not look up immediately though Simon was certain that his footsteps had been heard and recognized. Wolfe with his foreign-language reports—Mr. Important. Simon stood watching him, wondering if he spoke French with a British accent. He probably did. There was nothing Wolfe cherished so warmly as that accent he had acquired between his fifteenth and seventeenth years when Mama had handed him over to English schoolmasters.

Wolfe's eyes came away from the work laid out before him. "What's the matter?" he asked.

"Something's the matter?"

Wolfe said, "At this hour I'm busy and so are you. If nothing's the matter then what are you doing here?"

Simon sat down and stared at the pile of letters on Wolfe's desk. There was almost a law against interrupting Wolfe's morning hours. It was a thing nobody did. But it was important to plan something for Ruby's birthday. And to whom could a man turn if not to his brothers?

Wolfe's eyes had gone to a long sheet of paper covered with figures and notations written in French. "Can't you wait till lunch to see me?" he asked.

Simon said that he couldn't but he did not look at Wolfe. He was remembering that he had waited till lunch to tell Wolfe that Hannah had been taken to the hospital.

"Look, Kid, what are you and Enid doing tonight?"

Wolfe studied the figures and the French notations. His cold eyes gave no sign that he had heard. He was forty-three. Maybe it annoyed him to be called "Kid." Well, Simon thought, all his brothers were kids to him. Besides, it had an affectionate ring. It sounded good when you had come to ask a favor. A favor? He wanted to blow Wolfe and Enid to a dinner and an evening's entertainment. This was asking a favor? Yes, it was. Might as well face it. Enid would make the evening bright. She knew how to manufacture that certain artificial gaiety that no night-club table should ever be without. She could create belief that here, now, fun was being had.

"Listen, Kid, just give me a minute. Are you and Enid busy tonight?"

Wolfe nodded.

"You couldn't get out of whatever you'd planned to do?"

"No. Why should I?" Wolfe looked up now in some surprise. "What's special about tonight?"

Simon was embarrassed. "Well, as a matter of fact it's only special to me, Kid. You see it's—it's Ruby's birthday."

Wolfe said, "Tell her I send congratulations."

"I had hoped that you and Enid would have dinner with us and—"

Wolfe frowned. "Aren't you going to Mother's for dinner?"

"No, we're not. You see—" Simon fell silent. He was suddenly angry at himself. What in hell had come over him? He was acting like a bum who had sidled in to borrow a sawbuck. Just because Hannah had died and he had married a young girl he was behaving as though he owed an apology to everyone in the family. For what? He hadn't committed a crime. He had married Ruby. Were they hanging men for such things nowadays? Was his family doing something big for him? Hiding him from the police maybe?

"Why aren't you going to Mother's for dinner?" Wolfe demanded. "We all have dinner with Mother on our birthdays."

"I didn't tell Mama this was Ruby's birthday. Ruby doesn't want to go to Mama's."

"She doesn't *what?*" Wolfe laid the list of figures down and faced his brother. "Do you mean to tell me that *Ruby—?*"

"Now just a minute, Wolfe. Ruby has her rights, too, you know. If she doesn't want to—"

"You mean she can't be asked to do the ordinary, simple things that the rest of us do?" Wolfe's smooth face was suddenly white with suppressed anger.

Simon understood. He knew the things that Wolfe wanted to say of Ruby. He admired Wolfe's control. He was grateful to Wolfe for holding himself back, for not creating a situation in which Simon would have a choice between defending Ruby or agreeing that the girl should be groveling to a mother-in-law like Zeda Marcaboth.

His gratitude was such that he was willing to explain. "You see, Kid, Ruby hasn't had any advantages in life. The very thought of Mama scares her. She's afraid she'll make some kind of a social error. She's terrified at the thought of even meeting Mama. Sooner or later of course—but for now I thought—well, you know. Hell, Wolfe, when she heard Mama referred to as 'The Princess' she actually trembled at the idea of meeting her."

Wolfe smiled slightly. He was pleased. His mother was

17

a princess. People like Ruby *should* tremble at the thought
of her.

"I misunderstood," he said. "I thought she was—"

"Trying to snub Mama? God, no, Kid. Ruby's just scared
of her."

Wolfe's face melted into an almost sympathetic expression. "Who was it," he asked with gentle amusement, "who
referred to Mother as 'The Princess'?"

"Oh, some salesgirl. She was trying clothes on Ruby and
she said, 'The Princess will love you in that.' You know
how salesgirls go on. They like to use high-sounding terms
for people and—"

"Well, after all, Mother is a princess. She was the wife
of a prince, wasn't she?"

Simon said, "Yeah, Kid. He was a prince but he didn't
have a dollar. Not a penny for that matter. He was—"

"But he was a prince, wasn't he?"

"Oh, sure. He was a prince but you can't cash titles in
a bank."

Wolfe waved this observation aside. "There are more important things than those which can be cashed in a bank,
Simon."

"You may be right, Kid, but the Prince would be the last
to agree with you. He had the average man's interest in
dough."

For a moment Wolfe Marcaboth was quiet. His slightly
protruding gray eyes were full of the scorn he felt for such
vulgarity. His gaze traveled thoughtfully over this brother
of his whose clothes were as expensively tailored as his own,

whose nails were as well manicured, whose hair with its crisp, white streak gave him an air of dignity and patrician calm. Despite all these things there was a dash of commonness somewhere in Simon. Wolfe wondered how it had survived the years.

"I do not pretend to know how much interest the Prince had in money, and since he's been dead for some time an argument on that subject would be pretty futile. The whole point of the discussion anyway is simply this: You seemed to think it odd and slightly silly for a salesgirl to refer to Mother as 'The Princess.' Well, she *is* a princess."

"So all right, Wolfe. She's a princess. Sometime when you want to borrow a hundred thousand dollars or get a good table at the Stork Club or get a plumber up to your house in a hurry, tell them you're Prince Zleki's stepson. And when you get tired waiting, then tell them your name's Marcaboth."

"Well, of course the Marcaboth name—"

"Yes, Kid, it sure is. Are you and Enid going to have dinner with us tonight?"

"Can't do it, Simon. Sorry."

Simon shrugged. "Okay. I'll ask Garth and Judith."

Wolfe's eyes turned to his work. Simon stayed where he was, thinking about Garth and Judith. They'd be great fun for Ruby—the intellectual Marcaboths, lawyers, both of them, a woman lawyer yet—fine for Ruby. Of course Judith had never practiced but she was a lawyer just the same. She read up on everything and wrangled with Garth about it.

And when they weren't talking law, it was politics or books or the educational system.

"Or maybe I'll ask Rome and Solime," he said, dully.

Rome and Solime. They were young at least. Solime wasn't more than twenty-five and Rome was only—Simon made a swift calculation—cripes, the kid was thirty already. Well, they were young enough for Ruby, but Solime was a quiet little thing. And Rome had such damn fancy manners. If Ruby laughed too loud he would be embarrassed. If she wore a dress with a neckline that forgot to stop plunging he would take it as a personal insult like he had been blackjacked and dragged into Minsky's.

Simon got to his feet heavily. He'd have to ask Garth and Judith—or Rome and Solime. He'd have to ask somebody. Ruby and he couldn't just go out alone again and sit and sit and sit. Not on her birthday.

He was leaving the office when Wolfe spoke unexpectedly. "Let me know how you make out with the others," he said.

"Okay." Simon went back to his office feeling hopeful. Did Wolfe mean that if nobody else would go that he and Enid could be depended upon? They would certainly be the best bet. Not that Wolfe would be stimulating company for Ruby, but Enid would be there.

The secretary was still waiting in the office. "I'll buzz you later," he said and told the switchboard to get his brother Garth on the phone.

Garth was apologetic. "Couldn't do it, Simon. Sorry as

hell but Judith and I have a long-standing date for tonight that we couldn't possibly—"

"All right, Kid. Forget it."

Simon didn't care too much. Garth and Judith, the lawyers—fine company for Ruby on her birthday. Who needed them?

"Get me my brother Jerome."

Rome said, "Why did you wait till today to ask us? If you'd only called me yesterday it would have been fine. Last night Solime got us into a buffet and Canasta deal and now—"

"It's all right, Kid. I just thought maybe—"

"Why aren't you going up to Mother's for Ruby's birthday?"

Garth had asked that, too.

Simon gave the same answer he had given Garth. "It's best to let it slide this time. By Ruby's next birthday Mama and she will know each other better."

"I suppose," Rome said, vaguely. "Well—"

"Well."

Simon replaced the phone and walked back to Wolfe's office.

"Garth and Rome are both tied up for tonight," he reported. A thin note of complacency was in his voice. That left Wolfe no choice now but to cancel his other date. That was certainly what Wolfe had implied when he had asked to be notified of developments, wasn't it? Hadn't he meant that he and Enid would fill in if no one else was available?

Wolfe said, "That's very unfortunate." He was quiet and

thoughtful for a moment. Then, "Something should be done about Ruby's birthday. She is after all a member of the family. She is your wife, and regardless of your reasons for not wanting to spend the evening with Mother and regardless of how I may feel about that piece of rudeness, we just can't let the day slip by as though we have no interest in it."

"That's swell of you to feel that way, Wolfe."

"What other way is there to feel? If families don't stick together in small things, they're not going to stick together in big things. And we've always stuck together, haven't we?"

Simon made his responses fervently and without hesitation.

Wolfe nodded his satisfaction. "Well, I'll tell you what I've figured on doing, Simon. I'll have Garth and Rome get hold of Judith and Solime, and I'll call Enid. Then the three girls can meet somewhere and go up to see Ruby. They'll bring presents, and she'll see that the Marcaboths care that she's having a birthday."

"That'll be fine, Wolfe, but—"

"But what?"

"But it was *tonight* I was worried about. If you and Enid could—"

"Couldn't do it tonight, Simon. Couldn't possibly."

"All right, Wolfe."

Simon turned away and Wolfe said, "Simon, you know I'm not fond of Ruby."

"You hardly know her."

"Then let's say I'm not fond of the *idea* of Ruby. I just want you to understand something: Ruby has to be absorbed into this family. For *you*, we'll forget how we feel. You married her, and I'm not even going to say whether I think that was right or wrong. It's enough that for some silly reason you married her. She's your wife, and we have to make her one with us. Believe me I'll do everything I can to make her feel that she belongs."

Simon said, "Don't strain yourself. She belongs. She's one with us. The diamond bracelet she got this morning cost me a fortune. She's absorbed already. You shouldn't worry."

"If I could go this evening I would, but—"

"Enjoy your poker game," Simon said and went back to his office.

"Madame."

Zeda Marcaboth turned her glance away from the sea. Margaret, the cook, was standing beside her—short, squatty Margaret who always looked bewildered and reproachful.

Nobody, Zeda thought, behaves as Margaret was told people should behave. It hurts her but there's nothing she can do about it. If she was cracked she could write letters to the papers or maybe kill one or two people. But she's sane so there's nothing she can do.

"It's about dinner, Madame."

Zeda smiled at her cook. "Must you and I always talk

about dinner, Margaret? Let it go for a moment. Isn't it a beautiful day? You can see Catalina."

The cook squinted her blue eyes and looked out at Catalina Island. She was a very good cook. Zeda made it a point to chatter aimlessly now and then with a very good cook. You paid a high salary to such a person, but that was not sufficient. Other people paid high salaries, too. You had to offer the little something extra, the touch of warmth that made a cook know that in her employer's eyes she was something more than just an expensive kitchen fixture.

"Have you ever been to Catalina, Margaret?"

"Yes, Madame."

"I have never been. Is it nice over there?"

"Quite nice, Madame. There is the bird farm, you know, and a few other interesting sights."

"But it is such a tedious boat trip."

"I flew over, Madame."

"You flew? There are airplanes going to Catalina? How exciting."

Zeda Marcaboth sat back and permitted her cook to tell her about the airplanes going to Catalina. Did it hurt to let the poor woman feel that there was something about the great world that she knew and her employer did not? Was it wrong for Margaret to go back to her kitchen feeling a new, unexplained contentment with the day? Zeda Marcaboth knew the lovely feeling it was to tell someone about a place you had been, an experience you had known. It made you feel proud of yourself. I'm smart, you thought. Look, I have been there. She has not. I have seen things which she has not seen. She listens with such interest because I am smart.

But Zeda knew that when you became truly smart you did not say where you had been or what you had seen. You did the listening then, when you were really smart. You let the cook—if she was a really good cook—tell you about an airplane trip to Catalina, and you were silent about your own flight to Paris. Why should you speak of it?

And after Zeda asked all the questions she knew to ask about Catalina, and the subject had been pleasantly exhausted, Margaret asked again about dinner.

"Miss Blount said there was to be something special for tonight."

"Oh, yes." Zeda smiled faintly, but the smile was not for Margaret. It was a very personal thing, that smile. "It is a birthday again, Margaret. My son, Mr. Simon—his wife is having a birthday."

And her smile widened a little at the thought of how startled Simon would be. She would wait till five o'clock to call him, and she would speak very sweetly, very quietly.

"Simon, darling," she would say, "tell Ruby happy birthday, and please don't be late for dinner. I'm expecting you at seven-thirty sharp."

She'd wait till five o'clock because by then he and Ruby would probably have some plans made for the evening. It would serve him right to have to cancel and rearrange. It would serve him right to be forced into saying to Ruby, "My mother wants us there. What can I do?"

And indeed what could he do? It was Ruby's birthday,

and Ruby would do with it what every Marcaboth did with a birthday. She would spend it with Zeda Marcaboth. It was going to be fun to hear Simon splutter and try to explain. Zeda felt that she could scarcely wait till five o'clock.

When the knock came at the door Enid knew that Wolfe was on the phone. She had told the maid that she was not to be disturbed unless something important came up. Wolfe's telephone calls were always important—to Wolfe. If he only wanted to know what the temperature was in Bel-Air he would tell the maid that it was very important.

"Sorry to disturb you, Madame. It is Mr. Marcaboth on the phone. He says it's important."

Enid rose to a sitting position on the chaise longue and took the phone.

"Yes, Wolfe."

"Good morning. How are you?"

"Small talk? Or are you really interested?"

"Interested? Well, of course I'm interested. How are you?"

"I have a terrible toothache. I was up all night with it."

"Did you call the dentist?"

"Of course. He's trying to rearrange some appointments now so he can fit me in."

"Good. Good. That's fine. Listen, there's something I'd like you to do, Enid. Today is Ruby's birthday."

"Whoopee."

"Well, yes, sure. You know I don't care either except for Simon's sake. Look, Solime and Judith are going up there."

"What for?"

"To bring Ruby presents of course. It's her birthday. I want you to get her something nice. You know, something a little flashy, the kind of thing she'd like. You can call the girls and arrange to meet them—"

"Wolfe, this toothache is driving me crazy. I want to get to the dentist as soon as he can see me."

"Yes, of course. But perhaps lying around thinking about the pain doesn't help much either. There's a possibility that when you get shopping and talking with the girls, you'll forget the tooth. Now buy something really lovely for Simon."

"For Simon? I thought it was Ruby's birthday."

"You know what I mean. I wouldn't bother you or myself with this if it weren't for Simon. She *is* his wife, and we have to put ourselves out a little for her."

"How are you putting yourself out, dear?"

"If you could see the stack of work on my desk you wouldn't ask. I've spent an hour listening to Simon talk about poor little Ruby all alone up there, and now a call from London is waiting while I talk Ruby's birthday over with you—Ruby's birthday. Why, I can't even look at Simon without thinking of Hannah. I think of her all the time."

"So do I. In my thoughts I refer to her as 'the lucky Mrs. Marcaboth.' Go ahead, take your London call and after that

lie down a bit. You must be exhausted from the things
you've had to do for Ruby's birthday."

Enid lay back upon the chaise longue and closed her eyes.
She thought she could almost hear the throbbing ache of
her tooth. Or was it teeth? She couldn't tell any more. Oh,
God, out to buy a present for Ruby, then conversation with
Judith and Solime and finally with Ruby herself. What did
you say to Ruby? Lovely Ruby who had sunk her claws
into poor old Simon. You could say, "Oh, you should have
known Hannah. Such a sweet gal. On *her* birthdays she always got things that Simon had been wanting for a long
time." Or you could say, "Happy birthday, you little gut-
tersnipe. All right, so you hooked a Marcaboth. Stop
grinning."

It was the aching, aching tooth that made you think such
things. There was nothing wrong with Ruby. She was just
young and gorgeous and stupid. That was all. She couldn't
help being any of those things.

I was once all of them myself, Enid thought. And now
I am none of them. And she thought about getting up and
making herself presentable. It took time. It took a lot of
time when you were a hundred years old. And I am every
day of that. I must be. The calendar doesn't know best. I
know best. You could tell when you were old. You knew
it by the way you felt. And you knew it when you stood
before a mirror and fooled with the hair that had been
bleached too often or sat with the little mascara brush in
your hand hoping that your stiff, dark lashes would be so
intriguing that no one would notice the crow's feet or the

dry crisscross of tiny wrinkles on the eyelids. You looked at the skin that needed ice and lotions and creams and tonics in order to make it seem alive, and you were sorry for the skin because it didn't know why it was being tortured this way. It had been beautiful. It had earned its right to grow old peacefully, to go its way without being punished. It wanted to rest but it could not rest. Here is another day, old skin, pull yourself together. Remember how we used to look? Well, give me a reasonable facsimile.

Enid reached for the telephone and spoke to the nurse in the dentist's office.

"This is Mrs. Marcaboth again—"

"Oh, yes, Mrs. Marcaboth, I'm trying to cancel out an appointment now and—"

"That's what I called about. I'm not going to be able to come right away, as I thought. Could you find some time for me this afternoon?"

There was a moment of chilly silence. Then, "I guess your tooth doesn't ache quite as much as we thought, does it, Mrs. Marcaboth? We were so worried about you. We thought you were in real pain."

"Could you fit me in this afternoon?" Enid asked.

"Oh, I'm afraid that would be impossible. Doctor's just booked solid with really important things. I'm terribly sorry. How is Thursday, Mrs. Marcaboth?"

"Never mind. Forget Thursday."

How is Thursday? What a question. How do I know how Thursday is? I haven't seen Thursday in almost a week. Time for another aspirin perhaps. That might help.

But it was such a nuisance to get an aspirin. You had to get off the chaise longue. Well, you had to get up anyway. Ruby's birthday, remember. Happy birthday to you. Happy birthday, dear Ruby. Here's my toothache. I'd give you Wolfe, too, willingly, only you already have a Marcaboth, I see. Well, a Marcaboth is one thing that a woman can certainly have too many of so just take my toothache, pet. My, how nice it looks on you.

Enid got off the chaise longue and walked into her dressing room. Now to get dressed. Or should she call Judith first? Or should she call Solime? Or should she take an aspirin? Or should she make the whole thing as simple as possible and just shoot herself?

She slipped out of her pajamas and looked in the mirror. She did that every day. It was fine for morale. A hundred and ten pounds. A lovely figure on a small-boned frame. A girl's figure. What girl? Damn few of them had figures like that. Damn few of them had the control to eat as little as she ate or to take the poundings that she took to keep that figure so straight and firm.

"It is a beautiful figure, Mrs. Marcaboth," the masseuse always said. She never failed to say it. It went with the massage. "In fact, Mrs. Marcaboth, you are beautiful."

Well, she'd better be. Wolfe had no patience with things that deteriorated. He dealt in exquisite objects—marble and ivory and ebony and jade. From all over the world they came to him—treasures of lasting beauty. He bought them and sold them and some he kept, but whatever he did with

them, they did not deteriorate. Wolfe did not care for
things that deteriorated.

And after a while Enid took an aspirin and began to
brush her hair. And as she brushed she thought about Ruby
who was having a birthday. And she thought that Ruby was
a pretty lucky girl. When Ruby was ninety-seven years
old, she'd still be a kid to Simon. He'd be going on a hundred and twenty-eight.

Judith Marcaboth stood in the green-tiled kitchen of her
Beverly Hills house and waited for the new servants to
come out of their room. They had arrived a half hour
earlier with a dozen boxes and suitcases and bags, and obviously they were intending to unpack and make themselves at home before reporting for instructions.

Damn it, I should have told them to get into uniform at
once and to unpack later this afternoon, she thought. Now
what do I do? Stand here awaiting their pleasure, or do I
knock and say, "Come on out?" It occurred to her that if
she knocked they might become annoyed at her hounding
them. They might not unpack at all. They might just say,
"We don't like being hurried. Good-by, Mrs. Marcaboth."

She hadn't felt too happy about them during the inter-
view at the employment agency. They didn't seem bright
or eager. Their attitude had been definitely on the devil-
may-care side. They seemed to feel that if she was game
enough to try them, well, then they'd try her but, mind
you, they weren't promising anything.

31

The woman had, without enthusiasm, admitted to being a cook. The man had said yes, he had been a butler but he preferred gardening.

"We have a gardener," Judith had said. And the man had looked gloomy about that.

Judith waited in her kitchen for the couple to emerge. There was so much to tell them. She thought sadly of the last couple. When she had gotten them just nicely broken in they had torn off to Texas to run a ranch. She glanced at the clock. So much to tell the new servants, thousands and thousands of things. Even the immediate duty that lay before them involved a dozen instructions—lunch for the children—the plates are here, the silver there. This is what they'll eat. You serve them so. Here in the breakfast room. This is the electric mixer for their malted milks. This is how we fix malted milks in this house. Come out of that room, for God's sake. I have a million things to tell you. Do you realize that upstairs hasn't been done yet? Of course I haven't done it. That's your job, but I'll supervise this first day. Mr. Marcaboth's bed is the one nearest the window. Be careful how you make it. Don't touch his desk except to dust. He's a lawyer, you know. Never throw a piece of paper away if it has writing on it. Be careful of that bric-a-brac. It's very valuable. Here's the linen closet. Don't use the pile of sheets on this side. Don't vacuum the rug in the guest room. It has to be swept. Don't empty ash trays in the fireplace. Don't yank the curtains in the living room. We never like whipped cream. Be careful when you detach an electric plug. You might be disconnecting the clock. This is a television set. Don't bump the tube. Here are the back stairs. Do you know about garbage disposals? Never light the incinerator in the afternoon. Don't use wax on the floors. Oh, my God, come out of that room. There's so much you have to be told.

They came out of the room at last. The woman was wearing a uniform that was slightly soiled. The man was smoking a cigarette. Nice beginning, Judith thought. Added to everything else they would have to be taught simple things like cleanliness and manners. Oh, well, hop to it.

Judith opened her mouth to begin and at that moment the phone rang. The servants looked a little startled. Oh, come now, they must know about telephones.

"Mr. Marcaboth's residence," Judith said. First lesson—that was the way for a servant to answer a telephone. She hoped they had noticed.

"Oh, it is, is it? Well, how are you, Mrs. Marcaboth?"

"Hello, Garth."

"Say, Judith, what are you doing?"

"Anne and Frederick have just arrived and—"

"Oh, that's fine. You haven't anything to do then. Listen, it's Ruby's birthday and—"

"Just a minute, Garth, I'll go on the other phone."

Anne and Frederick were leaning against the stove watching her with bright-eyed interest.

"When I begin to speak from the other room, you hang up here," she said.

Frederick said, "What?"

Judith thought: Oh, to hell with it. Listen if you want to.

She raced into the living room and picked up the phone there.

"All right, Garth. What is it?"

"It's Ruby's birthday and Enid and Solime are going up to Simon's to sort of, you know, bring her presents and things."

"Oh, that's nice of them, isn't it?"

"You'll have to go, too, of course."

"I can't, Garth. I can't possibly."

"Why can't you? This is important, Judith. What have you got to do?"

"I've got new servants to break in."

"Oh, that isn't important. Listen, for my brother Simon I don't hesitate when he asks a favor. When it's for Simon it gets done."

"This is for Simon?"

"Of course it's for Simon. Do you think I care about Ruby? Besides, Enid and Solime are going. How would it look if you didn't go? It would be a snub to Simon."

"Oh, Garth, that's a lot of nonsense. I'm busy. Is that a snub for Simon if I'm busy?"

"Yes. In this case it is. I don't ask much of you, Judith, but now I'm asking something. You have to call Enid and Solime and arrange to go up there with them. I tell you, it's important."

"All right, Garth, if you think it's important."

"Well, I do think it is. Bring Ruby something nice—a good present."

"All right, Garth."

"And don't sound like a martyr. It's not so much I'm asking, you know."

"No, Garth."

"Okay then?"

"Okay."

"You'll call Enid and Solime?"

"Sure."

"You sound as though I had asked an incredibly difficult thing of you. I ask very little, Judith, and I think that when I ask a favor for my brother you could—"

"I'm going to do it, Garth."

"Yes, but the way you're going to do it! Like an abused wife, for God's sake. I ask—"

"I know, Garth. You ask very little of me. I'll call Enid right away."

Judith walked back to the kitchen thinking of the "very little" Garth Marcaboth had asked of her in the years since first they'd met. Practically nothing, she thought bitterly.

Anne and Frederick were sitting in the breakfast nook. They were thoroughly relaxed, utterly disinterested in what the day might offer.

"I expected to stay in and sort of get you started," Judith said, "but I find I have to go out. The children are at play school. They go there in the mornings during the summer. Now when they come home—"

She felt that she wasn't catching the couple's attention. Perhaps she wasn't presenting the subject matter in its most interesting aspect. She began again.

"Mr. Marcaboth and I," she said, "have grown very fond of our children. They've been around for a few years now and we've come to like them. We feed them well. We make a little ceremony of feeding them. We use plates and things. The children are served as carefully as adults are, the same china and silver as is used at the dinner hour. Now today I thought perhaps—"

Anne said, "On account of we didn't know we were starting here today I have an appointment with my chiropodist. I got trouble with my feet. Is it all right if we go out later this afternoon?"

Judith stared at the woman who had trouble with her feet. Would that woman run all over the back alley looking for little Lorna if someone left the gate open and Lorna wandered out? Yesterday at the employment agency it had seemed possible. Now it didn't.

"As I told you the children aren't allowed off the property alone—"

Frederick suddenly roused himself and spoke with reproach and surprise. "You don't have an electric dish washer, do you?"

"No," Judith said. "If we had, perhaps I'd do the dishes myself, and in that case— But about the children now—"

"I never worked anywhere before where they didn't have an electric dish washer," Anne remarked, sadly.

"Listen, Anne, the little girl—who incidentally is named Lorna—takes a nap after lunch and—"

"Everybody's putting in electric dish washers now and in some houses—you know what they got?"

"Yes," Judith said. "They got good help." She'd had to say it. She had found the urge irresistible, but now she was terrified that they would leap to their feet and be off. She smiled at them, warmly, deceitfully. "And I know you'll be good help, too. Won't you?"

Anne said, "You can't please everybody. Now in the last place we tried and tried, but it was no use. And they had so much company, and then my feet took to—"

"I have to go out," Judith said. "You'll find the silver and dishes, won't you? And watch the children? That's the most important of course, watching the children. You'll make out all right. Watch the children. See that they don't go in the pool. They're never allowed in without an adult. You'll be careful, won't you? About the children?"

Anne sighed. "I thought they were in school all day," she said.

Judith walked out of the kitchen. Behind her she could hear Anne's doleful voice commenting on the fact that this kitchen was terribly large. A person could get worn out just from mopping it.

They're not going to stay, Judith thought. They'll leave. They have no interest in the job, and because they have no interest maybe they won't watch the children. Maybe they won't even bother to feed them. Why can't I just send

Ruby some flowers? Why do I have to go up there? Why shouldn't I say, "To hell with Ruby and her birthday"?

She could. It was a good thought, but it was thoroughly impractical. After all, Garth asked so little of her.

Solime clutched at the telephone the second it rang. That was one way to be sure that a servant didn't get there first and hang on the line listening. You couldn't be too careful. You could never tell who was calling. This time it was Rome so it was all right.

"Hello, darling."

"Hello, Rome."

"Solime, will you do something for me?"

"It's highly possible. What had you in mind?"

"It's Ruby's birthday, and Enid and Judith are going up there to bring Ruby some presents. Will you get her something and string along with them?"

She hesitated a moment. "When?"

"Now, Solime. As soon as you three girls can get together. What's the matter? Have you got something else to do?"

"No, oh, no. Of course not."

"I know you can't want to call on Ruby, but on account of Simon I figured you wouldn't mind."

"Oh, I don't really mind, Rome. I'll do it."

"Buy Ruby something expensive—a mink-edged handkerchief perhaps."

Solime laughed and thought that a monkey wrench

would be a more appropriate gift. Ruby was certainly going to miss the one she had thrown in today's machinery.

When she had replaced the phone she sat for a moment staring out the window at June Street.

Damn, she said to herself. Damn. Damn. Damn.

She got up and walked across the hall to Rome's room. He had a private line without an extension so it was better to call from there.

"Mr. Galal's residence."

"This is Miss Solime, Roberts. Let me talk to my mother."

"Yes, Miss Solime."

Mother would be in the morning room answering her mail about now. It was easy to picture her reading a letter and holding a phone conversation at the same time. Solime had often wondered how that trick was done.

"Hello, dear."

"Hello, Mother. Mother, I'm in a predicament."

"In what way, Solime?"

"Well, Rome just called and he wants me to do something for him and—"

"I wouldn't consider doing something for my husband a predicament exactly."

"I know *you* wouldn't, Mother, but Rome thinks I've resigned from The Circle."

"Yes, Solime, I know he thinks you have."

"Sometimes I wonder if I shouldn't have."

Mother said, "Well, you didn't. Now what do you want of me?"

"I want you to tell Lisa Benrabnan that I won't get to the meeting in time for lunch but that I'll be there later."

"All right. I'll tell her."

"They never discuss anything important till lunch is over anyway. And I can rush through this other thing I have to do and be at Lisa's by the time they really get to talking."

Mother said, "You could miss the meeting. I'd tell Lisa that—"

"But I'm not going to miss the meeting, Mother. Are you listening to me or reading a letter? I'm just going to miss lunch. I told you that. Now, please, dear, tell Lisa I'll be there later."

"Very well, Solime. Very well."

Solime went back to her own room. She was feeling cross. This ducking and dodging and lying made a pretty tedious routine, and all because that upstart sister of Rome's had been blackballed in The Circle. He had said that her rejection was as much an insult to Solime as to the Marcaboths. Solime didn't see it that way. She detested keeping secrets from Rome, but how could she resign from The Circle? She had been enrolled as a member on the day of her birth—a compliment to Mother who had been The Circle's president at the time.

She thought of all the lies she had told Rome—black ones and white ones, lies of all colors, shapes, and sizes. Was it worth it? Probably not. What was The Circle after all? "An organization of snobs," according to Rome. Maybe so, but he'd have been immensely proud if his sister had been accepted.

I should have said, "Thy people shall be my people." And Solime wondered if Ruth would have said those words to Naomi if Ruth had had the problem of Naomi's people not being welcome in the most exclusive clubs. And she envied Ruth for having been spared the embarrassment of an in-law's trying to buy her way into The Circle with a five-thousand-dollar donation.

Solime thought about Rome's sister, and when she did it seemed that it was a miserable thing indeed to be a Marcaboth, to be one with that tribe of outlanders who had their origin in the dark, secret womb of a fifth-rate country. It wasn't fair that the Marcaboths had produced a son so handsome and appealing that she had been unable to resist him. It was some kind of a snide Eastern trick, something they had brought with them from that legendary land of theirs. They had wanted their blood and bone to blend with that of the Galals so they had conjured up a son, and, bewitched, she had melted into his arms.

Mother said the Marcaboths were barbarians—barbarians in custom-made slacks, barbarians who had happened to make good investments. Frightening, Mother said, just frightening. Of course Mother hadn't said anything like that in a long while—not since Solime had married Rome. It wouldn't be Mother's way to speak ill of the Marcaboths once she was mother-in-law to one of them and grandmother to another.

The thought of Adin drew Solime to the windows that

overlooked the garden. He was down there playing with his collie pup. Miss Trivers was on the job beaming upon the two beautiful young things, watching the child and the puppy, alert lest either in its innocence injure the other.

The sight of Adin always filled Solime with happiness and awe. She had caused this miracle to be. She had borne this healthy, handsome child. Her satisfaction was great as she looked at him though she knew that Adin was not Galal but Marcaboth. Adin was a barbarian, too—a barbarian with an English nanny.

Rome had said, "Why, God damn it, if you ever have a daughter she won't be welcome in The Circle. Do you realize that? Your daughter will be a Marcaboth just as my sister is."

Solime had not replied. She knew her daughter would not be as Rome's sister was. Her daughter would be gentle of voice, and she would have elegance without ostentation, pride without arrogance. The Circle would welcome her, and the members would think of the girl as Mrs. Galal's grandchild. They would think of her as the daughter of Mrs. Galal's daughter, and they would not concern themselves with the trivial detail that her name was Marcaboth.

Solime turned from the window. Today appropriations would be discussed—the charities and what amounts each should receive. But the Silver Star Ball would demand the most discussion. The planning of that was never a small matter.

But first there must be the visit to Ruby. That was more important than anything. As a Marcaboth it was customary and natural to deplore Ruby's very existence, but it was also understood that one would fight fire and flood to get to Ruby on her birthday. The ways of barbarians were strange ways and the laws of the tribe inexorable.

Simon had to go down to the warehouse and he had to go to the shop. Any day that week would have done, but he chose this morning because he wanted to get out of the office. He didn't want to wait for the answer to his telegram. He wanted the answer to be there, lying on his desk when he got back. The words of the wire he had sent to his son kept running over and over in his head. At first he had written, "Tonight is Ruby's birthday and I want to give her a small party. Do you mind if I invite Phil and Harry and their wives?"

He hadn't sent that wire. It sounded pleading and pathetic.

The final version had been, "Am giving small dinner tonight at Mocambo. Would you like me to invite Phil and Harry and their wives? Answer at once."

That had struck a more casual note. It was better but still it didn't convey exactly what Simon had in mind. There was really no way that it could. For Simon wanted to say—without saying it—that not for all the Rubys God had ever created would he hurt or embarrass his boy, Lawrence.

Of course there needn't have been a telegram at all. He could have telephoned, but he had swung too many deals in his day not to know the value of giving a man a chance to think your proposition over. Human beings were inclined to say no. They said it automatically without thought or reason, and once said, they were apt to consider a retraction a sign of weakness. So you didn't just explode a question on the telephone. You gave a man a second in which to think. You gave yourself a fighting chance.

The secretary glanced at the wire and said, "Oh, your son didn't come home for the summer."

"No, he's visiting with friends."

And his daughter was visiting with friends, too—six thousand miles away. He still remembered the wedding present she had sent him, the letter in which she had said that she would endeavor to forget Ruby's existence although it would of course be difficult and, Papa, how could you do it when Mama was such a wonderful woman and my husband feels the same as I do and, believe me, my children will never be encouraged to think of Ruby as anything but a terrible mistake their grandpapa made.

So grandpapa made a terrible mistake. You made one, too, sweetheart. But did I ever tell you that you did? Did I ever tell you that you married a slug who held me up for twenty thousand dollars when you were so happy, darling, getting fittings on your wedding gown and the invitations out already and the presents coming in? Did I ever tell you that he wanted Mara Laban then, and that he could only fall out of love with Mara and back in love with you if I paid a gambling debt for him? This I never told you, darling. This you shouldn't hear, but so stuck up with

Ruby you shouldn't be. I bought a husband for you and I bought a wife for myself. So? Are you happy, darling? Well, that's all that matters. Go ahead, look down your nose at Ruby. Things like this I can stand if you are happy.

His thoughts went back to Harry and Phil. They'd be fun for Ruby. They'd dance with her, and their wives wouldn't mind. Nice girls would be too polite to interfere with their hostess having a pleasant evening. Maybe they wouldn't accept a second invitation, but it was only tonight with which Simon was concerned. Just let them come tonight. If only Lawrence wouldn't object to his friends being dragged out to meet Ruby. If, in his telegram, Lawrence would only say, "Fine. Have fun. Wish I was there."

Simon shook his head wonderingly. All of a sudden—me —Santa Claus—who's always had to do things, buy things for people, all of a sudden I'm running around like crazy asking favors of everybody, getting down on my knees to little kids, begging them to let me buy them a dinner.

He got his hat and went out of the office. You could go batty sitting waiting for a telegram.

Not just any telegram. But this is an important one, he thought, grimly. When it comes I'll know who won the popularity contest.

He decided to take a taxi to the warehouse. Let the Cadillac sit cool and useless in its hole in the earth. This was no day for a sensible man to cope with downtown traffic. He got a cab at once and sat staring at the driver's back thinking how surprised the guy would be if he said to him, "You look fairly young and lively. Bring your wife or gal to Mocambo tonight and we'll have some fun. Meet me there about nine."

The cab driver wouldn't show up. He'd figure there was something fishy about a deal like that. He'd be too smart to fall for it. People were always that way. They only went for things they could thoroughly understand like the numbers racket or pyramid clubs or Wall Street.

At the warehouse there was a jade tree that Simon had to check on before it was sent to a New York dealer. There was also a teakwood bed that he was thinking of keeping to give Garth and Judith for their anniversary. Too, there was a talkative warehouse manager with a list of complaints about his help, about his responsibilities, and about the hardships the Chinese situation and the dock strikes had been to him.

"I don't know where I am from one day to the next. Everything's at sixes and sevens. Shipments, trans-shipments, delays, postponements, disappointments—you can't depend on anything."

"You can depend on disappointments," Simon said. He looked at the man's haggard face. People were wonderful, he thought. Here was a man who was actually suffering because shipments were no longer to be depended upon. His salary was the same if they were late or early. His salary was the same if everything ran with clocklike precision or with hectic uncertainty. But his salary shouldn't be the same. There should be compensation for that haggard look. The Marcaboths weren't running a business unless they were paying for what they received, and here in the warehouse they were getting a man's entire output of nervous energy, loyalty, and enthusiasm. All right, so the guy had too much conversation and too many complaints. He wasn't lonely with failings like that.

He'll get a raise, Simon thought, and then he'll be more conscientious than ever. He'll get new ulcers and deeper lines in his face and I'll feel sorry for how hard his job is and so I'll give him a raise and then he'll be more conscientious than ever and he'll get— Simon took off his hat and began fanning himself. Always you felt the heat more when you were standing around doing nothing.

He inspected the jade tree and the teakwood bed. He wasn't impressed with the tree.

"Mark it for Mr. Jerome's shop," he said. "I don't want that sent to New York. It's not good enough. I'll write to Kingle myself and explain."

"What's the matter with it, Mr. Marcaboth?"

Simon said, "It's a sporting-house ornament. Do you see what I mean?"

"No, I don't."

"Well, there are sporting houses that think they are pretty elegant: deep rugs, crystal chandeliers, rose quartz lamp bases—all that stuff. If you look close, if it's your business to know, you'll see that nothing is first-rate. Everything is just a little short of top-grade."

"And this jade tree—"

"Yes."

"But I don't see where—"

"When you've seen as many as I have you'll catch on."

"I suppose you have seen a lot of jade trees, Mr. Marcaboth."

"I don't mean jade trees. I mean sporting houses."

It took almost a lifetime to learn the things Simon Marcaboth knew about jade. Was he to tell it all standing there in the warehouse? "Keep that teakwood bed for me. And I want that whole shipment from Adzibah Brothers to go to the shop. The vases and screens that came from San Francisco can go on to Chicago, but don't include those Balinese carvings. They're strictly for the knickknack trade."

"Mr. Wolfe bought them."

"No. They were sold to Mr. Wolfe. It isn't the same thing."

"Ben has some rugs to show you."

"I can't look at rugs today."

You couldn't look at rugs unless you were in the mood for them. Rugs were something you didn't go near unless you could approach them with a peaceful, pleasant feeling inside of you. It was like visiting a woman you'd gone steady with when you'd both been young. Did you drop in on her when your humor was bad and you had things on your mind? No, you called when you had leisure and a smile for her and maybe a little bunch of flowers in your hand.

"I'm going to the shop now. I'll be back in the office in an hour or so if you want me."

Simon got another taxi and went on to the shop. There was no need for him to go there. Three or four times a month he went, but he had never been certain that Rome welcomed him. It was hard to tell whether the kid thought the visits represented a check-up or whether he'd feel slighted if Simon never came to look the shop over. Today Simon knew that the visit to Rome had a real reason. It would kill a little time while he waited for the telegram to come.

Simon dismissed the cab and stood for a moment on the sidewalk giving the shop a critical eye. The displays in the two large windows had been well conceived, he thought, only it was a mistake to exhibit Japanese swords. They were antique and of exquisite workmanship, but this the ordinary passer-by wouldn't know. Japanese swords still had a very special meaning to some people.

It wouldn't surprise me, Simon thought, if dopes seeing Japanese swords in a window would go in and try to buy a trench coat or a tent or some other war surplus things. What do dopes know of Tagumaki swords?

Simon thought about the Tagumaki swords and how strange it all was. Not long ago the Marcaboth family had been concerned with the question of how Rome would make out against Japanese bayonets. Simon took a moment to give thanks for Rome's safe return from the war. While he was about it he thanked his God for Garth's safe return, too. It would have seemed peculiar, he thought, to give no sign that he was grateful for Garth's safety, but he didn't consider that it had taken anything in the way of miracles to bring Garth back to his loved ones from a war spent in Washington, D.C.

It pleased Simon that Rome had this shop. Rome had never liked the idea of coming into the office, and in all truth there was nothing there for him to do. Simon and Wolfe would have had to create work for him. Instead they had created this. The Marcaboths were not piddling little dealers bothering with the whims of a housewife who wanted something bright for that spot beside the goldfish bowl. But Rome was the brother who had been to war so now the Marcaboth family had a shop. Rome had been in a hurry to get to work. And Mama had been in a hurry to see that he did.

"You shouldn't worry, Mama. Rome wants to work. What do you think? You think he wants to spend his time playing—?"

Simon had almost said polo. The Prince had been killed in a polo accident. You didn't mention polo around Mama. Papa had died of pneumonia, but pneumonia you could mention.

Simon opened the door and stepped into Rome's shop—nice atmosphere, rich and quiet, people talking in low tones to salesmen, well-dressed customers wandering about, casting admiring glances at the stock.

Simon signaled to a salesman that he was going upstairs to Rome's office. The salesman hurried over to him.

"I'm sorry, Mr. Simon. Mr. Jerome has just stepped out."

Simon felt a stab of disappointment. He had wanted to pass an hour with Rome. He liked being with Rome. The minutes flew when you sat with the kid and talked about this or that.

"It doesn't matter. It was nothing important. Just tell him I was here."

"I certainly will, Mr. Simon. Is there anything I can do for you?"

Simon shook his head. Maybe he should say, "Why, yes. Can you rumba? Do you know any shaggy dog stories? How are you on keeping a silence from falling?"

"No, there's nothing," he said.

The salesman waited politely, his clean-shaven young face turned interestedly toward Mr. Simon—Mr. Simon, the eldest Marcaboth, Mr. Simon who looked smooth and dignified on even the hottest day, Mr. Simon who— Cripes, I'd like to have his dough.

"I'll tell Mr. Jerome you were here."

Simon turned and walked out of the shop. Maybe he should have gone up to Rome's office and lain down for a while. Maybe he could have fallen asleep. And when he woke up it would be time for—

But the telegram was waiting for him when he got back to his own office.

"Wish you would not ask Harry and Phil. Letter follows. Lawrence."

Simon made a little yellow ball of the telegram and threw it in the wastebasket. Letter follows. He didn't need any letter. Lawrence didn't want his friends to meet Ruby. So okay. That was Lawrence's privilege of course. They were his friends. Lawrence had a right to protect them from being exploited for Ruby's entertainment. That was pretty decent of Lawrence. Loyal little guy, Lawrence. He wouldn't have Harry and Phil used in the name of friendship. Fine. Lawrence had standards.

Only, Simon thought, at what point does it get to be my turn? When does all this loyalty and youthful idealism pay off for me? When does the moment come when I'm the fellow whose feelings nobody wants to hurt?

SOMETIMES Zeda invited her secretary to have luncheon with her. Most times she ate alone. To-day was one of the days she invited Miss Blount. Miss Blount was so little nuisance that she could have lunched every day on the terrace were it not for the fact that Zeda allowed no habits to be formed that were not particularly advantageous to her.

"Will you be lying down this afternoon, Mrs. Marcaboth?"

"I don't know, but in any case I don't want you to count

on staying around here. You must go to the florist's and get flowers for Mr. Simon's wife."

"What kind?"

"That's right. We didn't decide, did we?"

Miss Blount shook her head. "You haven't even said what Mrs. Simon is like."

Zeda stared out at the ocean. "I have not met her," she said.

Miss Blount bit her lip. It was a mistake to remind an old lady that she had not met her eldest son's wife.

"But I know what she is like, Miss Blount."

"You do?"

"Oh, yes. She is as tall as I. She's a dark-eyed blonde."

"She sounds beautiful."

Zeda said, "They say she is."

Miss Blount did not ask who "they" were. Her employer's information could be expected to come from anywhere.

Mrs. Marcaboth suddenly chuckled. Miss Blount looked at her questioningly.

"Nothing. Nothing, child. I was only thinking that at sixteen he took his first drink. With whom did he take it? With a stranger? With a chance acquaintance? No. He took it with the janitor in his father's showroom, and he could not figure for the life of him how I found out."

Miss Blount said nothing. She frowned out at the ocean. She had not been expected to follow this train of thought, but it was like outsmarting Zeda Marcaboth if you could guess what she was thinking. And outsmarting Zeda Marcaboth was something you didn't do every day in the week.

"And he buys a diamond bracelet for his wife in a shop where I have dealt for years and years, and he does not expect me to hear about things like that. He is as simple and trusting now as he was at sixteen."

Miss Blount understood now that Mrs. Marcaboth was referring to Mr. Simon, her oldest son, and Miss Blount did not believe that Simon Marcaboth was as simple and trusting as he had been at sixteen. He had made too much money to be that kind of a ninny. Miss Blount was merely a social secretary. She didn't handle any of the details of the large, involved Marcaboth family interests, but she, too, had her sources of information. She knew that the boys had shares in the vast Marcaboth fortune. And she knew that Simon had long ago invested his profits in independent holdings and that he had become a wealthy man in his own right. Miss Blount wondered why he was permitted to use his money as he chose. It would cause horrible confusion if the balance of economic power should ever swing from his mother's grasp to his. Suppose he managed to build a fortune larger than the amalgamated family holdings? But Zeda did not seem concerned that such a thing could happen. And, Miss Blount conceded, maybe it could not.

"Are you still thinking of what kind of flowers to buy Mrs. Simon?"

"Yes, I'm thinking of gladioli."

"Naturally you were. Everybody thinks of gladioli. Get something nobody ever thinks of, my dear. And when you come back from the florist's, go into the vault and get me one of those golden goblets."

"Anything else I can do, Mrs. Marcaboth?"

"Certainly. There'll be lots of things you can do."

"I'm glad. I don't like being idle."

"Neither do I. But I have no choice. I am too old and too rich to do anything."

Miss Blount laughed. "You're never idle. Your mind is working every second."

Mrs. Marcaboth addressed the air and the ocean. "A fortuneteller. She knows what my mind is doing."

Miss Blount finished her parfait in a hurry. She had gone too far. She had been too familiar. When Mrs. Marcaboth was displeased she always spoke to the walls or the ocean as though nothing else in sight was more intelligent or more worthy of being addressed.

Miss Blount was pleased however at being sent to the vault. It thrilled her to think of carrying one of the magnificently wrought golden goblets to Mrs. Marcaboth. There was excitement in thinking about it. She felt like an acolyte taking part in some ancient ritual. She should wear a flowing robe of snowy white and upon her head a crown of silver leaves and— Miss Blount had a sudden, most prosaic thought. Would Hannah Marcaboth's golden goblet stand beside the new Mrs. Marcaboth's golden goblet? Had Mr. Simon hidden the first one? Maybe he'd given it back to his mother. Maybe Ruby was going to get the same one again, the one Hannah had been given.

Zeda Marcaboth was leaning back in her chair, her eyes

closed, her face turned toward the little breeze that rode in from the ocean.

She's asleep, Miss Blount thought and went silently away.

But Zeda Marcaboth was not asleep. She was thinking of the golden goblets. Each wife had received one on the first birthday following the marriage. It was a pleasant idea, Zeda thought. Like so many other Marcaboth customs it served to knit the family more closely together. Of course Hannah had received the first goblet. Poor Hannah—for all her stolid, unexciting soul—she had read meaning into the gift, and when Enid had joined the family and received the second goblet, Hannah had felt deep and abiding emotion, and the blonde, violet-eyed Enid had become as Hannah's sister.

Tonight I will give one to Ruby, Zeda thought. She had not given one in the past to a daughter-in-law who came as a stranger. The idea disturbed her. A stranger—Simon had a wife who was a stranger to his mother. What was she like, this Ruby, the dark-eyed blonde?

I have a thought on the subject, she said to herself. But it's only fair to reserve judgment on the little tramp until I've met her.

Zeda sat up and stared out at the ocean. If you looked at the ocean you could not think of Ruby or of anything else that was disturbing. You could only think how fortunate you were to be sitting upon the terrace, feeling the salt air upon your face. Here high on the cliff with the green sea below it was cool and pleasant and there was nothing in life more wonderful than solitude and a fresh breeze from the ocean. Only you had to be sixty-six before you knew that there was nothing better than this.

The ocean and the air were God's, and so by His kindness they belonged to everybody. But if you had no money you lay on a public beach and you felt hot, sweating bodies too close to you and there were orange peels and discarded lunchboxes and refuse that was animal, vegetable, and mineral. And long ago Zeda Marcaboth had known such a beach. Now she sat on a breeze-swept terrace and stared out at the ocean, and she was no fool so she did not think that life had been better on the crowded, dirty beach.

Her eyes, strong and sharp, undaunted by the intense sunlight, followed the line of automobiles below her on the ocean highway. She knew that people down there were raising their glances to her elegant aerie. Some of them, she supposed, were wondering who lived in the castle up there on the palisades.

"I live here," she whispered. "I live here." And she was not frightened that she was alone and had spoken to people who could not hear her. I could live a thousand years, she thought, and I would be tired but my mind would not be tired. I would be feeble but my mind would not be feeble. And she whispered again to the soft wind, "I live here." And she looked down at the calm sea and it seemed blue now, and she looked at the dainty white foam that edged the length of the blue and it reminded Zeda Marcaboth of a dress she had once owned—a wonderful dress. Blue it had been, trimmed with white lace. And she smiled because blue hadn't been her color. It had taken years to learn that.

The Marcaboth Women

First she'd had a husband and eleven children and then she'd learned that blue wasn't her color. She laughed a little thinking about that and she wished that there was someone to whom she could tell it. But there was no one.

She closed her eyes for a moment and sat quietly in the sunlight, a tall, aging woman with long, narrow eyes and a high-bridged nose, a woman whose white hair was of such startling beauty that the first thought of each beholder was: It must be a wig. And of course it was.

Perhaps among my children who died there might have been one to laugh at the things that amuse me, she thought.

And she summoned to mind the five that were gone, and they stood there in her memory vague and shadowy and she bade them be gone again.

I had too many children, she thought. It must be too many when I knew some of them so slightly that I cannot remember them. They are not real at all. It was too many children.

The best of her children had survived. Of that she was certain. The two girls—one in Paris, one in New York—were fine girls. Daughters you could love forever and never exchange a cross word with them providing they stayed in Paris and New York.

Sons were different. You wanted them close to you. Sons you could understand. You could even quarrel with a son, and when the quarrel was over, it was over—no tears, no sulks. With daughters it was different. You had a disagreement and for six months afterward you were still explaining or listening to explanations. Daughters!

She thought about her sons: Jerome so handsome and smooth; clever Garth, the lawyer; Wolfe, the ambitious; and of course Simon—Simon, the eldest, Simon who had almost been born in the old country.

Maybe she should have let him be born there and maybe she should have left him in that God-forsaken hole. She smiled as these thoughts drifted through her mind. She kept smiling as though Simon were with her there on the terrace, as though she were teasing him, and as though the smile was necessary lest poor Simon believe her serious.

And she thought about the old country and how its name was always linked with hers. It amused her to think of herself as an exotic female from an ancient, golden land of legend, a figure as mysterious and bizarre as the veiled lady upon a package of cigarettes. It amused her as it would have amused anyone else who had been born in Jersey City.

And she thought of the past with interest but without longing. It was gone. It had been but it was gone. And she thought of Marcaboth, the husband, who had also been and was now gone—Marcaboth, so young, so stupid, his popping gray eyes full of sadness and homesickness.

She thought about Jersey City and the rooms in back of her father's store. She had been born in one of those two little rooms and she had lived there till the day she had left as Marcaboth's bride. She had slept on a cot beside the stove. The family had cooked and eaten in that room, and she had lived her youth as the poor always live the years of their youth, without privacy, without dignity.

She had gone to school and had learned that the Mississippi River rises in Lake Itasca and that George the Third was a tyrant, and she had learned a great many other things, too. But she had not been part of America nor even part of Jersey City for she was a foreigner. Many, many years would have to pass before she found it funny that a girl born in Jersey City was a foreigner.

It was a bad thing to be a foreigner. You ate foods cooked with almonds and honey though nobody else did. Your parents spoke English haltingly, almost unintelligibly, and you were forced to translate for them. You had no friends, no standing, for you were an especially foreign kind of a foreigner in a neighborhood where Irish and Germans were familiar and comprehensible. She knew she looked different for her eyes were too black, too long, and they had that peculiar little lift at the corners that one did not find in Irish or German eyes. Her hair was blacker and silkier than the hair of other girls, and after a while she stopped caring and struggling. She knew she was a foreigner. She stopped fighting against the clothes her mother made for her, against the aromatic foods she was forced to carry in her lunchbox, against her parents' unwillingness to live as Americans lived. And finally when a young man came to the store and talked in her father's language of making her his wife, she hardly protested at all.

"I don't love Marcaboth."

Her mother paused in her stirring of the ever-present pot of soup. "Who mentioned love?" she asked. "Who can afford it?"

And so at fifteen Zeda married Marcaboth, the young man from her parents' homeland. He took her to live in a room on the island of Manhattan. It was a small room, dim and almost airless, and in that room Marcaboth, the lusty peasant boy who had never before had a woman, stilled his restless dreams. And in that first week of her marriage she learned to hate Marcaboth.

"Why did you come to America?" she asked him.

"I heard it was better here, that a man could get rich."

"But he gets rich by working. What have you done so far in America except marry the daughter of your father's friend and live here in a dingy room?"

"I do not like America," Marcaboth said. "I am thinking of going home."

Her heart gave a flutter of fear. She thought of an alien wilderness and herself stranded there with Marcaboth. "The fare for the boat, Marcaboth—"

He smiled at her, a smug, secret smile she had learned to hate and fear. The smile said that he had the money to go home and to take her with him.

"We'll stay here, Marcaboth, won't we?"

But he took her home with him to that strange land, and she wept as she saw the United States fading from her view. And she did not weep because she would stand no more in an assembly hall of an American public school with Lincoln and Washington beaming benevolently upon her. And she did not weep because she loved the rocks and rills of the great new world. She wept because she was alone with Marcaboth and she was seasick and she was remembering the terrible stories her father had told her of life in the old country.

The voyage was a nightmare of sour odors and vile food, but it was no worse than the section of his homeland to which Marcaboth brought her.

"This!" she cried. "You brought me all that way for this?"

And she was appalled at the dirt and poverty she saw, for with all the evils of Jersey City and Manhattan there was nothing to match this. And she looked at the narrow, crooked streets and smelled filth, and she saw people with sore and running eyes and children bony and diseased. She saw figures lurking in the darkness of sagging doorways, and she did not know whether they would beg or murder for the penny they desired.

"This is your homeland, Marcaboth!"

"And the homeland of your parents."

Her mother-in-law was a flabby-fleshed woman with slack jowls and greasy skin. She smelled unclean, and Zeda did not like being crushed against the enormous bosom and greeted as "Daughter." Zeda knew that even in the lowest strata of social existence there were caste lines, and she looked at her mother-in-law and saw that it had been possible to step down even from living in back of her father's store.

She gazed at the room in which she would sleep with her husband and his mother and his young sisters and brothers, and she shook her head. She had a silver bracelet her father had given her as a wedding present. For the bracelet she got a year's use of a room in a house next door to the Marcaboth family.

And the people on the street laughed at her as she passed for she was a foreigner with strange and peculiar ways. It was well known that she wanted one whole room for just herself and her husband. And nobody liked her for she was a foreigner.

She wrote to her father, "Help me. Help me," but he did not answer for she was Marcaboth's problem now. Zeda knew that she was pregnant, and she was determined that her child should not be born in this dreary, hopeless country of the terrible Marcaboths.

"We are not city people really," her husband said. "We could go back to the land, you and I."

"What land?" she demanded. "Connecticut? Ohio?"

"These are American places? No, I mean here. Back toward the hills we could farm and raise our children—"

"No," she said. "We'll have no children here."

He smiled and placed his hand upon her rounding belly. "What can you do?" he asked.

And for the first time she gave him back a smug and secret smile much like his own.

"We'll have no children here," she said again. "I promise you there'll be no children here."

The child within her she would name Simon, she thought, for it would surely be a son. And she planned for the child, great things she planned for this, her first-born, but to the stupid boy whom she had married she spoke of death.

"As he comes from my womb I will strangle him," she

64

said. And she thought how she would set Simon in a wash basket in the Jersey City sunshine and how she would feed him the fine, rich milk that would come from her heavy breasts, and she would sew and make for him a long, white dress with lace upon it. And she thought how he would kick his chubby little pink legs and laugh in the gurgly way that babies laugh. And she said to her husband, "And I will fling his crushed body at you, and you can feed it to the mad and hungry dogs upon these filthy streets of your homeland."

She knew that she had frightened Marcaboth when he stayed for an entire night upon his own side of the bed.

"You tease your husband about the child," her mother-in-law said to her. "Young wives sometimes do. You wish him to think you do not want his child. It is a harmless joke perhaps but not when carried too far."

Zeda looked at the woman sadly. "I do not tease," she said. "I long for the child so that I may murder it. Perhaps I am crazy. Who knows? I dream over and over that I have strangled Marcaboth's child. I dream that I see Marcaboth's blood running from his throat, and I see myself standing with a bloody knife. And it is such a good, fine feeling. It is such joy, such bliss."

Zeda watched the gray, protruding eyes of her husband's mother roll in terror.

"And in my dreams I have ripped your heart out. I see it tossed into the street and the birds pecking at it. I see you lying right there where you are standing now, and you are lying in your own blood and the walls are splattered with your blood and the doorstep is wet and slippery with your blood."

Marcaboth's mother swayed slightly, and Zeda reached a hand out to steady her but the woman stepped back to avoid the contact.

"And," Zeda continued, her voice quiet and hypnotic as before, "I hear the people in the streets crying and all of them are saying, 'If he had taken her home his mother would have lived. He would have lived. His child would have lived, but he did not take her home and they are dead for she went mad and did this awful thing.'"

The Marcaboths were simple—simple and superstitious and, Zeda thought with irony, like most other people they were afraid of foreigners.

Marcaboth was concerned about the boat fare for two to America. He need not have worried. His mother furnished the money. From between her large, greasy breasts she drew a small, greasy bag and counted the money into her son's hand.

"Now take that devil away from me," she said. "Take her far away."

That was how Simon came to be born in the United States. Zeda Marcaboth on her terrace overlooking Santa Monica Bay smiled a little to herself. It seemed very odd that tonight she would give a golden goblet to the wife of that same Simon—Simon who might have been born in a filthy, God-forsaken country and lived his life in wretched rags had he not had a mother who, no matter where she went, was always a foreigner—but a foreigner who thoroughly understood the natives.

And she thought how far she had come from the early days of her marriage, those days when Simon had been a soft little baby in her arms.

He was a sweet baby, she thought, and she sighed. She did not sigh for the streak of white in Simon's hair nor for remembering that he himself was a grandfather now. She sighed because of those first years with Marcaboth and how there had been nothing sweet about them save the baby, Simon.

That flat, she thought. It is almost impossible to believe that I ever lived in such a place.

The flat had three rooms, she remembered. It had a parlor overlooking the street. There were two windows in the parlor. As a matter of fact there were two windows in the flat, for those two parlor windows were all there were. The room behind the parlor was the kitchen-dining room. The windows in the parlor lighted the kitchen-dining room. The stove in the kitchen-dining room heated the parlor. Behind the kitchen-dining room there was the bedroom. It had no windows and no stove. It was neither lighted nor heated.

There was no bathroom in the flat. On each floor of the four-story tenement there were three flats. On each floor there was one lavatory. This was enough. No one expected more comfort or convenience. It was enough to keep warm and fed.

The Marcaboths paid eight dollars a month for the flat. It was too expensive. The landlord reduced the rent to

seven when Zeda began scrubbing down the stairs. She had
lived better than this in the room behind her father's store
but she had been a child then. After marriage one works
harder and has less. Only why should one have less? Worry,
pain, and anguish. Yes, these things were all part of being
married. But there should be compensations. One should
get for one's heartaches a new set of dishes perhaps with
little blue flowers painted upon them. For the backache that
came with the scrubbing one should get a picture for the
parlor wall, a picture of sunset on the ocean maybe. And in
return for the broken nails and rough hands there should
certainly be a pillow on the bed. She thought these things
as she stood stirring a pot of soup, and she thought of her
mother who had stood so for years stirring, stirring. And
she thought of the contents of that other pot as "Mother's
soup" and she thought of this as her soup, and she was
proud of it and she thought she had made it alone because
she was smart and industrious and more worth while than
other people. But a week passed when Marcaboth was unable to bring her any money. And when Marcaboth did not
bring her any money she was not able to make the soup.
She was not smart enough or industrious enough or worth
while enough to make the soup without meat and vege-
tables. So there all by herself in the kitchen-dining room of
the flat in Jersey City she learned not to have contempt for
money. She learned that the onion you can't afford is important enough to make you forget how clever you are,
how superior and lofty. And after that she was less boastful

of the soup. She no longer thought that she, alone and un-
assisted, had brought to the table this fine and fragrant meal.

She learned a great deal in that week when Marcaboth
brought home no money. She learned what it was to be
hungry and what it was to humble oneself to a relative. And
when money came again she learned what it was for her
family to eat once more a meal for which they need thank
no one but God. And she thanked Him fervently, and she
said to Him, "I'll never come whining to You for anything.
I did not whine this time, did I? I'll only come with thanks.
I'll never be a nuisance to You for I will never throw away
what You give me."

And she hoped that He understood what she was trying
to tell Him. She was trying to tell Him that though she dis-
approved of praying for material riches still she would appreciate His giving her a goodly share. She was trying to
tell Him that if, in His wisdom, He saw fit to bestow wealth
upon her, that she wouldn't be fool enough to squander it
and come back whimpering to ask for more. She hoped
that He understood for she had come to desire money. She
had come to believe that the nobility of poverty was a
myth. She did not believe that want developed character or
added to one's spiritual stature. She studied her neighbors
and decided that a hand-to-mouth existence made people
mean and narrow. And because she was now a wife and
mother she looked without coquetry at the boys who stood
on street corners. She looked at them with fear and hatred
for she thought that Simon might one day stand with them

and learn evil ways and die in prison. And she thought of money as her salvation.

The rich are not always angels, she thought, but let me lay my hands upon money and I will guarantee the character of my children. Give me money to keep them off street corners and away from poolrooms and I will raise fine sons.

The more she thought of money the more resentment she felt toward Marcaboth. He was so stupid, so slow about learning English.

"Look, Marcaboth, this is a chair. Say it. Chair. Oh, for God's sake, it's not that hard. Say it! Chair!"

She knew that there should be laughter running through the English lessons—two young people and a new language. There should be jokes about Marcaboth's pronunciations and his funny mistakes. They should be able to scream together at his errors. But there was no laughter. There was only a dogged determination on her part that the dull, empty-headed peasant she had married would one day speak English. As for Marcaboth, he was reconciled. He had come to realize that in America most people spoke American.

"English, Marcaboth. They don't speak American. They speak English."

"But we are not in England."

"How do you know? How could *you* possibly know?"

They sat in the parlor with the gas turned low to save expenses and they talked in whispers so that Simon, in his little bed beside the stove, would not awaken. Zeda showed her husband pictures from the newspaper.

"What's this, Marcaboth?"

"Boy."

"What kind of a boy? A big boy?"

"Little boy."

"Good. Now if he's a little boy what else is he? You know. Think a minute. What is a little boy? He's a child, Marcaboth! A child! I've told you a million times."

And she was going to have another one. Another child. She was pregnant again—pregnant though no words of love had ever passed between herself and Marcaboth. There was nothing between them save their incessant quarreling, the English lessons, and the dark moments of the night in which he reached out for her.

It had frightened her for the children—the way she felt about him. Could it hurt the children? Could her horror of Marcaboth place upon them a mark or cause strange, black fancies to haunt their minds? Though she had no illusions concerning her mother's worldly intelligence she had a superstitious belief in the wisdom of such women. Her mother, she felt, knew all there was to know of assisting a baby into the world or of preparing the dead for burial. This, Zeda thought, left a very noticeable hiatus in her mother's knowledge, but she went to her just the same for there was no one else to whom she could go.

She sat on a low stool in the room behind her father's store. She sat close to the stove where her mother was busy with the cooking. She sat close because she was cold and because she did not wish her father to hear.

She raised her face to her mother and said, "I hate my husband."

"So?" Her mother's face was expressionless. She did not feel or think. She only stirred the soup. That was after all the whole business of life.

"I hate Marcaboth."

Her mother said, "I asked you before you married him, 'Who can afford love?' "

"I did not need a husband. I did not want a husband. I married to please you and my father. I could have run away. I could earn a living and work less than I work now, and at nights I would not have to submit to Marcaboth."

"This is perhaps the truth. What do you want? Do you want I should say a magic word and make this Marcaboth of yours disappear?"

"No."

"What then?"

"I want only the answer to a question. These children of Marcaboth's—they are conceived in hatred."

"So?"

"Will it hurt them?"

"Who will tell them?"

"I do not mean will it hurt their feelings." She looked at her mother in some surprise. She would not have guessed that her mother had heard of such delicate anguish as wounded feelings. "I mean will it make monsters of them? Could I deliver a half-wit or a deformed one or a murderer

72

as a result of the disgust I feel while my husband is putting these children into my body?"

Her mother never once paused in the important task of stirring the soup. She said, "If I believed that such could happen I would have killed myself when I first knew I was to have a child."

Zeda sat on the low stool beside the stove for an hour more but no further words passed between the two women. She knew now why she had not surprised her mother when she had said that she hated Marcaboth. Her mother expected women to hate their husbands. And Zeda looked at her mother and wondered if she felt robbed.

I do, Zeda thought. I feel robbed. There must be something for women as well as men. If this were not so then why should wives sometimes be unfaithful? Surely no woman would submit to a stranger if there were no pleasure in it. It's bad enough having one man paw you. No woman would have two unless there was pleasure to be had.

She would have liked to mention this to her mother, but it would be a pity to speak of things both evil and unattainable. Her mother was too old.

And she thought about all the men she had ever known and she saw no likelihood of her being unfaithful. All the men she had ever seen, as they paraded through her mind, seemed much the same as Marcaboth. On the bed in the stuffy little room behind the kitchen-dining room with any of those men it would be the same for her. The lying in the dark thinking of this, that and the other thing, waiting for the moment when he would allow her to sleep—it would be the same with any man she had ever met.

But at least, she thought, some of the others have brains enough to learn English.

Marcaboth made his living by cleaning windows, hallways, cellars. There was a little card in her father's shop that informed customers that a young man named Marcaboth would work at almost anything for fifteen cents an hour.

"Do you want to do that kind of work all your life?"

"It is not so bad. And if I am too dumb to learn English—"

"You can learn," she said, swiftly. "You can learn."

He was grinning at her. He had a new weapon. She thought what an idiot she had been to place it in his hands. She should have feigned a complete indifference as to whether or not he absorbed the English language. But she had let him know that she could not endure her children to live their lives without having gained an inch on their mother's Jersey City standing.

But finally Marcaboth learned enough English to satisfy her. Little Simon had a sister now and Zeda was pregnant again but Marcaboth knew as much English as her father knew and Zeda was certain that at last he could get some kind of a regular job.

"It must be something," she told him, "with a chance for advancement."

She spoke in English to him now and he did not understand the word "advancement." She explained it painstakingly for this was important to her—very important.

"And it must be a job where you get a chance to learn something."

"What shall I try to learn?"

"Something. Anything. Baking or brewing or carpentry or harness-making. Anything. I do not care as long as you learn something."

"I would like to be a farmer," he said.

She shook her head. "This is not for you. Now say again what you said so well last night."

His face assumed a mask of wooden solemnity. "I am honest. I am—"

"Take off your hat when you say it, and try to stand with your shoulders back and your head up."

He thrust out his chin and squared his shoulders. "I am honest. I am bright and I am not lazy. I will work hard if you will give me a chance."

Zeda surveyed him, her long, dark eyes cold and disdainful. "I don't believe you," she said.

"What do you mean?"

"You must say it as though you meant it, not as though you were a parrot."

"What is a parrot?"

"It's a big green and red bird that talks."

"It's what? No, Zeda. Birds cannot talk. You have really seen such? Oh, this I must see. It is called what? Say the word again."

"Parrot, you dope. It's a talking bird and so are you. You must speak to a possible employer with meaning. You must

75

not speak as though the pretty words had merely been taught to you."

"But they were taught to me. You taught them to me. Don't you remember?"

She said, "God help the family of a stupid man." And she went to attend to her children.

As it turned out Marcaboth didn't actually need the English his wife had so laboriously taught him. During the second week of job-hunting he saw a name on a warehouse. It was a familiar name, a name from the old country. He did not know anyone of that family personally but he felt that he did. Standing in this alien country staring up at the warehouse with the familiar name upon it, young Marcaboth felt that all his troubles were over. Strangely enough they were.

Inside the warehouse he could forget that he was honest and bright and not lazy and that he would work hard if he were given the chance. Inside the warehouse he could forget English. The tongue of Marcaboth's native land greeted him on every side.

"You can perhaps use me?" he asked.

Sure. Sure, but first—what town are you from? Indeed? And what street? Truly? When have you seen it last? You don't say? Do you know my uncle? What have they done about the tree that was struck by lightning? Did the fire take my grandfather's house? And is the man who was bitten by the mad dog still living? Did the sickness come the season you were there? Have they started the new burial ground?

76

"What can I learn here?" Marcaboth asked them.

They laughed. "You can learn to unpack rugs and to pack them again. To roll and bind them and to lift them upon wagons."

"My wife wants me to become a great success."

"You can develop large muscles."

"That will not be enough to please her. My wife is an American. She wants me to grow rich."

"You can begin at six dollars a week."

"And progress to?"

"Seven," they said and hooted with laughter.

He took the job because he could work with men who spoke his language.

"I have a job," he said to Zeda that evening.

"Doing what?" She scowled at him because she was not pleased. It could not be a good job nor a promising one. He was a fool and he seemed happy about the job. Fools were only happy when they were doing something that could not possibly have any importance.

"Something with rugs. Just what, I am not sure yet."

"Is there a chance to advance?"

"Oh, yes. I will learn all about rugs, and in time this knowledge will make me a very rich man." He thought he was lying to her.

Zeda well remembered the day that Marcaboth had taken the six-dollar job. And now she lived in a castle on the ocean.

It only goes to show what you can make of a six-dollar job, she thought, if you are honest and bright and not lazy and will work hard if given a chance. And if, on top of everything else, you are lucky and shrewd and have a lot more business sense than anyone in Jersey City ever thought possible.

And she said to herself: But Marcaboth is not living in a castle on the ocean. Marcaboth is dead. So what good does it do him that he was lucky and shrewd and had good business sense? Never did he get anything better out of life than the apartment on Cathedral Parkway.

Her mind lingered upon the Cathedral Parkway apartment. She could picture it vividly. It was the largest, most luxurious apartment she had ever seen up to that time—seven rooms in a building that had an elevator. It had been a tremendous step forward from the flat on Eighth Avenue that had been the stepping stone to all this Cathedral Parkway splendor.

Marcaboth said, "The rent is high so be careful with the table. Do not buy butter or expensive cuts of meat."

"But the children—"

"That is why you must be so saving. There are too many children."

She hated him for his unfeeling remark. She had buried two children that year. But she obeyed him in the matter of keeping the bills down. Marcaboth was boss now, and she did not challenge his right to hold that position. He had overtaken and passed her. He knew everything that she had learned in her seven years at school and beyond that he knew the rug business and had solved the mystery of how money is made. These things he was not willing to teach

her. She was a woman and a woman was useful to have
about but one could not treat a woman as though she were
a man's equal. Zeda did not argue. She was content to do as
she was told. Marcaboth would do better for her children
than she had ever dreamed possible so she held her peace.
She was an old-country wife, little more than a servant. She
waited upon Marcaboth and his friends. He had many
friends and he brought them home but he did not introduce
his wife. She cooked and brought the food to them. They
never looked up from their plates or in any way at all acknowledged her presence. She ate in the kitchen with her
children and cautioned them to keep their voices low so as
not to disturb Marcaboth and his guests.

She tried to keep the apartment presentable but it was
not easy to do. The place always looked unsettled as though
the family had just moved in or was preparing to leave. The
long hall was forever jammed with rugs and in the living
room there were more rugs, leaning against the walls like
lazy, loose-jointed idlers with no place to go.

Sometimes when Marcaboth's guests left they would
carry a rug or two away with them. She never knew
whether Marcaboth had made a business transaction or a
gift. She just did the cooking.

Once in a while her eyes flashed fire but it did no good to
fight Marcaboth. He was cruel with the peculiar, invincible
cruelty of a stupid man.

"Simon will have to quit loafing now. He is fourteen and
can get his working papers."

"Marcaboth, at least let him graduate from grammar school."

"For what? They are not teaching him anything."

"That is because he is absent so much. Three days last week you made him stay out to run errands for you, and the week before—"

"It is as I'm telling you. I need him to work for me."

"Hire a boy. Surely if we can live here you can afford to—"

"I cannot afford to. I am a poor man. Besides Simon must learn the rug business."

"Now? At fourteen? My God, Marcaboth—"

He had narrowed his protruding, gray eyes at her. "If you shut up now I will forget that you stood against me. If you go on arguing I will make the girl get her working papers, too, next year."

So Simon went to work without wages. He grew lean and nervous, and Marcaboth never said that he worked hard or learned well. Marcaboth never bought him a decent suit or a tie that a boy could put on and get a sudden, joyous lift from its color or texture. He gave Simon carfare and fifteen cents a day for lunch and on Sundays he reviewed the mistakes that Simon had made in the week gone by.

"You treat that boy miserably," Zeda said to her husband. "You are not a kind man, Marcaboth."

The next day he brought a skinny little Negress to her. "Here is a girl who will wash all your dishes for you and help you clean the house. Don't say I am not a kind man."

"How much do we pay her?"

"This is not your business."

"I can wash my own dishes. Take her away and give Simon what you would have paid the girl."

"Simon is not your business either. You tend to the children. Simon is a man now."

The little Negress remained. She was young and inexperienced for Marcaboth would not have paid the wages of a capable servant. Zeda taught the girl something of the household routine and let her watch the baby, Garth.

Simon reported on the Marcaboth rug business. Zeda had never seen the loft that her husband had rented in the beginning. She was amazed to hear that there was an office and a showroom and that Simon was not the lone employee.

"It's a good-sized business, Mama. He imports fine rugs and they sell for a lot of money. I think there is even more to his business than I know about. He goes out a lot and he talks on the phone about things I don't understand and men come to see him and he talks to them in corners where nobody can hear."

"Yes, dear, I think Papa is doing very well."

She was sure that he was when he announced that they needed more room in which to live. Marcaboth said, "Sometimes I must ask a man to remain overnight with us. It is impossible as crowded as we are. I think we will take the apartment across the hall and then we will have fourteen rooms."

"But the people won't move out just because you want their apartment."

He grinned at her in that smug, superior way of his.

"Marcaboth, what will we do with two kitchens?"

"Stop worrying."

The people across the hall moved away and Marcaboth had a wall torn out and now the Marcaboth family had fourteen rooms on the fifth floor of an apartment house on Cathedral Parkway.

The elevator operators and the doorman treated them with great respect, and Zeda said to the children, "No doubt they never before knew any family who lived in such a large apartment." But for all their fourteen rooms and the fact that now they had two servants, the Marcaboths were a shabby crew. Not one of them owned a garment that wasn't either old or shamefully cheap.

"I do not dress well myself," Marcaboth said. "When I start buying fancy things for myself and not for you, then you can complain."

She pretended to the girls that Papa was right and that new clothes were merely vanity and folly. But of herself she asked, "What will I do when they realize that they will be invited nowhere dressed the way they are?"

Marcaboth said to her, "My expenses are terrible now that I have given you such a lovely home. You must help me economize. We will stop drinking coffee. Have it only for my friends."

She nodded. It was easier not to protest. She looked about the "lovely home" he had given her. She hated it. It was a large, depressing jigsaw puzzle of rooms. It was filled with noise and disorganization. In the halls and in most of the rooms the rugs piled high against the walls, and she never

82

understood why they must be there in Marcaboth's home.
There were two parrots that screamed incessantly. Marcaboth would look at them and grin, and she had an uncomfortable feeling that there was something she should remember about Marcaboth and parrots, but though she
searched her mind for the clue it had been lost somewhere
in the crowded years.

The children and the colored girls wrangled in the cor-
ridors and in the distant rooms of the sprawling apartment.
The girls slapped the children and the children slapped the
girls. Everybody cried and the girls quit and new girls came
to take their places. There was always new help in the
Marcaboth family. It changed but it remained the same for
the help was always inexperienced and incompetent. Wages
were low in the big, noisy apartment.

And in that apartment Zeda wept for three more dead
children. She had lost five now and she was pregnant again.
She sat listening numbly to the squawking parrots and to
the complaints of her servants and she thought, I shouldn't
have this child. My state of mind is such that I should not
have it. I am too depressed. This is all there will ever be to
my life and I wish myself dead.

In this pregnancy she was huge and clumsy. A neighbor
said to her, "Mrs. Marcaboth, do you know what doctors
are doing nowadays? They're making you keep weight
down so that later your figure will return to normal."

Zeda said, "That's very important. Thank you."

Garth was four years old when the new baby came. It
was the longest span of time that had passed between Zeda's

confinements. They named the baby Jerome, and Zeda hoped that this would be her last child. He was born in the autumn, a cold, bleak autumn with rain and wind. Marcaboth came into the room where Zeda lay with her infant and she said to him, "What are you doing here at this hour of the day?"

"I am sick," he said. "My head is burning."

He coughed and she said, "Do not cough on the child, you pig."

"Zeda, I am very sick." He knelt down beside her and buried his face in the blanket. She put her hand on the back of his neck and withdrew it thoughtfully. Then she got up and placed the baby in the crib and turned her attention to Marcaboth. She padded about in her bare feet, her flannel nightgown billowing out from her fleshy figure as she prepared Marcaboth for bed.

When the doctor came his examination was swift and he made it with a solemn face.

"Bad?" Zeda asked him in the hallway.

It was very bad. Marcaboth died before another day had passed. Zeda was stunned. It had never occurred to her that Marcaboth could die. He was a healthy, husky peasant. They lived to bury their grandchildren, men like Marcaboth did. Only he would never see his grandchildren. He was dead. She forgot to go back to bed. She sat in a chair in the front room with her five-day-old baby in her arms and she thought: I am a widow. I am alone in the world with six children. But she looked at Simon, the eldest, and she did not really feel that she was alone.

And the renting agent came to bring his doleful face and his sympathies to her. She wondered uncomfortably if it were rent day and if he would be kind enough to wait till she discovered how to find Marcaboth's money.

"Is there anything I can do to help, Mrs. Marcaboth?"

"Thank you. There is nothing."

"Perhaps not now but if you need me later, please feel free to call on me. If you want to sell the building, for instance, I put my experience at your disposal."

She blinked her puzzled eyes at him.

Later in the month she sat in a lawyer's office and stared in silent amazement as figures were read to her. She owned more than the apartment house. She owned a fine, thriving rug business and the building that housed it. She owned four rows of tenements, a cheap hotel, and a movie theater. She owned a drug store in Jersey City and a thousand acres of ground in a Long Island community of which she had never heard.

"This is all excellent property, Mrs. Marcaboth. Your husband was a brilliant man."

Brilliant? Marcaboth who had taken three years to learn English? Marcaboth who had shoveled his food into his mouth with a knife? Marcaboth who had never won the love of any person on earth? This was brilliance?

"He made remarkable investments. Often he took very long chances but he won, and he deserved his winnings because he had tremendous courage."

She looked at the trim, well-tailored, well-barbered man who had admired Marcaboth.

"He was a phenomenon, Mrs. Marcaboth."

"Yes, indeed."

She went back to the apartment on Cathedral Parkway and studied the lawyer's figures. After a while she got up and began to live.

The first thing she did was buy clothes for her children. She bought none for herself. She was not yet ready for clothes. She would buy massages first.

"I am only thirty-six," she said to herself. "Only thirty-six."

That night she and Simon talked about the rug business.

"Can you run it?"

"Yes, Mama."

"Do you want to?"

"It's the only thing I do want. For some reason I find I love rugs."

She squeezed his hand. "I make you manager. You're head of the Marcaboth Importing Company."

They laughed together, two people suddenly young and free.

Simon said, "Do you understand that all this money didn't come from rugs?"

"From where then?"

"Well, in a way it's from rugs, of course, but Papa didn't sell rugs to a store and then put that money in a bank, you know. This way you don't get rich. He took chances with the money."

"So?"

"So am I to do that, too? Shall I invest like Papa did?"

She shook her head. "Not yet, Simon. For a while you just sell rugs, darling. For ten years maybe. During that time you and I will grow up a little. We will learn things. We will teach each other what we learn, then after a while we take a few chances like Papa did."

"Sure, Mama."

"But, Simon, darling, we'll always remember, won't we, that I'm Papa's widow? I'll make all the final decisions and sign all the big checks."

He said, "Yes, Mama, that is the way it should be and I know you will always be generous and fair. With you it won't be carfare and fifteen-cent lunches. It will be—"

"Simon! With me it'll be five dollars a day just for your lunches. You'll go to work in a taxi, and I'll buy you all the suits you want and all the theater tickets and everything else. You've got a big job."

He smiled at her and he said very softly, "Yes, Mama, I've got a big job and I want two hundred dollars a week to start and I want commissions on all business that I bring in. I'll buy my own suits and theater tickets."

Zeda took off forty pounds that year and she learned how to make up those long, half-slanted eyes of hers so that they appeared to be smoldering behind their dark lashes. She bought three fur coats and filled the closets with new clothes. Then abruptly she broke up housekeeping.

"I'm going to travel," she said to Simon. "I'm going to take a big trip. I may even go back to your father's country for a visit."

"What do you want there?"

She did not say what she wanted there. She could not explain why she needed to go back to Marcaboth's homeland. She could not have told her son or anyone else why she longed to return to that miserable country from whence her parents and her husband had come.

"I'll take the children with me of course. Will you go to a hotel or take a small apartment?"

"One or the other, Mama. Don't worry about me. I'll send you regular statements of course, and if anything unusual comes up I'll cable you. How long will you be gone?"

"I don't know, Simon."

It surprised her to find that Marcaboth's country was not as she remembered it. It had a gorgeous hotel filled with wonderful servants who quarreled among themselves for the privilege of serving the American lady and her family. The city was beautiful and picturesque, and everywhere there was light and gaiety. The sheen of romantic intrigue lay upon the city like a silken veil, and Zeda said, "Why, it is beautiful."

But when she walked alone one afternoon down into the streets that she remembered it was the same—the filthy, sickly children starving in their rags; desperate-looking beggars with their skinny shanks and long, matted hair. She found the house in which she had lived with Marcaboth and she found his family. The mother was dead. Two sisters and a brother still lived. She remembered them as small, dirty scraps of humanity. They had changed. They were large now. She gave them each a hundred dollars and went back to her hotel.

"We will go to Paris," she said to the children.

But she did not go immediately for she had met a man, a man who resembled no one Zeda Marcaboth had ever seen even in a dream. His English was awful and he had no sense of humor, but he was big and broad-shouldered and his hair was black and straight. This was a blue-eyed man who rode a horse like a fiend and spoke the soft, sweet words of angels to a woman who had borne eleven children and had never been called by a pet name.

What a pity, people said, that conditions in his country were as they were. He was a prince of royal blood, they said. Zeda shrugged. So he was a prince. That was perhaps a fine thing, but she could not help noticing that the hotel employees did not give him the attention that she herself received. She knew what that meant. And she knew what it meant to her. And she looked into Zleki's blue eyes and thought of the question her mother had asked so long ago: Who can afford love?

She cabled Simon that she was to be married and that he should come for the wedding. He was her favorite child, the first-born. He could take a vacation to see his mother married. And you could depend on Simon. You could depend on him not to notice that Zleki was several years younger than Mama.

And you could depend on Simon to know that an invitation to a wedding didn't mean a person was welcome on the honeymoon. Simon knew when it was time to leave.

"So good-by, Mama. Good-by, Zleki. Long and happy life together."

"But where are you going, Simon?"

"I'm going to the train. I have to catch it to make my boat."

"You could have a drink with us."

"A drink I could have—a quick one."

She and Zleki toured Europe. Zleki had seen it all before of course, and it was his familiarity with it that made the trip so wonderful.

"We will come to Europe every year," she told him. "I love Europe."

"It is your spiritual home," he said. "And confidentially I will be glad to get away from New York. I hate it."

"Do you hate America?" she asked, fearfully.

"Oh, no. Only New York. Have you ever seen California, Zeda?"

"No."

"I have. There I could be happy with Europe forever forgotten. It's a wonderful place. Polo twelve months a year."

She had begun to buy things for a home they would build one day. Two marble mantels, a statue, and a pair of vases were sent to the warehouse of the Marcaboth Importing Company. Simon cabled that he had a chance to sell them at 500 per cent profit.

She cabled back, "We're in the rug business."

His reply was brief. "So?"

After that the Marcaboth Importing Company was no longer simply interested in rugs. Zeda bought and bought and left buyers behind her in Venice and Rome, in Paris and Madrid. She found a set of golden goblets that bewitched her with their magnificence. The merchants drew close to her and whispered in reverent voices. "We think, Madame, that Cellini—"

She nodded and could not resist a twist of humor that she had brought straight from Jersey City.

"So it's only eleven goblets! Not even a full set."

"Oh, Madame."

She paid for her joke by not haggling over price. She carried her eleven goblets back to the hotel. She did not send them to Simon. She was afraid to trust him with them. He would sell them.

And so at last the trip was over and she and Zleki and the children and their new stylish servants sailed for New York. On the pier they were photographed by newspaper men, and Zeda was Princess Zleki to New Yorkers who glanced at her picture across their breakfast coffee. It amused her to be a foreign princess to the people of her own homeland. Abroad she was an American lady.

Zeda, on the terrace that overlooked the Pacific, remembered how Simon had been waiting at the pier. He had grinned but he had kept silent while the reporters had chattered with Zleki, throwing out their usual questions and shaping Zleki's almost unintelligible replies into grave comments on Europe's relationship to the United States. The reporters had not spoken to Zeda. The Princess Zleki with her long, black eyes and sullen, red mouth would of course speak less English than her husband. They only smiled at the foreign woman and said nothing. And as they had walked away Simon had winked at her and called, "Glad to be home, Mama?" And he bustled her into a hired limousine before the newspaper men could turn back to rectify their mistake.

Zeda laughed aloud remembering. That Simon! Her laughter ended in a sigh. Simon. Ruby. Ruby who was coming tonight as a stranger.

They met in the perfume department and stood for a moment in the air-conditioned comfort of the store wondering what they should buy for Ruby. Nobody was very much interested. They were not interested in Ruby, and they were not particularly interested in being together. They would not have chosen each other as friends or companions. They were simply three women named Marcaboth.

"I'm going to buy her a nightgown," Enid said at length.

"That doesn't seem very spectacular," Judith remarked.

"Never mind spectacular. My tooth is killing me."

Solime said, "Did you call the dentist?"

"Yes, dear, several things. Of course I wouldn't dream of seeing him today. I wouldn't miss Ruby's birthday for anything."

Solime's yellow eyes that were usually soft and dreamy looked slightly disapproving now. Solime was *too* perfect, *too* good. Solime was a sister-in-law that a mortal shouldn't have to put up with on a hot day. Enid knew what she had done to earn Solime's disapproval. Solime didn't like the flip way she had spoken of Ruby's birthday. Solime was conventional to an alarming degree. Ruby was Mrs. Simon Marcaboth and Solime would be in there pitching for her till long after dark.

"You should have gone to the dentist," Judith said.

Enid sighed. "You know how it is."

"Oh, I know all right. I have new servants but here I am."

Solime said nothing, and the sister-in-law with the new servants and the sister-in-law with the toothache felt themselves different and apart from her.

"Maybe we won't have to stay long," Judith said.

"I don't know. Wolfe seemed to think that Ruby was lonely. We may be there all day."

Solime raised her hand to the golden chain at her throat, and she stood twisting it and staring at Enid. "All day?" she asked.

"Why, yes. If a girl is lonely on her birthday you stay and keep her company, don't you?"

Solime said, "Of course. I was only thinking that we know Ruby so little."

The Marcaboth women fell silent remembering the one and only time they had seen Ruby. It had been five months earlier, the night after Simon had come back from Las Vegas with his bride. They had all been invited to the house to meet Ruby, and they had gone and sat at the table where on other evenings they had sat with Hannah, and they had looked at Ruby and had come away wondering if Simon had really meant it all to end in marriage.

"We'll find things to talk about," Judith said. "Don't worry. There'll be clothes or movies or something."

"The legal mind at work," Enid said. "Even I could have figured out that Ruby would talk clothes or movies. Well, I'm going upstairs and buy her a nightgown."

Solime said, "I'm going to get her perfume."

Judith stayed with Solime. She was more comfortable with Enid but always she felt a curious compulsion to remain with Solime, always she felt that she was on the brink of a discovery, always about to find what she had been seeking, the secret knowledge that Solime possessed, the thing that made Solime calm and poised and quiet within herself. It was a secret worth having. When it was yours, you moved in tranquillity and loveliness.

I am not like that, Judith thought and she asked aloud, "What kind of perfume will you get her?"

"I haven't decided yet."

Judith said, "Get her a big shiny bottle of something that costs a lot and she'll love it."

Solime said nothing to Judith. She talked to the salesgirl in low tones, and the salesgirl brought bottles and packages for her approval. Solime gave her attention to the things which were before her, looking at them through the slanted, shell-rimmed glasses she had slipped on so that she could see as well as smell the fragrant display.

Judith said, "Oh, quit sniffing. She won't know the difference between one perfume and another."

This time Solime turned and looked at Judith. There was an absent-minded, hazy expression in the eyes behind the provocatively tilted glasses and Judith flushed. Solime certainly couldn't have meant anything by that look and yet—

Suppose she had said it? Judith thought. Suppose she had said, "And when did *you* learn?"

Judith wanted to go away from Solime and the perfume counter. She wanted to hide but when one was a Marcaboth there was no place to hide. She could not lose Solime. Solime would be part of her life forever, and Solime would be remembering that Judith had been vulgar enough to make remarks about Mrs. Simon Marcaboth in the presence of a salesgirl.

Judith thought: I have learned something from you, Solime. Just standing here these last few minutes I have learned that you are buying for Ruby as you would buy for yourself. If I were buying I would buy a strong, sweet scent for her, an overwhelming scent, but you buy a delicate fragrance, one that you would like yourself. I know why, Solime. It is because you want her to suppose that you think of her as a woman who prefers a gentle fragrance. This is a nice gesture. Today I have learned a nice gesture. Oh, lucky me, from my fine sister-in-law, Solime, I have today learned a nice gesture. And I have also learned that your rapt concentration on Ruby's present, your complete absorption is meant as a gentle reprimand to me. You are saying to me, "Ruby is important, Judith. Watch how carefully I select her gift. She is a Mrs. Marcaboth, too."

Judith stood at the counter gazing down at the splendid array of soaps and sachets in the case. The sunlight knifing through the glass caught and flung shimmering ghosts of colored bottles across a smoky mirror, and there was a moment when suddenly Judith felt the fragrance and the dancing reflections were all too much and she turned away.

"Are you all right, Judith?"

"Yes. I'm all right. What made you ask?"

"You looked so odd."

Judith said again, "I'm all right."

Sweet Solime with the shining black hair and soft, yellow eyes. When you looked at her you felt your hands were too big and you thought your lipstick was a glaring mess of orange goo upon your mouth and you looked at Solime and you hated yourself for being awkward and probably ugly. And she reprimanded you in her own way for your gaucheries and you hated her because all you wanted in the world was to be exactly like her. And you knew you never would be. Suddenly Judith wandered away to look for a present for Ruby because she couldn't bear to stand any longer at Solime's side, feeling herself a foil for the beauty and graciousness of the other Mrs. Marcaboth.

And Judith wanted to go upstairs to find Enid for Enid was easy to be with. Long ago Enid had stopped caring how anyone behaved. She had no interest in building character or raising standards. She didn't care what was said of any Marcaboth. She only made one tiny stipulation and that was that you must be a Marcaboth to say it.

"What shall I buy for Ruby? What shall I buy?"

Judith paused at the scarf bar and she thought how complicated the choosing of Ruby's gift might become. It was

96

all right for Solime to flatter Ruby by pretending that they shared the same tastes but suppose one actually did like the sort of thing that Ruby liked? How did one make the nice gesture then? By buying something you personally wouldn't wear to a dog fight? It was a puzzle.

She glanced toward the perfume counter and could not see Solime. Now they were all scattered. Suppose they kept missing each other throughout the morning?

But they came together at last, each with a package.

"What did you buy, Judith?" they asked.

Judith said, "Something perfectly silly. Boots."

"Boots?"

"Yes, they're gold cloth boots—sort of Russian military style. They come to just above the ankles, high heels, gold kid fringe at the top. They're bedroom slippers, you know."

Solime said, "They sound gay. I think that's very nice if Ruby is lonely."

"They're really ridiculous. I bought them for laughs," Judith said.

Judith had no actual distaste for lies. Lies were an integral part of civilization and could be eliminated only when man reverted to the cave and had no further need for imagination, sympathy, or tact. But there were certain kinds of lies that Judith hated, the kind that were part of the numbness that lay within her. She had just told that kind of lie.

I didn't buy them for laughs at all, she thought. I like them. I wish I dared to wear them. But I don't dare to

wear them. And there were so many things she didn't dare
to wear, so many things she didn't dare to do. I don't even
dare to say I like them.

"Well, I guess we're ready to go," Enid said.

Judith thought the children would be home from play
school by now. What am I doing here? They are there
with strangers. Maybe they'll play too close to the pool.
Maybe the servants won't watch them at all. Maybe—well,
she'd have to forget all that for now. She'd been elected
chauffeur. She always was. Other girls always said, "You
take your car, Judith."

"Let's stop on Beverly Drive and buy some flowers for
Ruby," Enid suggested.

Judith said, "Okay."

"And," Enid went on, "let's get candy, too. What's a
birthday without flowers and candy? Since we have to do
this thing we might as well do it in style."

Solime nodded.

"Enid always thinks of everything," Judith said.

"Oh, but everything," Enid agreed.

She watched the younger women as they went off to
buy the flowers and candy. She watched till they were
safely hidden within a florist's shop, then she jumped out
of the car and into another air-conditioned corner of the
hot, bright day. This was a dim little corner and rather
lonely at the moment.

Enid did not sit down and she took the whisky straight,
letting it rest for a moment, hot and stinging, against her
aching tooth.

98

I have to. I can't get through this visit to Ruby without it, she thought. I'm jittery enough to scream. In the bar mirror she considered her reflection. Interesting. From this distance you'd say the woman was maybe thirty, she thought. Shoulder-length blonde hair was a gamble when you were no longer a girl. It aged you ridiculously or it created an illusion of youth.

I think I look young, Enid thought. Of course I could be as crazy as hell. All those poor old chromos with their dyed hair and made-up eyes think they look young.

She studied the slim figure in the sleeveless, black blouse and shepherd's plaid skirt.

You're fine, she thought. Just fine, you with the tooth-ache. What a thing to be doing at this hour of the day! What a place to be! Suppose you were seen? She thought of the shame it would be to the Marcaboths—Wolfe's wife drinking by herself in a barroom. The sooner she got out of here the better.

It wouldn't help to say she'd never done such a thing before. It wouldn't help to say she was a soft-drink fancier from way back. It wouldn't help to say that the tooth was killing her, that every nerve in her body was jumping, and that she could easily take to screaming right here on Beverly Drive.

She paid for her drink and went back to the car. I should have had the courage to say no, she thought. I should have gone to the dentist but Wolfe would have been sore. Even with the aching tooth it's easier this way, I guess.

The girls were coming back. Solime was carrying the

flowers. Judith had a large box of candy clasped against her striped cotton dress. Poor Judith. God help any average brunette who had to walk beside Solime, Enid thought. It didn't help a bit to look clear-eyed and intelligent.

"Now I guess we have everything we need," Solime said. Enid nodded solemnly. "I guess we have."

They drove north on Beverly Drive, crossed Sunset, and continued on into the canyon for a way. Then Judith made an abrupt swing, climbed a hill, rounded a curve, and they were there. The girls stared at the house for a moment.

Solime said, "Why, it's been painted pink."

"Pink," Judith sighed. "Hannah's house!"

Enid said, "Don't be silly. Hannah's house is marble. This is Ruby's house."

They got out of the car and approached the wide front door. Judith was looking about her with distaste. "If there's anything I hate," she said, "it's a pink house."

Enid rang the bell. After a time she rang the bell again but still there was no answer. They looked at each other in surprise.

"She could have gone out," Solime said. "If I were lonely I would go out."

"But would you take the servants with you?" Judith asked.

Enid rang the bell again. "The servants can't be off today," she said. "Nobody's servants are ever off on Tuesdays."

The three Marcaboth women carrying the roses, the candy, and the other gifts wandered in puzzlement out to the driveway. For a second they stood irresolute, then Enid began walking toward the back door. The girls followed her. At the back door they rang again. They rang and rang and they stared through the windows, and they saw Hannah's enormous double-sized refrigerator and Hannah's stove and Hannah's deep-freeze unit all standing there in Ruby's kitchen.

"Well," said Judith, "nobody's home." They looked at each other and at the presents and they felt pretty silly.

"If the servants were here we could leave the things but—"

"I know," Enid said, suddenly. "The pool. On a day like this she'd be down at the pool."

They crossed the kitchen garden and opened the gate that led into the little diamond-shaped lawn space that had been the children's playground. Enid remembered Simon's son and daughter as children romping here on this stretch of green. Only yesterday. Maybe. But if it were only yesterday then the night had been very long.

They walked on through the rock garden and down the rough stone steps toward the hollow where the pool lay, a green sparkle in the sunlight. They could see no sign of Ruby but they walked on. She might be in the bar or in the ping pong room or the dressing quarters. She could be anywhere. They walked past the brightly colored furniture that surrounded the pool, the scarlet chairs, the royal-blue sofas. They paid no attention to the rubber floats, the grotesque sea horses and small bobbing lifesavers.

Suddenly Judith said, "Oh, there she is."

Their eyes went to a yellow mattress on wheels. It had been rolled some distance from the pool, and because of its curved awning that formed a private shady little world, it had been difficult to see Ruby. But now they saw her. At least they saw her legs. They saw the ten painted toenails, the golden anklet, the tanned insteps.

By the time they noticed the second pair of legs it was too late to retreat. They had already called a greeting, and Ruby was scrambling off the mattress and coming toward them.

She was wearing one of those incredible bra and G-string outfits that permitted you to see at a glance that she'd never had an appendectomy. Behind her, walking a little slowly, a little doubtfully, came a large blond god in a pair of white trunks.

"This is Jim Clare," Ruby said.

Not for a moment had any of the visiting Marcaboths mistaken him for Simon.

"He's a friend of mine," Ruby said.

It hadn't occurred to them that he was an enemy.

"He was passing by and dropped in for a moment," Ruby said.

They looked at the little yellow world under the curved awning.

"I'm sure surprised to see you," Ruby said.

They believed her, but like good children at a birthday party they handed the presents over.

"This is sure nice of you," Ruby said.

The visitors said nothing. They were thinking that they

needn't have come at all. Ruby wasn't lonely. Ruby had company.

Her company took the flowers and looked questioningly at Ruby. "Shall I put them in water for you?" he asked.

"That would be fine," she said, but as he started toward the dressing room she shook her head at him. "There's no vase in there, Jim. You'll have to take them up to the butler's pantry."

"Okay." He picked up the large cardboard box of roses and departed on his errand.

Solime was impressed by the fact that he did not have to ask any questions about the butler's pantry.

Ruby noticed that another box contained candy. "Maybe I should have had him take that up, too," she said. "It'll get all melted in the sun."

"You could put it in the shade," Enid suggested.

"Yeah, but it would be better up at the house." She raised her voice and shouted for Jim. She called twice but there was no answer. She smiled at her sisters-in-law. "I guess he didn't hear me."

She opened Enid's present and said, "A nightgown. That's swell. Thanks a million."

She opened Judith's present and said, "What's this?"

She opened Solime's present and said, "Perfume. What do you know!"

She put the presents on a white iron chair and crumpled the fancy paper and birthday bows into a noisy, untidy ball.

She smiled and said, "It was sure nice of you to come."

They could think of things to say but they didn't say them. They smiled back at Ruby. Enid wished that she could say, "I see you have a man. And what a dandy one he is. He must be quite a comfort to you."

Maybe she could say it at that. Later she could blame it on the toothache. It was going great right now.

Judith thought: Slut. That's what you are, Ruby Marca-both, a slut. Why don't I tell you so?

But she couldn't say such a thing to Ruby. Not she. If Enid and Solime could tolerate Ruby, then where did she, Judith, have any right to burn?

Solime thought: We needn't stay long. She will not beg us to linger. We will stay a short while, then we will say good-by to our dear sister-in-law and to that nice Mr. Clare and we will walk away as though nothing out of place was going on. And we'll look back over our shoulders and wave to her—no, we'd better not look back.

Ruby said, "Well, you might as well sit down."

They sat down side by side on a wide, tufted couch. It was red and had a red awning over it. They looked at each other and resolved never to buy red umbrellas. The bright reflection of the red from top to bottom enclosed them in a hideously unbecoming light. Flesh took on an unhealthy lavender glow, and a small, blue vein in Judith's temple was all of a sudden almost unbearably evident.

They turned their eyes upon Ruby. Ruby was blonde but not blonde as Enid had once been. Enid had been sleekly, fastidiously blonde. Ruby's hair was wild and tousled. It was twenty shades of gold, all of them natural, all of them sun-bleached on the sands of the most popular, most crowded beaches. Her eyes were brown and she had long, black lashes, and her figure was no stingy little thing but the de luxe package, the economy size all shapely, generous curves. And she was very nearly naked in the expensive scraps of material that she wore about her middle and her bust. The sisters-in-law stared at her and saw that she was perfect, without flaw or blemish, and they dropped their eyes and thought that it would have been fantastic to suppose that all this magnificence had ever been meant for Simon.

Upon Ruby's wrist there blazed a diamond bracelet, and they knew it was her birthday present from her husband and they did not think it was bad taste for Ruby to wear a diamond bracelet at high noon in a swimming pool. This was to be expected of Ruby.

"I got this," she said but she took no notice of the bracelet. Instead she reached over to a small table and picked up a box. She handed it to Enid. Enid opened it, and the three visiting Marcaboths stared at a gray velvet French poodle who wore around his neck a narrow collar of fake rubies. "Jim gave it to me," she said.

They looked away from the stuffed animal. Judith's eyes followed a spider who moved slowly toward some spidery destination. Solime studied the great glare of sunlight in the center of the pool. Enid thought: My tooth aches. It aches too much for me to bother with such things today. Let us stick to simple things like Ruby being an unprincipled, unfeeling little she-pup. Let us not get complicated and take to imagining that she has emotions or sentiments or that the gray velvet poodle will one day remind her of a guy who—no, my tooth aches too much for all that.

Ruby said, "Would you like something to drink? There's stuff in there." She gestured toward the bar. "All kinds of stuff. Soft drinks, too. There's an icebox in case you want—" She broke off and laughed. "Here I am telling you what's in there. You probably used that bar before I was born."

Enid said, "Oh, it's darling of you to say so."

Solime remarked that it must be lunchtime.

"You can stay if you want," Ruby said a little sadly.

They assured her that they wouldn't stay.

"We're going to have a picnic, Jim and me," Ruby said.

Enid thought: I'll just bet you are.

"I figured it would be fun for my birthday to do something different so I gave the servants the day off. You know I figured it would be nice for them to celebrate a little, too. Besides, what did I need them around for? I just had them pack me a lot of sandwiches and stuff and I came down here and then Jim dropped in."

"How convenient," Judith said.

"And then," Ruby went on, "you dropped in." She said it with her dark eyes leveled upon Judith, the lawyer. You dropped in. You did, didn't you? People do drop in, don't they? Then isn't it possible that Jim Clare dropped in? Can you say that, beyond a shadow of a doubt, this meeting was arranged, contrived, designed?

He was back, Ruby's company. He walked toward them

smiling self-consciously. He had the roses most inexpertly bundled into a vase completely unsuited to them. But he had meant well. You could see he meant well. Enid remembered how he had walked toward them when they had first arrived. He had been uncertain how he could help but he had known it wasn't a good moment for Ruby and so he had tagged after her in case she needed him.

"I didn't mean that you should bring them back down here," Ruby said in exasperation. "They look like hell in that thing. You might as well have used a milk bottle."

"You know I thought of using a milk bottle," he said. He set the flowers down on a table in the shade. "They don't look bad there."

Enid got to her feet. So did the others.

Ruby looked at them hopefully.

Solime said, "I suppose you're going up to The House tonight."

"Where?" Ruby asked.

Enid said, "Simon's mother's house." She felt like adding, "You do remember Simon, don't you?"

"Oh, no," Ruby said. "We're not going there."

"We all go on our birthdays."

"I know," Ruby said. "But I'm not going. I'm scared."

Solime said, "You'll find Simon's mother very pleasant when you get to know her."

"I'm scared," Ruby said again.

"But there's nothing to be scared of. She's—" Solime fell silent as she became aware that Ruby was laughing at her.

Ruby was shaking her head and grinning. "I couldn't

go," she said. "I'm too scared." And then she laughed aloud and her eyes met Jim Clare's and she said to him, "You know how scared I am of meeting people, don't you, Jim? I'm a coward."

They looked at Ruby as she stood leaning against the outer wall of the rumpus room and they knew that she was not a coward. They looked at her red mouth and at the brazen, dark eyes. Then they looked away from her and they thought that this one would do as she pleased with her birthday. She had no intention of being bound to spend it with her mother-in-law.

"I'm scared," she said but she was not scared. She was only determined not to be drawn into a plan of traditional behavior. "I'm a coward," she said but she laughed when she said it and they knew that she was laughing at them for they had been great fools and all of them had lost the right to celebrate their birthdays as they chose.

Enid thought that Ruby might be able to postpone a meeting with Zeda Marcaboth forever. A Marcaboth wife who refused to call on Zeda might well be dragged by the hair of her head into her mother-in-law's presence. But a girl who stood in awe of Zeda, who thus implied her own inferiority might well be regarded with sympathetic understanding. Such an attitude could easily win a girl complete freedom from having to spend each and every holiday at The House.

Enid thought that Judith could continue to be known as the clever Mrs. Marcaboth if that gave her any pleasure, but it was Ruby who had figured out how to duck the birthday dinner with Zeda.

Funny thing about a girl like Ruby, Enid thought. She gets what she wants and nobody's ever told her how to get it. She has a natural instinct for doing the very best she can for Ruby. And Enid thought of the furry little animals of the woods who keep themselves fed and sheltered. She thought how right it was that they were not expected to complicate the process by adhering to a code of ethics. She wondered how long it had taken Ruby to learn her way around. Not long, she decided. The furry little animals learned fast and they survived. It was the same with kids like Ruby, kids who were pushed out into the world to make their own way as best they could.

"Shall we go now?" Enid asked the others.

They walked back up the steep little stone steps and past the rock garden. They did not look behind them, down into the hollow where the pool lay green and cool beneath the sun. They walked on across the diamond-shaped lawn where Simon's son and daughter had played as children and they walked through Hannah's kitchen garden and out to the car.

Nobody said a word until they had left the pink house behind them and were almost to Sunset Boulevard. Then Enid spoke.

"I hope you will not mind my suggestion but—but, well, do you see any sense in our telling Wolfe or Garth or Rome that Ruby had a caller this afternoon?"

She looked at Solime as she asked the question, Solime

who was apt to feel it her duty to tell everything she'd thought and seen throughout the day.

It was Judith who surprised Enid. She said, "What are we supposed to do? Play cover up for that chippy?"

Enid thought Judith's choice of words regrettable. They were worse than merely common. They were dated as though Judith had heard such words on the street as a child.

She said, "It's not a matter of covering up, Judith. It's a matter of sex loyalty. Men—and the Marcaboths are no exception—do not think too highly of women. Why should we say to them, 'You're so right. Women are faithless and cheap'?"

Judith said, "I have no objection to saying that Ruby is faithless and cheap."

Enid shrugged. "Say it then. I only thought that Ruby is young. She has adjustments to make with life and maybe she'll make them. Maybe she'll be a good Mrs. Marcaboth one day. She'll have children—"

"Yes. But whose?" Judith demanded.

Enid thought that Judith was almost ugly in that moment. There was a hard, twisted curve to her mouth. Hatred. It could be nothing else but hatred. Enid was disturbed at the thought that Judith wasn't quite hitting on all cylinders. Normal women didn't take to hating a gal just because the gal had a lover.

"What do you think, Solime?" Enid asked. "Are you going to tell Rome?"

Solime shook her head. "Not without reason surely. I'd tell him if I had a reason but—"

"There now, Judith, Solime won't tell and I won't tell so why should you—?"

"Well," Judith said, "Ruby will tell Simon. She's going to figure that we'll talk and that she'll be in deeper hot water if he gets the story through us."

Enid said, "I have a toothache. Kick Ruby's situation around as you choose. I don't give a damn."

Judith was silent. They crossed Wilshire Boulevard and she rolled the car into the parking space of the department store where the cars of the other girls were waiting. They said good-by to her and to each other, and the Marcaboth women scattered—north, east, and west. They made no plans for reuniting. Their husbands would tell them when it was again time for that.

Simon had an appointment at two o'clock. It was an important appointment. Had it been otherwise he would have called it off. It was, after all, Ruby's birthday. He thought that it would have been pleasant to telephone her and say that on account of its being her birthday he was coming home early. Well, he'd telephone her anyhow. He was surprised when the phone didn't answer. Where was Ruby? Where were the servants? Perhaps the phone was out of order. That had to be the reason for his not getting an answer. He thought that he'd wait a bit and try again. If there was still no answer, then he'd have the operator check the line.

The second time Ruby replied.

"Hello, darling."

"Hello, Simon."

"Where were you a few minutes ago?"

She was silent a second. Then, "I must have been in the pool."

He pictured her lying in the sunlight. His imagination traveled slowly over the length of her as she lay spread upon a canvas mattress. He thought that she might be lying on the yellow one. She would be wearing one of those French bathing suit affairs.

"Are you coming home?" Ruby asked.

"I can't. I have an appointment."

"Oh, well," she said.

"Where are the servants?"

"I let them have the day off."

He thought of her lying spread out on the yellow mattress. He heard the soft, contented purr in her voice. He had often heard women sound like that—often. Why did Ruby sound like that just now? He couldn't take the chance. It had been meant as a surprise, but he couldn't take the chance. He said, "Enid and Judith and Solime are coming to see you. They'll be there any minute."

She said, "They've been here and gone."

"Oh."

"They brought presents."

"That was nice of them."

"Yeah."

He said, "I'll come home as soon as I can."

"Okay," Ruby said.

When he had replaced the phone he smiled a small, bitter smile to himself. There was one fine thing about being fifty years old and married to a supercharged organism like Ruby. A man never got sick. At least he never got sick in the middle of the day. He couldn't go home unexpectedly.

But it was all right. If there was anything wrong she'd have told him that she wasn't alone. She'd have to tell him. She couldn't run the risk of Enid and the others telling him. She'd have to say, "Oh, by the way, when the girls dropped in so-and-so was here."

That's the kind of thing she would say if anyone was with her. But it was hard to forget the purring note in her voice.

Miss Cass walked into the office and said, "Mr. Simon, Mr. Iscanun phoned and said he would be a little late for his appointment."

Simon shrugged and did not answer.

"Is it all right, Mr. Simon?"

"You told him it was, didn't you?"

"Yes, I did. With Mr. Iscanun I thought that—"

"And you were right. Quit bothering me already."

Miss Cass went away. Simon was thinking that never before had Mr. Iscanun been late for an appointment but when he was late it had to be on Ruby's birthday. Things always happened like that. With some people you could arrange that they should see Wolfe but not with Iscanun.

He didn't like Wolfe. You could tell when a man didn't like Wolfe. He always said so.

"So today I got Iscanun. On Ruby's birthday I got Iscanun and he has to be late yet."

He thought about Mr. Iscanun and sighed remembering that it had been this Iscanun's father with whom he had once done business. The years waited for no one. Young Iscanun was about twenty-nine, Simon thought. A good-looking fellow—maybe he could dance. Maybe he'd like to go to Mocambo. Simon thought of saying to him, "What are you and Mrs. Iscanun doing tonight?" No, it wouldn't work. Simon remembered that Mrs. Iscanun spoke no English. Still, was that such a drawback? What would Ruby and Mrs. Iscanun have to say to each other anyway?

He wondered how the little visit had gone up at his house. Ruby and her sisters-in-law—he tried to picture what it had been like. It was pretty hard to do. He had no trouble imagining the sort of things the other girls had said, their expressions, their attitudes. He could easily guess in what manner each of his sisters-in-law would react to anything and everything under the sun.

Well, he thought, I know those girls better than I know Ruby. He sighed again. I'm getting old. Like my mother, I welcomed each girl into the family. It seemed to him, as he sat there thinking, that he was as old as Zeda. She was only sixteen when I was born, he thought. The gap is closing between us. We are of the same generation now—my mother and I. To Rome and Solime, to Garth and Judith, I am no younger than my mother. And to Ruby—with a son and daughter older than she is and with grandchildren yet, I shouldn't even think how I must seem to Ruby.

His lips twisted into a small smile as he remembered that he had even seen his mother as a bride—her second marriage of course. He had been twenty-two years old at the time.

He remembered his mother's wedding. It had been in one of those places that had a new name now. He could never remember the new name. His mother had worn velvet of a deep jewel tone and a small hat with sweeping plumes upon it. Simon remembered how the Prince had thrown coins to the poor after the ceremony.

My sense of humor, Simon thought, regretfully. But I couldn't help it. He threw the money so freely, with such wide gestures, and there were such showers of silver coins. All I could think of was my old man whirling in his grave.

But he had been a nice guy, the Prince—such a nice guy. Simon, aged fifty, sitting in his office, felt sudden shame for the twenty-two-year-old Simon who had been suspicious of the Prince's motives in marrying the widow Marcaboth. He shook his head remembering how he had bribed bell-hops and chauffeurs and chambermaids to keep him informed of the Prince's activities.

Such a lovely kid I was, he reflected. And how happy I'd have made my Mama if I could have gone screaming to her with the news that the Prince had a dame and that he was only marrying Mama for her money. I'd have done it, too, if I'd ever gotten anything on Zleki. Kids have such noble ideals. They don't care whose heart they break if only they're being honest little heroes. But there was nothing bad to say of Zleki. He was a good fellow.

And Simon got up from behind his desk and paced the room nervously. It always made him uncomfortable to realize that no one knew how he had felt about Zleki. Wolfe had never appreciated Zleki. He had only appreciated Prince Zleki, and Wolfe's snobbish delight in having his mother a princess had always deviled Simon into belittling the title.

I never belittled Zleki, he thought. But no one ever noticed that I didn't. It's easy for them to be mistaken, to confuse my indifference to the title with indifference to the man.

He thought that he would like to tell his mother how he had felt about Zleki, but he knew that he would never mention Zleki to her except in the most offhand fashion. When she spoke the Prince's name it was always in a stilted, unnatural manner as though she were trying to be someone else in that moment, someone who didn't care that Zleki was dead.

He couldn't talk to Ruby about Zleki either. She hadn't known him. Known him? For God's sake, Ruby had been six years old at the time of Zleki's death.

But Enid had know Zleki. Sometime he'd talk to Enid about him. It would be nice to know that someone would be able to say, "Why, Simon thought the world of Zleki."

Simon suddenly shivered. So where am I going that I want to leave someone behind to tell how I felt about things? I'll do my own talking, please God. He knocked three times on the rosewood table and then knocked three times again just to be on the safe side.

He went back to his desk and sat down. A man of fifty should take it easy. Why? Was fifty so old? Certainly not. A man was still young at fifty, still young even if he was as old as his mother, even if he had seen all the women of the family as brides. He thought about Enid. How old was Enid? He didn't know. She never said how old she was. But he had known her as a bride.

It was the year he had taken Hannah for her first trip to Europe—1930. Simon remembered 1930. People were still reeling from the blow of the stock-market crash. Some were stunned, others hysterical. Later they would learn to accept the depression, but in 1930 they were not yet able to realize that there would be slow, bleak years ahead. They were still looking backward, still trembling with shock. The Marcaboths had had their losses, but they were small losses. The Marcaboths would not need to retrench. Business would decline of course, but costs would decline, too. There was no need to worry. They had lost nothing essential to basic stability.

Zeda and the Prince were in Paris that season. Wolfe had followed them over. He had been expected to stand his first watch as top man in the business so that Simon could take Hannah to Europe. But Wolfe had not considered himself quite ready for so large an assignment.

"Look, Wolfe, Hannah's never been to Europe and I promised her that this year—"

"You can take her next year, Simon."

"But maybe Mama and Zleki won't be there next year. You know Hannah will have a bigger time for herself if Zleki's there to introduce her around."

Wolfe said, "I hadn't thought about that."

"Like hell you hadn't. That's why you want to go so that you can use Zleki to make yourself look important."

"Really, Simon, that's awfully small-minded thinking."

"Listen, you squirt, you give me that phony British accent once more and I'll push your teeth down your throat."

But Wolfe had gone to France that year. He had been quite indifferent as to whether or not Hannah got her trip.

"Don't you worry, Hannah. We'll go," Simon had promised.

"Who's worrying? Europe I can do without, Simon, darling."

Mama had backed Simon up. Hannah should have her trip, Mama said. Hannah was a good girl, and if she had been promised a trip that was all there was to it.

"For six weeks the office can run without a Marcaboth," Mama had written. "With business so slow you could even close the office and no one would notice. But that I only mean jokingly, Simon. Don't close the office. Let that little Mr. Harnizi handle things for you."

So Hannah and he had gone to Paris in 1930. Hannah, Simon liked to remember, had had a wonderful time. Wolfe wasn't in Paris when they arrived. Mama had been fearful that there was bad feeling between the boys and she had packed Wolfe off to visit friends of Zleki's in Nice.

Simon thought about the fun he and Hannah had had in

118

Paris. Vividly it all came back to him: the tremendous suite
in the hotel; the shopping Hannah and Mama had done; the
way they had all laughed that year; how he had sat one day
on the piano bench in Mama's salon and had realized for the
first time that Mama never used to laugh. Her laughter was
new. It was something that had just somehow come along
with Zleki.

Funny how things came back to you. He could see himself again sitting on that piano bench in a room that had
rose-colored draperies and a great many slim, gilt chairs.
Hannah was trying on hats and Mama was laughing and
laughing at some ridiculous mispronunciation of Zleki's. She
had gone on laughing long after everyone else had stopped.
She had laughed as though there was something secret and
delightful about having a husband who couldn't learn
English.

Funny how a thing like that came back to you after
twenty years.

And Simon remembered that it was that day that they
had first read the news about Wolfe. Mama's maid had
brought the Paris paper in, and Simon idly scanning the
front page had seen the words: "Caldwell Beasley denies
daughter's engagement."

This was interesting already. Caldwell Beasley was an
important American. If you were home you wouldn't
bother to read an item about him and a scrap he was having
with a daughter you hadn't even known existed till now.
But you were an American in a strange country, and things
that went on with other Americans was serious business.

"Interviewed last night Mr. Beasley said, 'My daughter is certainly not engaged. If she were I would have announced it.' When informed by a representative of this newspaper that Mr. Wolfe Marcaboth had confided to intimates that he and Mr. Beasley's beautiful daughter, Enid, would be married some time this month Mr. Beasley replied, 'This young man is dreaming. He's an opportunist from the slums of New York and I strongly advise him to refrain from giving his imagination such free rein.' "

Simon remembered Mama drawing him into her room to discuss the situation.

"You believe this is all true, Simon?"

"Yes, I believe it is."

"And Wolfe is going to marry this Beasley girl?"

"Sure. It's a big romance. The whole world loves a lover. All Paris will be crazy about a boy from the slums and a girl brave enough to defy her papa. It'll be the talk of the town. Sure, Wolfe will marry her."

"You think they could be happy?"

"Her I don't know, Mama, but Wolfe will be happy. He saw a girl and because she was Caldwell Beasley's daughter he had to have her. I always knew Wolfe would find a wife who'd go with that accent of his."

"Perhaps he loves her."

"Mama, wake up. We're talking about Wolfe. He could love somebody? Who are you trying to fool?"

He remembered Mama standing there in that room in Paris, looking worried and sad. "I want him to be happy," she said. "I wouldn't care if he married a beggar girl, God forbid, if only he was happy."

"He'll be. He'll be. Wolfe's a man of very simple tastes. All he wants out of life are the things that he thinks were meant for somebody bigger and better than himself."

Wolfe had returned from Nice unexpectedly. He had simply walked into the suite one morning when they were all having breakfast. And he had Enid with him. Even after all this time Simon hadn't forgotten his first glimpse of Enid.

There may have been a more beautiful girl, he thought, but I don't know where.

They had, all four of them, eyed Enid in startled amazement, the Prince even losing a split second in getting to his feet at her entrance.

If he hadn't stood up I never would have thought of it. I was like a fellow who'd been hypnotized.

Simon recalled the large, violet eyes, the pale and lovely complexion. None of them had ever seen hair like Enid's. It was pure moonlight.

And he had thought as he had looked at her: This can't be any good. She couldn't be that beautiful and be someone you could like.

He remembered how, after a time, he had managed to tear his eyes away from Enid. He had looked at his brother and had seen the smug contentment upon Wolfe's face—the guy who just filled an inside straight, Mr. Self-Satisfied. Simon's heart hurt for the radiance, the quiet joy in the eyes of the girl whom Wolfe had brought to them. She was in love. She had given up her family and fortune for Wolfe.

This was what she had been born for, to feel alive, to be living and giving for someone. And that someone was Wolfe, and Wolfe could only look smug and feel nothing but a curious, reverse pride in having won a woman who was too good for him.

And Simon had looked at Enid and thought: Why are you marrying him? Don't be a fool. You can have anybody you want, sweetheart, and this brother of mine is no prize. His disposition, believe me, a hyena would be ashamed to have.

"And I told Enid that she could stay here with you, Mother, until the wedding."

Mama had kept nodding and saying, "Sure. Sure." Mama had liked Enid right away. In that first moment she had been satisfied that Wolfe had made no mistake. It never occurred to Mama to worry that perhaps Enid had made one. It was a lie that women stick together.

And Simon remembered what Hannah had said when she and he were alone: "Darling, it is a good world, you know. For all his cynicism, Simon, your brother was able to recognize true sweetness when he saw it and he fell in love just like anybody else and it wouldn't have mattered to him if Enid had been a nobody."

Simon had said, "Sure, sure, Hannah, and tomorrow being Easter why don't you hurry down to the Place Vendome and watch the bunny rabbits lay a few pink eggs?"

"Tomorrow's not Easter, Simon."

"No, and rabbits don't lay eggs, but I'll tell you something, Hannah, it would be a better world if they did."

"Why, Simon?"

"I don't know. Today it just seems to me like it would be a better world if just once on an Easter Sunday morning a rabbit would lay an egg."

It didn't happen. No rabbits laid any eggs and Enid and Wolfe were married in Paris that year—1930.

And the Marcaboths had gone to the wedding and had beamed upon the bride and groom and Zeda had folded the blonde girl in her arms and her embrace had been as warm as the one in which she had held Hannah.

They had accepted Enid. And Enid had accepted the Marcaboths and all the good and all the bad that came with them. She had accepted the petty tyrannies and the warmth of their affection, the demands upon her time and the loyalty they gave her. She had accepted the idea of Zeda as high priestess and herself as the new and therefore least worthy member of the tribe. In short, Enid had accepted her golden goblet.

Quite a gal, Simon thought. He was thinking now of how gently, how sweetly Enid had always greeted Hannah's little foolish comments and ideas. Never once did Hannah guess how smart Enid was. Poor Hannah thought that she and Enid were both two little dumbbells together. Enid was wonderful to her right to the end. And who did Hannah speak of that last night? Her kids? Me? No. She spoke of her sister Enid. Her sister yet.

And he thought of the other brides he had welcomed into the family—Judith and Solime. To mention them in the same breath was ridiculous. Solime was an angel, but an angel. Judith was— Simon shrugged. His brother Garth had married her. Who could tell why? Maybe it was because everybody didn't look the same to everybody else. Maybe to some people Solime would be just another girl and Judith something sensational. No, that couldn't be. So cockeyed as that nobody was.

He thought of the thing his son referred to as "Human Relations." The words amused Simon. Who didn't have human relations? Everybody's relations were human. Or was there somewhere a guy whose uncle was maybe a bull-finch? Human relations didn't mean that though, he remembered. It meant something else. It meant how you got along with this one or that one—how they seemed to you, what you felt about them, how, for instance, Judith could look like nothing to him and like heaven to Garth.

Things can be that way, he said to himself. It's the truth. What my brother Wolfe thinks I am is not what my brother Garth or my brother Jerome thinks. To my Mama I probably stack up as something between Little Boy Blue and Master-mind. We look different to different people. Maybe I am the only one who knows that Enid is wonderful. Maybe the girls dislike her. Who can tell? And Mama has her faults and maybe some people could hold them against her.

And he thought that maybe it wouldn't be too hard to find Mama a little tough to like if you hadn't known her for fifty years, if you didn't know all that an old friend like Mama's first-born knew about Mama.

She's got faults. So all right, Mama's got faults. Has

she got any big, terrible ones? Sure, she has. So what? And he thought that it was funny that Mama was able to browbeat him, scare him, make him feel like a bad kid and still remain a woman who somehow needed his protection and his superior masculine mind.

This trick is not done with mirrors, he thought. It's that thing again—human relations. Maybe to some people Mama would just be—like any other old woman. Maybe. But such people I would like to meet. They might be interesting to talk to.

One man's opinion was different from another man's. That was human relations—pure and simple. It was the same old thing again—Judith and Garth. To Garth, Judith was one thing, to Simon another.

He was not proud of the part he had played where Judith was concerned. He had never been too crazy about Judith. He had never completely understood what had attracted Garth to her. She was a brilliant girl no doubt, but this had never seemed to Simon a satisfactory explanation. Was it possible that a man ever married a girl because she had a fine mind?

This I do not believe. It is against Nature for a man to think, "With this woman I want to sleep for the rest of my life because she has the finest mind I ever encountered." No, it can't be.

But still, what had Garth seen in Judith? Not that Judith was ugly. She wasn't. She looked like everybody else. That was the whole trouble as Simon saw it. Judith was the kind of girl about whom people always said, "Doesn't she remind you of so-and-so?" She had dark hair that she parted on the side. If only in the middle just once. But no, it was always parted on the side, and it looked nice and it had the gleam that thirty-five-dollar permanents give to the hair of neat, dark women. She had brown eyes—naturally. She had good teeth, a straight nose, and an average complexion. She wore a clear red lipstick on a mouth that was neither large nor small, and in the summertime when she got tanned she always peeled a little bit.

When Simon had first seen her he had thought: She's the kind that when she disappears, the police can never find her. And this was Garth's beloved.

Garth had said, "She's dark and very, very good-looking." That was before Simon had met Judith.

Afterward Garth had asked excitedly, "Well, Simon, what do you think of her?"

Simon had replied, "You're absolutely right, Garth. She's dark."

And Simon had asked his mother, "What gives? What's with that girl that makes Garth think she's so terrific?"

His mother had said, "Simon, you're forty years old now. I'm ashamed that you still ask simple questions."

"What do you mean simple questions? Do you know what he sees in her?"

"Yes, I know. He sees what you saw in Hannah."

"Well, for God's sake, at that age Hannah was pretty and she had a good figure and a cute smile."

Mama had said, "Sure, and that love affair involved Simon and Hannah and therefore is very understandable. Whereas this one merely concerns itself with Garth and Judith, two completely uninteresting people."

"Mama—frankly I'm not crazy about Judith."

"Frankly nobody asked you. Frankly you're not going to marry her and I'll give you another frankly, Simon. She's not a girl I'd have picked for Garth, but if Garth would let me pick a girl for him or if he'd let his big brother, Simon, pick a girl for him I'd die at the embarrassment of having such a jellyfish for a son."

"Okay, Mama, I can take a hint."

But Judith had no poise or polish. She wore the wrong clothes and said the wrong things. She always seemed nervous and possessed by a terrible fear that she would upset her water glass or burn a hole in the rug.

He had asked Hannah about Judith. "What's the matter with her?"

"Honey, there's nothing wrong with Judith. She's as sweet as she can be. She's just trying too hard."

"What's she trying?"

"To please everybody. It's a hard thing for a girl, Simon. She thinks we're all looking at her and judging her and wondering if she's good enough for Garth."

"Well, of course that's exactly what we're doing."

"Oh, we are not. We know what a fine girl Judith is."

"We do?"

"Of course. She's just so nervous—"

"Now wait a minute, Hannah. Do you think she was nervous when she was all alone in the store picking out that lousy pink dress she wore the other night?"

127

"Simon, didn't you ever buy anything that you later regretted buying?"

"Sure, I did. Did she say she was sorry about that pink dress?"

"No," Hannah admitted. "But I'm sure she must be."

Judith never wore the pink dress again. She was from a family where money was scarce. With them a dress would not ordinarily be worn once and then discarded. Simon's curiosity had been aroused, and he had questioned Hannah.

"Did you tell Judith not to wear that dress again?"

"I, Simon?" Hannah's soft, velvety eyes looked at him in wonder. "You know I could not have hurt her feelings so. How could I have told her that it was not suitable or becoming?"

He had asked his mother, and she had gazed up at him from the ebony and ivory chess table at which she was solving a problem.

"No, Simon, I did not concern myself with the pink dress. I looked at it and then I looked away. It was in bad taste and what was worse than bad taste was the way it robbed the girl of any beauty she may possess. But I did not tell her to stop wearing it."

"It would have been a kindness to tell her."

"So kind I am not, Simon."

"An intelligent girl would welcome someone telling her that she looked awful in it."

"No, Simon, no. When people say, 'Oh, I'm so glad you told me,' they do not mean it. They are hurt and they go away and cry and after a while they stop crying. They dry their eyes and they see the sense of what you said and they don't make the same mistake again. They are better for what you have told them. They have improved a little bit, and everything is fine except that all the rest of their lives they hate you."

"She wouldn't hate you, Mama."

"Strictly a Marcaboth viewpoint." Her eyes had gone back to the ivory figures on the chess table. Thoughtfully she moved a bishop and sat turning over in her mind the wisdom of what she had done.

"Mama, you think Judith realized the dress was wrong?"

Zeda had not looked up from the chess table. "Only after she was told."

"Who told her?"

"Garth."

"He told her?"

"Yes. And she will not hate him because she cannot hate him. Garth told her, and now I understand why she is not easy with herself when she is with us. A girl can rest even among enemies if she knows that there is one man present who thinks her perfect. But there is no rest for a girl whose man says, 'Of course I love you, but why don't you dress as my brother's wife does?' "

Simon had taken a moment to think that over. Then he had said, "Garth can't be crazy about her if he—"

"Life isn't that simple. Things get mixed up in men's minds. He's crazy about her and she looks beautiful to him, but he knows that everyone is not crazy about her and that she does not look beautiful to everyone. He will pester her and torment her and maybe drive her mad all because he loves her and wants his judgment vindicated. He wants his family and his friends to say, 'Behold the wonderful woman Garth Marcaboth has married.' No one will ever say it, and he will always believe they would have if only Judith had tried a little harder."

Mama had stood up and walked away from the chess table. "Judith is going to New York. Garth is sending her to your sister's house as a child is sent away to school. She will stay a few weeks, and when she comes back she is expected to be a perfect carbon copy of a thirty-nine-year-old woman who took fifteen years to learn all that she knows today."

"That's not fair. Someone ought to tell Garth that it's not fair."

"Somebody already told him and he said, 'Mama, Judith is grateful for the chance to go.'"

"Well," Simon had said, "after all it's their business."

"Sure, but there's more to it. He's got a whole plan. It amounts to a plot against the girl."

"As long as it doesn't concern me I guess I'd better—"

"It'll concern you but we stick with Garth. Right or wrong we stick with Garth."

Judith had gone to New York. On a visit, Garth had said, but presently Garth had followed her to his sister's house, and then one day Zeda had called Hannah.

"Hannah, darling, would you and Simon like a trip to New York? Just the three of us. I thought it would be fun. You're my guests."

130

They had accepted the invitation and had wound up as members of Garth's wedding party.

"I had no idea," Hannah said, "that Garth and Judith were going to be married. When we left here it never entered my mind that they'd be married in New York. It only goes to show you how things happen. You never know, do you?"

Zeda had smiled. "No, Hannah, darling, everything in life is a surprise, especially to you."

Now as Simon thought back to the wedding of Judith and Garth he felt pity for Judith. Judith had never had a chance to state what she might have liked in the way of a wedding. She was surrounded by Marcaboths, beaten down by them, taken over completely.

I'll bet she didn't even get a chance to pick out her own wedding dress, he thought. She was in awe of us. She didn't dare open her mouth to say no. We really took over.

He remembered how bewildered Judith had looked at the reception. She hadn't know a single guest. She had stood with a little stiff smile on her face doing her best to look happy.

I was a help to her, he thought, bitterly. I gave her that extra glass of champagne, the one that started her crying. He remembered that he had wondered what she was crying about.

Hannah had said, "All brides cry."

"Oh, they do not. You just made that up."

"So it hurts somebody if I just made it up? Simon, you are

always looking for some fault to find with Judith. Wouldn't you cry if you were a bride in a room full of strangers?"

"We're not strangers."

"No, we're friends with everybody here. But who is Judith's friend? Look at the poor girl. She doesn't know whether it's proper to shake hands or give kisses or just say, 'How do you do.' She doesn't know anybody, and nothing that she learned at law school is going to help her today and so she cries, and to me it seems like she's doing the sensible thing."

"She's crying because she's had too much champagne."

"Too much champagne, he says. Believe me, Simon, she's had too much of everything."

Simon remembered that Hannah had gone to Judith then and had spirited her away to a quiet corner of the house. Nobody had missed Judith. She was the kind of a girl who even on her wedding day, even wearing her white satin and veil, could walk away without her departure being marked.

The wedding had taken place in 1940 and Judith still hadn't learned to take her position with casual calm. She was still trying, still straining, but she made no real blunders and she fulfilled her obligations to the family.

We are not ashamed of Judith, Simon thought. We have had no cause to be. She is Garth's wife and we are all very proud of her. And he thought about Garth's beautiful children and the house in Beverly Hills that was certainly not under inspirational management but where everything ran efficiently and smoothly.

There, Simon thought, the servants serve a well-cooked

roast. You know what you're going to get. Never will you find in Judith's house one of those fancy, imaginative dinners that can turn out to be either wonderful or terrible. With her it's roast, and you're not going to be thrilled but you're not going to be starved either. With Judith there's no surprises and there's no disappointments.

And he wondered if at last he had stumbled upon the clue to Judith's charm. Was this what Garth had seen in her? Were there men who hated surprises, who despised the unattainable woman, who had no interest in a drawn curtain? Maybe Garth was such a man. It could be that Judith had won her golden goblet on her talent for being predictable and more than a little boresome.

Go figure people, Simon thought. Garth wanted Judith, and as it turns out it wasn't a bad choice, but I would never have wanted Judith. Me, I'm a fellow who sometimes likes to go home wondering what's going to be for dinner.

And he thought of Solime, the latest bride—if one didn't count Ruby. Solime had been the 1942 model. Of course the Marcaboths had known long before 1942 that Solime would marry Rome. She was the natural choice, the daughter of David Galal. They had known it long before Solime had known it, Simon thought. As Galal's daughter any family would hope to take Solime to their hearts, but the Marcaboths had looked at their handsome Rome with great satisfaction. Any girl would want him, even David Galal's daughter.

Simon thought how he had watched Solime grow up. He

remembered that at twelve years old she had been a long-legged little thing in pigtails. He had sat with David Galal on the patio of the Galal house sipping a Cuba Libre and discussing the new wing of the hospital. The Marcaboths would naturally contribute. The Marcaboths could be depended upon for any figure David named.

"With hospitals we don't ask for terms, David. What is needed?"

They had sat there, he and David, with their cool drinks and, below them on the lawn, Solime in dungarees had frolicked with a family of red Irish setters. And when she smiled up at her father Simon had seen the braces on her teeth and he had laughed quietly to himself. My sister-in-law, he had thought. My sister-in-law.

He had watched her grow, approving the way that the Galals raised her. And through the years as Solime grew Simon had reported faithfully to his mother on her progress.

"The Galal daughter has gone away to school. David showed me a picture of her today."

"So?"

"So she is beautiful."

"Yes, I know. She has those yellow eyes like her mother."

"With kind of a misty, dreamy look."

Zeda said, "I bet she needs glasses. Nearsighted people always look like they're thinking poetic thoughts."

"Glasses she don't need, Mama. If she needed them, she'd wear them."

"Well, maybe just for reading or close work."

"Close work! Like when the daughter of David Galal darns socks, I suppose."

"I'd be surprised if she didn't know how. What do you think of that?"

Simon had said, "Maybe, Mama. Maybe. But if you want Rome to like her it's more important about the yellow eyes. She is very slim and she has a soft line to her mouth like she was gentle and sweet."

"Well, isn't she?"

Simon had smiled. "Mama, I don't know her. With me it's always 'Good evening, Mr. Marcaboth' or 'Good night, Mr. Marcaboth.' She's a little distant with me. You know we haven't told her yet that I'm going to be her brother-in-law."

Zeda had said, "No. We haven't told Rome yet either. He doesn't even know the girl is alive. He only goes over there to visit her brother."

"At his age he isn't thinking about girls."

Simon reached over to the silver box on his desk and selected a cigarette. He chose it carefully as though there was a difference between one or the other of the same brand. He lit the cigarette and drew on it without being aware of it at all. He was remembering how Rome's interest in girls had awakened long before Mama had known anything about it. There was no way Mama could know. Rome wasn't interested in the kind of girls Mama knew.

It scared hell out of me, Simon remembered. He shook his head recalling the fears he had had. Such girls he chased around with. Honest tramps. They never tried to fool anybody. A block away you could look at one of Rome's girls and know already that she was a tramp.

Simon thought how he had considered the problem of Rome's behavior too big for him to handle alone. He remembered that he had even had a faint suspicion that it was officious of him to think it his right to deal with the situation singlehanded. He had naturally turned to Wolfe, the second oldest male Marcaboth. He had drawn a brief outline of Rome's recent activities.

"I've run into him with a couple of these gals. I tell you they're something. It's a disgrace. Anything could happen when a fellow takes up with tarts like he's running with."

Wolfe had listened, his face impassive and cold. Once he had smiled icily, and Simon had been prepared by the smile for what had followed.

"Aren't you making an awful lot out of nothing, Simon? Rome is a brother, you know, not a sister. Custom doesn't require him to be virtuous."

"It isn't his virtue I'm worried about. A man needs virtue like he needs an appendix but, for God's sake, he can be a little careful, can't he?"

"I wouldn't worry, Simon."

"Why wouldn't you worry? Is he carrying some kind of a magic charm? A rabbit's foot maybe from a lucky rabbit who happened to have five feet? Cripes, this is to worry."

In the end Simon had had to handle the matter alone. Not that there had been anything to handle. Rome had simply said, "Simon, I'm not ready to marry yet."

"No, but couldn't you go with nice girls even so?"

"I'll go with nice girls when I'm looking for a wife. Right now I'm not interested in nice girls."

"You should be ashamed."

"Quit knocking yourself out about me, Simon. When I marry you'll be proud of my wife. I'll bring home a girl as pretty as Enid, as sweet as Hannah, and as intelligent as Judith. How will that be?"

Simon thought back to that conversation and smiled. Rome had almost made good his promise. Certainly Solime came awfully close to filling the bill. He remembered how Solime had looked on her wedding day—those yellow eyes of hers. And what a wedding it had been. A war wedding with the sadness of imminent parting upon it, but there was no denying that war also touched a wedding with a little extra glamor.

He remembered how he had looked at Solime that day and had thought of the kid in pigtails and dungarees, and when he kissed his new sister-in-law he had said to her, "God bless you, darling," and he had felt that she was his daughter, and he had been almost resentful of David Galal who was claiming Solime as his own.

He had wanted to say to Rome, "Be careful of this gentle young thing."

But he had not said it, and he knew now that it had not needed saying. A man could guess how Rome treated his wife. A man could guess it by the way Rome never used a strong word in the presence of Solime, by the way he was so

137

careful about what sort of people were presented to her.

Simon was startled by the thought that came to him then. Had Rome refused the invitation for tonight because he considered Ruby an unsuitable associate for Solime? Oh, no, this couldn't be. Ruby was a member of the family. She belonged. Besides, Rome had sent Solime with a present to Ruby. It must be that Rome had spoken the truth when he had said that he and Solime had another engagement. Ruby was a Marcaboth. Rome would realize that. Rome would know that even Solime must accept another Mrs. Marcaboth, even Solime, whose golden goblet had been the one given with the greatest joy, could not be rated too fine for the woman whom Simon, the first-born, had married.

And Simon thought about Ruby's golden goblet. Tonight it should have been given. But Ruby had pled with him to spare her the ordeal.

"Simon, the thought of your mother terrifies me. I can't go. Please don't tell her when my birthday comes. I am nobody, Simon, and she is so wonderful, from all I hear, so elegant."

What could you do when a girl was nervous about a thing? Could you force her? Could you make her miserable by dragging her where she did not want to go? No, a thing like this you couldn't do to a poor young girl. Next year she'd get her golden goblet. Next year he'd tell his mother how frightened Ruby had been and they'd all laugh together about it.

Sure. We'll laugh. Ha ha. I can hear my mother laughing

now as she pulls the bloody knife out of my heart. God, is she going to be furious! But still, what can I do?

It was a good thing that Mama didn't know it was Ruby's birthday. There was dismal satisfaction in knowing that though his brothers had been unable—or unwilling—to help him entertain Ruby tonight, at least none of them would tattle to Mama. None of them or their wives would ever carry a tale to Mama.

We got a union, he thought, a fine union. We're organized against Mama, and we're so strong we can always do what we want unless she says no.

The thought struck him funny and he laughed, but his face sobered immediately. He still hadn't settled the problem of where to take Ruby tonight, what to do with her so that at bedtime he might ask, "Well, was it a nice birthday?" without fearing that she would reply, "How the hell could it be a nice birthday? What did we do?"

Well, what was there to do? It was growing late. Some preparations would have to be made. What was there to do? After all, in Los Angeles there were only a certain number of things— But why stay in Los Angeles? Of course. Why hadn't he thought of it before? He could get away. Why didn't they go out of town for a couple of days? They could go anywhere, and if the trip started this evening it would take care of the big question of doing something that would please Ruby on her birthday.

He picked up the phone and called her. She answered lazily, sleepily, "Yes."

"This is the chairman of the entertainment committee."

"Who?"

All right, so she wasn't sharp.

"This is Simon."

"Oh, hello."

"I just had a thought. How would you like to go on a trip?"

"Where?"

"Anywhere. Canada maybe."

"What's up there?"

"Canadians. Or maybe you'd like to go to San Francisco. It's a good town. We could fly or take the train—whatever you wanted. What do you say?"

"Let me think about it."

"What's there to think about?"

"How do I know whether I want to go or not if you don't give me time to think it over? I'll tell you when you get home."

"Okay."

"What time will you be here?"

"I don't know. I'll call you before I leave."

"That's a good idea."

"Why? Why is it a good idea?"

"Because I want to know when to expect you. I'm lonely."

Maybe she was lonely. It was possible. A thing like this could happen. He went over and looked at himself in the mirror. The white streak in his hair was certainly a distinguished touch. He wasn't a bad-looking guy. He wasn't fat or droopy-jowled. Certainly he didn't look fifty.

Not bad, he thought, eying himself in the glass. Not bad at all. Say, maybe she could be lonely.

It had grown chilly on the terrace and Zeda Marcaboth had come indoors. She was in her private sitting room now, checking over in her mind the details attendant upon Ruby's birthday dinner. The menu had been arranged and Miss Blount had brought the flowers. She had selected those curious little leopard-spotted orchids for Ruby, and Zeda had not protested the choice. They were probably as good as anything for Ruby. At The House gardenias were Solime's flower, violets were for Judith, and of course roses for Enid. Zeda had no doubt that orchids were for Ruby. At any rate Miss Blount was busy at the moment creating a design for the table. In the center of the design there would be a heap of these little leopard-spotted things. To Zeda the flower looked both wicked and jolly. She had no quarrel with such a flower. She had met people like that, only not enough of them. She doubted that Ruby was wicked and jolly. She was probably a very dull young woman.

She wondered what she would discuss with Ruby. As she had flowers for her daughters-in-law so she had topics. World conditions were for Judith. That was an easy one. You could let your mind wander and just groan at suitable intervals. Solime liked to hear family stories to remember for Adin and some day for Adin's children. This was harder. Zeda made up most of the stories and attributed them to Marcaboth or his father or sometimes she gave her family

141

a little credit. Since they were complete tissues of lies, it was difficult to keep the stories from contradicting each other. Enid was the easiest of all three. She liked music. Zeda played records for her and then they discussed the composition or the performance. Poor Hannah. She, of course, had talked children and home. Well, Zeda had known how to talk her language. But Hannah would not come to visit any more. Ruby would come instead. And what would she speak of to Ruby?

Zeda wondered who would tell Ruby that she was expected to call on her mother-in-law two or three afternoons a month.

And, Zeda thought, what will Ruby and I talk about if anyone does tell her that she's expected?

Well, the menu and the flowers were settled. What else now? Of course there was the golden goblet. Miss Blount had brought that from the vault. Zeda sat with her fingers twined around the slim, golden stem. For the thousandth time she studied the minute details of the workmanship, the wonder of proportion and balance.

I will give one to each of my boy's wives, she thought, and to the wives of my grandsons as long as the goblets hold out.

And she turned the goblet that would be Ruby's in her hand and she thought that this was the second to the Simon Marcaboth branch. She could have taken Hannah's back, she thought, but Hannah's son had wanted it.

I'll have him give it to his wife when he marries, she thought. That will save me one goblet there.

142

She wondered if any of her other sons would ever have a second wife. No. Enid would probably outlive Wolfe. She was the type who either took an overdose of sleeping pills or lived to be a hundred. With women like Enid it was always one or the other. Enid wouldn't take an overdose. She would live forever. And of course Judith and Solime were young.

Before either of them die, I'll have given up worrying about the goblets, Zeda thought, drearily.

As well as the goblet there would have to be a birthday present for Ruby. What should it be? Zeda had no need to shop in the ordinary way. The house was filled with precious objects. She could give Ruby a golden candelabrum or a jade necklace, an ivory figurine or a fan of priceless lace. What should it be?

"What shall it be?" she asked as she heard Miss Blount's step behind her.

"I was thinking of that," Miss Blount said. "You mean of course what will you give Mrs. Simon for a present?"

"Of course."

"What about that dear little picture frame with the pearls and brilliants?"

Zeda grunted. "What will she put in it? A picture of Mr. Simon?"

"Why not?"

"Because I am going to give it to Mr. Jerome one day. His Solime will look well in it."

"Yes, she certainly will." Miss Blount drew her brows together and concentrated. "Now let me see—would Mrs.

Simon like one of those high-backed carved chairs for her dressing room?"

Zeda gave her a withering glance. "That would be fine," she said. "Mr. Simon can drive one of the trucks up here tonight instead of his car. And he can bring two moving men with him to dinner."

"I just thought—"

Zeda said, "You just thought! You mean you just spoke. It isn't the same thing."

Miss Blount lowered her eyes. She counted ten very slowly, and as she counted she told herself that all elderly ladies were difficult.

When she raised her eyes she said, "What about jewelry?"

"What about it?"

"Her name is Ruby—Mrs. Simon's name, you know. Would you like to give her something from your jewel box? You have several things with rubies."

Zeda nodded. "That's right. I have."

"There's a little pinky ring with rubies and there's a couple of pins. Then of course there's that pendant with the single ruby in it." Miss Blount's speech ended in a rising inflection. In this way she managed to state what was in the jewel box and at the same time, with the same words suggest the question: "Shall I go get them?"

"Yes, go get them," Zeda said.

Miss Blount scampered away. Zeda sat quietly, her fingers still twined about the stem of the golden goblet. She thought that probably she would give Ruby the pendant, or maybe one of the pins. It was a good idea to give her something with a ruby, Zeda thought. It was the obvious thing. That was one of Miss Blount's most engaging qualities, her penchant for never overlooking the obvious.

I will give her the pendant or maybe one of the pins. Whichever I give her it will have rubies in it and it will have cost a lot of money.

And to think that Ruby did not even know that she was coming here tonight. Soon I will call Simon and tell him. It was maddening that she would not be able to see the expression on Simon's face. It was a grave injustice that she should be cheated of seeing his astonishment.

Who could have expected such childish goings-on with Simon? At his age a man should be sensible. He should be able to meet all contingencies with utter composure. It was unthinkable that a man of fifty should behave like a schoolboy, hiding things from his mother and trying to avoid natural family obligations.

The idea of trying to keep Ruby's birthday a secret. All he had to do was phone and say, "Look, Mama, Ruby's birthday is coming up but we're going to spend it doing thus and such." I wouldn't have been mad at them. I would have simply, calmly explained that they had to come here. That's all. I wouldn't have shouted or made a scene. So why didn't he let me know he was trying to get out of coming?

Simon, she thought, had been smarter as a boy than he was now. He must have been smarter. A loony couldn't have learned all that he learned.

No, he was no loony, she thought. And she remembered

Simon as a boy learning the rug business, working so hard but always somehow holding back enough reserve energy to do for her anything that she asked of him. It had always been Simon who ran to the store for the forgotten loaf of bread or moved the piano or carried the heavy wash baskets down from the roof. And the memory of the boy who had been Simon softened her and she thought: He is no loony now. He is a fine man but I must have my little fun with him today.

And she thought about having her little fun with Simon. She would pretend that everything was as usual, that he had not tried to avoid spending the evening with her. That would be more nerve-wracking for him than a scene, she thought. It would teach him a lesson. What kind of a lesson? Simon was never again going to have a new wife. When a man of fifty married a girl twenty years old, the chances of his outliving her were slight. Simon would die before Ruby. It was not pleasant to think of Simon dying. Zeda sat quietly listening to the tick of the clock. It was not the first time in her life that she had realized that each relentless tick brought them all closer to the grave—herself, Simon, even young Jerome and his pretty Solime.

But there are Adin and Kenneth and Lorna and the other grandchildren.

Tick tock. Tick tock.

Yes, I know, but they will have children before they die. The Marcaboths as a family will survive.

Tick tock. Tick tock.

Of course. But time is not always the conqueror. We

live in other ways aside from the mere business of breathing and existing in the flesh.

Tick tock. Tick tock.

She turned away from the clock already bored with the discussion. At six Annette would come from the beauty shop. I will wear black velvet, she thought. And I will have beautiful, thick white braids wound about my head. They were once black braids, shining black braids, and they were mine. That, after all, is the important thing. They were mine.

And she thought that her thick, black braids had not been stylish at all. They had been foreign-looking, and for that reason they had made people think of greenhorn servant girls, immigrants who had come carrying all their worldly possessions in their hands.

But I was an American, Zeda Marcaboth thought. And I have lived long enough to see all kinds of girls buying false hair so that they can have braids as I had them. Perhaps everything in life is only a matter of living long enough.

But how long could a person live? Only a short span of time, a miserably short span of time. Not long enough. Not long enough.

Tick tock. Tick tock.

Enid drove through the green quiet of Bel-Air thinking that if the whisky had helped her toothache she would have had another drink the minute she got home. But the whisky hadn't helped. The tooth was still aching.

She entered the large, white Colonial house by the door that opened into the sun room. She wanted no lunch and she did not care to be coaxed. But as she crept stealthily toward the back stairs there was Katherine.

"Have you had your lunch, Mrs. Marcaboth?"

"Yes, thank you."

"I could bring you a little something on a tray."

"I've had my lunch, Katherine."

"A little sandwich perhaps. I could bring it to your room."

Enid climbed the back stairs without replying. In another moment she would snap at poor Katherine. Why was it that people who had only your interests at heart were often so damned irritating?

Enid walked along the upstairs corridor to her room. She went in and shut the door behind her and immediately removed her clothes. She slipped into a dressing gown and collapsed on the chaise longue. She lay perfectly quiet giving herself up to the throbbing tooth. It was operating on some mechanical system all its own. Off. On. Off. On. Like a neon sign.

Maybe it's even lighting up, she thought. It was silly to have undressed. She had to see a dentist—if not her own, then somebody else's. But first she would try the one she knew. There was just a chance that— This time she actually managed to get him on the phone.

"Gosh," he said with repulsive boyishness, "I wish I could fit you in today but I'm absolutely swamped."

She knew he didn't believe that she was in real pain. She

knew that if he believed it he would either find time for her now or else keep the office open past the regular hour. She knew that dentists were, as a general thing, decent, understanding fellows. She didn't blame him for not crediting her story of a throbbing ache that felt as though little men with red-hot knives were playing mumbledy-peg in her mouth.

He knew her husband. He knew Wolfe as a dentist knows a patient—Mr. Wolfe Marcaboth, pleasant gentleman, two gold inlays, inclination toward heavy tartar but very conscientious about having it removed. Prompt at keeping appointments—and excellent pay. That's the way the dentist knew Wolfe.

He wouldn't understand or believe if she said, "Listen, when I called this morning I was in agony. I'm still in agony but I had to go see my sister-in-law, Ruby. Now you think the tooth couldn't have ached much if I went skylarking off to see Ruby, don't you? That's because you don't know Wolfe. He'd have made my life miserable if I hadn't gone. He's mean. He's cold and he's mean and when he says, 'Jump,' I jump. Now, for God's sake, break down."

No, she didn't blame the dentist for thinking she had ridiculously exaggerated her pain. She'd better try doing a few of the things he'd suggested. She could start with another aspirin anyhow. That might help. Why? It hadn't helped up to now. But if she held the little aspirin in her hand and told it about Wolfe, maybe it would get to feeling sorry for her and really go to work.

Later I'll take a sleeping pill, she thought. If I take it now

I'll be up all night. So what? Why is it nicer to be in misery during the daylight hours? I don't know but it is. Anyone will tell you the same thing. The dark hours are the worst. Always the dark hours are the worst.

After she had taken the aspirin she went back to the chaise longue. Maybe the pain would let up. Maybe she wouldn't have to bother with a strange dentist. If it hadn't been for Ruby's birthday, everything would be all right now. The damn tooth would probably be out.

She touched her cheek and discovered that there was swelling. Infection. Infection, blood poison, death—that was the regular thing. And next week a really sad play about a girl who died from a hangnail. Oh, hell. You didn't die from a toothache. You only wished you would. She had been such a fool not to have told Wolfe that she couldn't possibly go to Ruby's. She imagined what the conversation between Simon and Ruby would have been under similar conditions.

Ruby: I can't do it. I'm going to the dentist.

Simon: But this is Enid's birthday.

Ruby: So she should drop dead and you, too. I've got a toothache and I'm going to the dentist.

And that would be the end of it. That would be the end if Ruby were involved. But it hadn't been Ruby. It had been Enid, and Enid wasn't like Ruby. Enid did as she was told. From the beginning she had done as she was told. And marriage was a peculiar sort of deal. It began as a significant drama and slid into a farce. You worked downward from the crashing cymbal to the silly wheeze of a kazoo. You started in a tangle of deep emotion and wound up with a toothache. You stood on a windy hill and cried out to God to help you, and you ended up begging a dentist for thirty minutes of his time.

And, she thought, you were surprised when these things happened to you. You were surprised because you had placed too much importance upon yourself and upon the decisions you would make. You thought you were Medea and you were really only a minor character in a road company comedy.

I was such an intense little thing, she thought. It seemed odd and faintly ridiculous to think of herself that way, for she was Enid Marcaboth, more than twenty years married, more than a hundred years weary.

But I am not thinking of Enid Marcaboth. I am thinking of Enid Beasley. And she thought of that other Enid with envy. I was so well loved, so protected and cherished.

Still, that had been her undoing. Perhaps Wolfe would have seemed less fascinating had he not been the very first man of his kind whom she had ever met.

That Enid Beasley, the intense little thing, thought of him as a merchant prince with flashing, scornful eyes, a character out of Arabian Nights, a ruthless man who was capable of wonderful tenderness. She pictured him as he might have been in another age, an elegant figure riding hard across burning desert sands, outdistancing misadventure and death to arrive at last at the side of his love. He was secretive, subtle, mysterious. She thought of him as a man who possessed locked closets behind which lay fabulous treasures, concealed from the eyes of infidels for a thousand years. She thought of him so because she had never before known a man whose grandfather's personal history was not interwoven into the personal history of her own grandfather. He was a new experience, a quiet stranger who said he loved her though she was forbidden to give her love to him.

"He's no good for you," her father said. "Forget him. He's no good."

"Don't say that, Papa. You'll regret it because he's going to marry into this family."

"Oh, no, he isn't. He might marry you if you're that big a fool, but he won't have any contact with this family. You might tell him that. It could possibly cool his ardor."

"I don't think so. He isn't looking for a rich wife."

"In that case he won't regret that you'll have nothing but the three thousand a year your grandfather left you."

"No, he won't regret it."

She told Wolfe that her father would disown her. It was his right to know and it was her right to watch the expression on his face when she told him.

"Your father can't disown you," he said. "He can only discontinue your allowance. He can only cut you out of his will. He can't change the fact that you're his daughter."

How comforting he was, how sweet and how different from the way Papa imagined him.

"I love him," Enid Beasley said. "I'll never love anyone else. That's all that really counts."

And in the end that's the way it came out, the way it

152

had to come out. Enid took her tears and her heartache out of her father's house one night. She climbed a little hill and stood there watching the trees bend, and she listened to them sigh and she lifted her eyes to the stars and she prayed. She prayed that she would do the right thing, the thing that God wanted her to do. She felt very young and tragic as she asked for guidance. It was wonderful standing there in the warm wind conscious of the important decision God was making. How puckered His brow must be, how carefully He must be thinking. And after a time she walked over to the Hotel Negresco and met Wolfe in the bar. She felt at peace, the storm behind her. God had decided against Papa. God had evidently known what was right for her. He had known how wonderful Wolfe was.

She hadn't guessed what fun it would be to have a husband, to have someone so intensely interested in her. Wolfe even liked to follow along on shopping tours. He never wearied of helping her make selections, complaining only when she hesitated over a price tag.

"Remember me?" she asked him. "The bride who came without even a cow or a feather bed? Three thousand a year, darling. That's all. Well, it will keep me in shoes and stockings. I promise that you'll never have to buy me any shoes or stockings."

His mother's wedding present to them was a house. It was a bigger house than Enid wanted. She was still nurturing her dream about the merchant prince galloping wildly across the sands to fold her in his arms. She wanted to domesticate that half-civilized love of hers. She dreamed of doing it in a little house that had gingham curtains and pots of red geraniums set on the window sills. She had never lived in a little house. She wanted to live in one with Wolfe.

"Frankly," he said, "I thought there'd be a tennis court as well as a pool. Do you think we can do without a court?"

"I don't know," Enid answered. "It's a question whether or not a marriage can succeed without one. Can people be happy and well adjusted with nothing but a pool?"

"I'm serious," he said. "We'll want to entertain."

"I suppose we will entertain, darling," she said. "We'll undoubtedly have to. As far as *wanting* to, that's something else. I've been my father's hostess for five years, and I can tell you that when it's done right, it's exhausting."

He smiled. "And I'll bet you always did it right."

"I think I did. I didn't hear any angry mutterings."

They began to entertain almost at once. Wolfe waited only for Enid to say that she had assembled a butler, cook, and waitress that satisfied her. There were small gatherings and of course the larger ones with extra help and extra responsibilities.

"Sometimes I like to rest, Wolfe."

"Well, you're not always busy. Half of the time we're dining out."

"That isn't resting. For God's sake, don't you ever read a book or listen to the radio or just sit thinking of nothing?"

She learned to entertain in Bangkok and Saigon, in Shanghai and Tokyo.

"I've been thinking, Wolfe, you won't be in the Orient more than six weeks this coming trip. We could be separated that long. The doctor thinks I should have my appendix out."

"Well, he said there was no rush about it, didn't he?"

"That's right. There's no rush about it, but I'd hate to be in mid-ocean or in one of those fabulously interesting Chinese towns when—"

"Doctors are always trying to frighten people. I like you with me, Enid."

"I know, dear, but—"

The appendix didn't burst. It just hurt from time to time. There was always ice to put on it and somebody gave her some pills that dulled the pain. Wolfe said she shouldn't take them. They were probably habit-forming, and besides, she wouldn't be in pain if some fool doctor hadn't put the idea into her head that she ought to be.

She took the pills secretly. It was probably because of their soothing qualities that she hardly felt the blow of her father's death. She was in Hong Kong when it happened. An English gentleman said, "So fine of you to come tonight, Mrs. Marcaboth. We thought in view of your loss that—"

"How did you know I lost someone?"

"I saw it in the paper. I knew Caldwell Beasley was your father. Wolfe mentioned it a long while ago—when you were first married as a matter of fact."

She had the appendix out the week she returned from the Orient. She loved the hospital. It was so nice there, so quiet. It was going to be nice at home, too. She planned on staying in her room for two whole weeks—no company, nothing but peace.

Wolfe didn't think that would be good for her. He had heard that after an operation a person had a tendency toward falling in love with invalidism. He had asked her doctor and, just as he had supposed, the doctor agreed with him. They'd been invited for a week end on the sixteenth and there was no reason Enid couldn't go.

It was that winter that Wolfe bought the dog, Sari. Enid remembered Sari well, lovely, golden Sari, best of breed, best of show, Sari with the roguish eyes and the passion for tearing bedroom slippers into tiny bits, Sari, the happy tail-wagger.

Wolfe adored Sari. He took her everywhere in the car with him, showing her off, reciting her blood lines to anyone who would listen. They'd even taken Sari to New York with them because Wolfe didn't like leaving her behind.

"I love her. I want her with me wherever I go."

Sari had been beautiful strolling down Fifth Avenue. Wolfe had never once complained that she was a nuisance. He never tired of having her with him nor of telling people how Sari's owner had not wanted to sell.

"But, as you see, I finally got her. Didn't I, baby? Whose pretty dog are you? That's right. Now heel, Sari. Good girl. Heel."

In the summer Sari came down with a skin disease and she didn't look very pretty. She walked about morosely, shamed by the bare patches of sore flesh and the purple splotches of medicine. The veterinarian said, "It'll take time. These things don't go away overnight."

Enid said, "Now, Sari, don't let's look so melancholy. Here's a pretty rubber bone I bought for you. Try to play, honey. Try not to be so sad. Enid'll get you all cured, sweetheart. Don't worry. We'll use the medicine and get you all cured."

Sari was missing the second week of her illness. Enid called the police but they had nothing to report. The chauffeur said that Mr. Marcaboth had taken Sari with him when he'd left for the office. Enid felt sure the man was mistaken. Wolfe knew that Sari needed treatments through the day.

At noon the vet called. "Mrs. Marcaboth, I feel I should tell you that I'm giving Sari to a lady I know. She won't mind working on the dog's coat and Sari'll have a good home and—"

"I don't understand. What do you mean about giving Sari away? You can't give— Is Sari there with you?"

"Yes, she's here with me."

"How did she get there?"

"Mr. Marcaboth brought her. He said I was to put her to sleep. Never before have I heard of killing a dog who had a minor ailment and who can be cured and enjoy a good life for years to come. If you won't permit me to give the dog away, then please come and get her because I am not going to do as Mr. Marcaboth asked."

Enid said nothing.

"Mrs. Marcaboth."

"I'm here."

"Are you coming to get Sari or aren't you? I'd like to put her in a good home."

Enid said, "I'm not coming to get her. By all means put her in a good home."

Many a year had passed since that day, but Enid still thought of Sari from time to time.

JUDITH walked into the house and directly out to the kitchen. Everything was quiet. When she had put the car away she had glanced into the play yard and there was no sign of the children and now she did not hear their voices anywhere inside the house. Anne and Frederick were sitting at the kitchen table, looking at the morning papers as they lingered over their luncheon coffee.

"Where are the children?" she demanded.

Anne said, "A man came for them."

"A man! What man?"

Anne looked questioningly at Frederick. He said, "A neighbor. I didn't get his name."

"What!"

"I guess he's a friend of yours. The children knew him all right. He seemed like a nice man."

Judith knew who the man was. He was the father of the Felton twins. He often drove over and picked Lorna and Kenneth up of an afternoon. But the servants shouldn't have let them go with a stranger. The man could have been anybody. The kitchen was a blur before her angry eyes and she felt her rage choking her as she said, "Get the hell out of here. Pack your things and get the hell out!"

They stared at her. "Mrs. Marcaboth, the man said—"

"Don't argue with me. Get the hell out."

She turned and fled from the kitchen. She ran upstairs and called the Felton house. Yes, the children were there. They were playing with the twins. Do you want to speak to Kenneth, Mrs. Marcaboth? No, it was all right as long as he was there. She replaced the phone and paced back and forth across the marbleized squares of linoleum in the upstairs sun room. She could feel the blood pounding in her temples, and she knew that she was not furious because Anne and Frederick had permitted the children to go with Mr. Felton. That had been the release. Something else lay at the root of her fury.

And as she passed an ornament that had sat for years on the shelf beside the clock she picked it up and flung it to the floor where it splintered into a hundred pieces. She stood looking down at it. But she did not really see it. She

saw Ruby Marcaboth scrambling off the yellow mattress
where she had been lying. She had no shame. She had been
annoyed at their arrival. But she had not been shamed. She
had not been shamed because she was a slut. Garth's brother
was married to a slut, but she, Judith, had to drop whatever she was doing to bring a birthday present to the
woman. She, Judith, had to humiliate herself before Ruby
Marcaboth.

"Because she is the wife of Garth's brother she is ac-
ceptable. She is all right, and I must wait upon her because
she is Mrs. Simon Marcaboth."

Judith picked up another ornament and flung it across
the room. It did not break and she went to the corner in
which it lay and stamped upon it.

She found that she was not only furious with Garth but
with herself as well. She had been so docile, so willing to
accept the value placed by Garth upon the business of
being a Marcaboth. She had wordlessly acknowledged that
few could be worthy of such an honor, that she herself,
though certainly unworthy, would strive ever upward, onward, toward perfection. He had pointed out a few of the
things that she could do to compensate for her unworthi-
ness, and despite what it cost her, she had not flinched.

She hadn't minded putting aside the matter of practicing
law. It was something else. It was that her parents had
spent so much money on her education, so much more
money than they could afford. They had made sacrifices,
terrible sacrifices. She had meant to make it all up to them
some day. She had meant to be a prosperous lawyer with a

good, comfortable home, and to that home she had intended to take her father and mother and they were never again to know worry or self-denial. But if she was not to practice law—

She told all this to Garth, and he held her close and patted her reassuringly. "We'll take care of them, honey. They'll get a regular check from me every week. Everything's all right now, isn't it?"

But it wasn't quite all right because Judith's father dismissed all talk of Garth's weekly check.

"I don't know Garth Marcaboth," her father said. "Who is this stranger who wants to give me money every week?"

Judith looked into her father's pale eyes and pretended to miss the sarcasm.

"He will be my husband," she said. "When the checks start to arrive he will be my husband."

"So? That makes him a man I know? Do I know what color his hair is, or how tall he is, or whether he eats strawberries or drinks tea? I don't want any money from strangers. And who asked for money? I work. I did not ask for anything."

So it wasn't quite all right. Sometimes Judith wished she had never met Garth, but she did not wish it often. She remembered how it had been in the beginning when she had first met him, how from the first moment she had wanted him and how unattainable he had seemed. She knew she was not beautiful. She was aware of her cleverness, but she had no faith in her sort of cleverness catching a man. Hers was only the harsh, clear-minded kind that had nothing to do with knowing when to sigh or how to look misty-eyed at the right moment. She had no wiles with which to enslave him. She had only her earnest young self. She had nothing to offer him, only love. In the end these things had been enough and Garth had chosen her as his bride.

But he said to her, "You've got a good mind, Judith. There's no damn nonsense about you so I can talk to you without being afraid that you'll cry or that you'll walk away. You can be realistic. I know you can be."

And he talked to her. He talked about advantages that she'd not had. He talked about the way she dressed, the way she spoke, the way she stood, and the way she thought. And she wondered why he wanted to marry her and she wondered if he wasn't terribly sorry that he did want to. But she listened and she was realistic. She did not cry or walk away. She had been touched by fate and she would marry into the Marcaboth family and she must be sensible and realize that it wasn't just anyone to whom such an honor came. It only came to superior people and to people who were willing to work toward the day when they, too, would be superior.

Garth gave her a large and brilliant diamond to wear, and she was invited to visit his sister in New York. She was slightly alarmed by the thought of Garth's sister but he reassured her.

"Darling, it's only by being with people like my sister that you'll become accustomed to getting around. She'll give a few parties and you'll meet people, and little by little you'll get over your inferiority complex."

She stared at Garth. Her inferiority complex? She'd thought herself a fairly self-confident person, a girl with a good brain and an astonishing amount of drive. When had she acquired an inferiority complex? Well, maybe he was right. Maybe she did have one.

When she packed to go on her visit to New York, Judith's parents stood in the hallway and watched her with stricken eyes. They never came into her room any more. It had become a room rented to a stranger, a room that could no longer be approached with an easy feeling that it was part of their home and of them.

"Mama, are you crying? Why should you cry? I'm going to visit Garth's sister and I'll be back."

Papa said, "Back." He pronounced the word as though it were a humbug word, as though it had no meaning, as though there was no such thing as "back."

"Of course I'll be back. They won't eat me, you know. Now, Mama, please."

Mama said nothing. She stood in the doorway, her plump arms crossed, her little fat hands holding onto the old red shawl that she liked to wear. It made no difference what you gave Mama in the way of scarfs or jackets, she hung onto the old red shawl.

"This Garth's sister, she has an address maybe?" Papa asked.

"Naturally. I'll leave it for you. I'll leave a telephone number, too, in case—"

"Telephone numbers I don't need. So rich I'm not."

"But in case of emergency—"

"They had emergencies before telephones. All our lives Mama and I have lived and never telephoned New York. So big a job I don't have. So much money I don't earn."

Judith choked down her exasperation. She folded a slim, black dress and placed it carefully in her suitcase. She said, "When I get back—"

"Back," Papa said.

As it turned out Papa was right. There was no such word as "back." Of course Judith returned to California but she never returned to the house on Silso Street. It so happened that while she was staying with Garth's sister, Garth came to New York. His mother arrived later the same week and Hannah and Simon Marcaboth with her. Then somebody noticed that Garth's sister had a perfect home for a wedding.

Judith said, "I don't think my father and mother could come, but my brother and his wife might be able to." And when nobody answered her she turned her suddenly hot face away from them and she was silent. Not until that moment had she understood why Zeda and the Simon Marcaboths had come to New York.

She had said nothing. She had married Garth accepting without protest a house filled with guests who were strangers to her, accepting the fact that only Garth's relatives were present, accepting a wedding gown selected and paid for by Zeda so that the Marcaboths would not be shamed.

All this she had accepted because it was understood that

she was not as good as the Marcaboths. This there was no
gainsaying. Her inferiority to the Marcaboths was there
for all to see. To question it would be idiotic. It was apparent and it was accepted.

She had been accepting it since the moment when she
had first fallen in love with Garth Marcaboth. She had accepted the fact that she must be married far, far away from
her family because they were not good enough to be invited to her wedding. Her father and mother were not
good enough for Garth Marcaboth. This a woman could
learn to accept. But Garth's brother had married a slut,
and Judith was asked now to accept this woman as a sister
though none of Judith's people had been sluts.

You could go on resenting it but you couldn't go on
breaking ornaments or acting like a child in a tantrum.
You had to calm down. You had to be reasonable and take
up once more the reasonable concerns of life. And after a
time Judith went downstairs and settled with the servants.
There was a certain amount of money coming to them
though they had done nothing in her home except eat their
lunch. She realized that they had been put to inconvenience
by having to move twice in a day so she gave them what
she thought fair and they were satisfied.

She was not sorry that she had discharged the couple.
There'd be other servants, and if there weren't—

I'm not so helpless, she thought, that anybody is better
than nobody. I can always get a day worker to do heavy
things, and even if I couldn't, I'd be able to manage.

She stared down at her strong, bony hands. They were

not pretty but they were capable. Solime's hands now, they were pretty hands. If Solime had no servants she would be in trouble. She would be completely bewildered. She would be—that wasn't the truth.

I'm making it up, Judith thought. Solime would always rise to the occasion. She would put on a gingham dress and pin her hair on top of her head and she would get down on her knees and scrub and never rest till her floor was shining clean. She would do the same as I, only when she straightened up she would still look crisp in her gingham dress and her hair would be neat.

And Judith knew that it was consolation propaganda that ladies were helpless. Ladies could do whatever they had to do, and maybe when all the arguments and discussions were settled that was the true definition of a lady.

But Ruby now.

Why the hell can't I get Ruby out of my mind?

Ruby hadn't married Simon to scrub floors, and she wouldn't do it if grass grew in Hannah's kitchen. Ruby would shrug and say, "I can't get servants so the kitchen's filthy." And that would end it.

How do I know that? Why am I so sure?

Judith looked back at her hands and thought about Garth. Suppose they couldn't get servants right away? How would he feel about her scrubbing floors? Perhaps he would rather that the linoleum became a mass of footprints and grime than see his wife slopping around in soapy water. It would depend of course. If Solime were scrubbing floors then he would not object, but otherwise it might only serve to remind him that Judith's background had not conditioned her to expect servants to perform this task for her.

She felt anger rising within her again. Her people had been unable to afford servants. That was true. But none of them were sluts like Simon's wife. None of them were—

Easy now, she said to herself. What are you getting so sore about? It hasn't happened, you know. Garth hasn't come home and found you scrubbing the floor and he hasn't said anything that reflects upon your family.

But hadn't he? What else had he done since first she'd met him? Had he ever said or done anything that hadn't reflected upon her family? Once he'd visited them—once. And yet she was supposed to drop everything and trot on down to see Ruby the moment he gave the order.

I'll start throwing things again in a minute, she thought. This is silly. I have to control myself.

But it was true. Only once had he visited her parents— right after the wedding when they had first come back to California.

She had said to him, "I wrote and told my parents I was going to be married of course. And then I wrote and described the wedding and I wired that we were coming home today, Garth. If you don't mind I'd like you to go with me to visit them tonight."

"Of course, honey. We'll go."

He was nice about it. She thought it was lovely of him the way he raised no objections. The whole family was at Mama's house. When they weren't there they were generally expected. Judith's brother, Kevi, lived just across the street with his wife, Brina, and they popped in and out the same as Uncle Eli and Aunt Gulda did. Everybody was there when she and Garth arrived.

Mama was a little frightened of Garth. He was so elegant. Papa wasn't frightened. Kevi and Brina didn't like Garth. Judith could feel their dislike. She wanted to say, "You're wrong about him. He's wonderful," but there was no chance to say it. Kevi stared at the floor and Brina stared at Garth, her bold, black eyes full of a sort of contemptuous amusement. Judith knew what Brina was thinking. Brina was thinking, "Mr. Big. A Mr. Big already she's got to marry."

Aunt Gulda said to Uncle Eli, "Look at Judith's husband. Such a fine man she got. Look at him."

And Uncle Eli said, "I'm looking. I'm looking."

Mama took a cushion off the best chair in the room and brushed it carefully and then replaced it. "You should sit there, Mr. Marcaboth," she said.

Judith laughed gaily. "Mr. Marcaboth! Mama, my husband is Mr. Marcaboth with you?"

Papa said, "What else? Did she ever see the man before?"

That made the situation a little tense. Garth was really truly sweet about it. He managed a smile.

"We've been neglectful, I know," he said. "Only we were dashing around so and there was the trip to New York and everything and—"

"Why did you get married there?" Brina asked. "You can't get married in Los Angeles?"

"It just worked out that way," Judith explained. "Garth

came unexpectedly to New York, and his sister thought that—"

Brina said, "Say, your mother would have liked to see you married."

"Where they got married is their business," Kevi said to her. "You keep quiet."

Mama said, "You'll have some tea and a little cake? Papa, in the milk pitcher in the kitchen you'll find change. Go down to the corner and bring maybe a little cheesecake or a sweet nut roll. No, Papa? You don't feel like it? Then maybe Uncle Eli'll go."

"Don't bother," Judith said. "Really, we just had dinner."

"Please don't bother," Garth echoed.

"It's no bother," Uncle Eli said. "It's a pleasure. Every day in the week we don't get fancy callers here on Silso Street."

Judith made a fresh start. She turned to her mother with an affectionate smile. "How have you been, Ma?"

"Good. Good."

"She's had pains in her heart," Brina said.

"Has she, Papa?"

"Three weeks ago she had pains in her heart. What do you want to do? Call the doctor now?"

"You did call the doctor, didn't you?"

Papa twisted his mouth into a hard, bitter line. "No, of course not," he said. "I waited till you got back from New York so you could tell me what to do."

"What did the doctor say?"

"He said she had pains in her heart."

170

"It was nothing," Mama said. "Indigestion. Maybe I ate a little piece fish not so good or—"

Kevi said, "He gave her medicine and told her to slow down."

"So next day," Brina said, "she did the washing. Four sheets, four pillow cases, six towels, four shirts, three—"

"What did you do that for, Mama?"

"The laundry's no good. They tear your things to pieces and—"

"But your health comes first."

Mama laughed. "By me now the washing is a joke. When you and Kevi were little and I had all that washing, then it was something. Now it's like a holiday to me. I'm through it in no time. You shouldn't worry."

"And she gets headaches," Brina said.

Aunt Gulda groaned. "Do *I* get headaches!"

"I get some good ones myself," Garth said. "I get migraines."

They all stared at him for a moment. Then Papa said, "Mr. Marcaboth doesn't get headaches. He gets *migraines*."

"Well, they are worse than ordinary headaches," Judith said.

"Oh, sure," Papa agreed. "This I know. They're bigger headaches, better headaches."

Garth smiled. "Okay," he said. "I'm wrong. What's the beef? That Judith got married in New York?"

Aunt Gulda said, "It was like a slap in the face to us."

Mama leaned forward and touched her sister on the knee.

171

"So this is your business, Gulda? I didn't mind but you're complaining."

"I'm complaining for you. I know how you felt about it."

Judith looked out the window at the pulley lines stretched across the court. She was thinking of her wedding and of how Mama would have enjoyed it. She was thinking of her wedding gown and of how Mama's life would have been enriched and brightened had she seen it and if she had it now in memory to recall and describe to her friends.

Garth said, "It was not Judith's fault. It was mine."

"That makes it better?" Papa asked. "Judith can't talk? She can't say to you, 'Look, I want to be married where my Mama can see me'?"

"She did say it but I was so anxious to hurry the wedding that I talked her into it."

Papa said, "An only daughter, and her Mama can't see her married."

Mama sighed. "So now it's done. Let's forget it. Judith, you shouldn't look so sad. What's done is done. Ah, here comes Uncle Eli with the cake. You got maybe a nut roll, Eli?"

Kevi excused himself and went home before the tea was ready. Brina stayed.

"I hear your Mama's a princess," she said to Garth.

He nodded. "We've almost forgotten that. She calls herself Mrs. Marcaboth since the Prince's death."

"Such a thing," Mama said. "Imagine being married to a prince. Your Mama liked that?"

Garth said, "I think she did. He was a fine man."

"But so funny I'd feel. Married to a prince! This I don't think I would like."

Judith looked at Mama's sweet little fat face with its shoe-button eyes and pudgy nose. She felt sorry for Mama because Mama seemed to think that she had just rejected a prince. Into Judith's mind came the memory of photographs she had seen of Zeda Marcaboth, photographs taken at the time of her marriage to Prince Zleki. Zeda had been lovely in a dark, dramatic way. She had held herself imperiously, and her flashing tilted eyes and high-bridged nose had made her look more royal than her groom. Judith hoped that Garth was not secretly laughing at Mama who didn't think she'd like being married to a prince.

And at last the evening was over. She was glad because it had been painful, but she was dreading to be alone with Garth, dreading to hear the things he would say of her people.

I will defend them, she thought, for they are right. They have every reason to be angry and hurt but, dear God, I love Garth, I don't want to quarrel with him. I never want to quarrel with Garth.

They walked out on Silso Street and she looked back to wave at Mama. Only Mama was standing there in the doorway. The others did not feel impelled to spin this evening with Judith out to its very utmost. She was aware of Mama in the doorway, and as she walked toward Garth's car she was terribly conscious of Silso Street—the shabby houses, the Chinese laundry, the delicatessen store that looked as though it might be improved by a good cleaning.

She pointed to the flat above the meat market. "Kevi and Brina live there," she said.

Garth squeezed her hand. "All right, darling," he said. "Calm down. You're the only one who cares that they do."

And she realized that she had given this uninteresting piece of information as though it were a challenge to a duel.

They got in the car and drove away, Judith looking back to see Mama turn and re-enter the house. Mama would cry now, for Papa would say dreadful things and Mama was not smart enough to know that Papa would say them only because he was as hurt as she was.

We might as well have it over, Judith thought. We might as well have it over. She lit a cigarette and said, "They gave you a bad time, didn't they, Garth?"

He smiled at her. "Forget it."

She blessed him because he did not say any of the things that he might have said.

"You understand them, don't you, Garth? You understand how disappointed they are that we were married in New York."

"Of course I understand. I told you to forget it, honey."

She didn't quite want to forget it. She wanted to pursue the subject a little further. She wanted to pursue it far enough to assure herself that Garth did understand, but she knew this was not wise. There had been just the tiniest

touch of sharpness in his tone the second time he had said
that she should forget it.

He had never gone again to Silso Street. She had never
found the courage to ask him to throw himself again against
the barrier of her father's bitterness. She knew she was a
coward. There was a way to right the wrong that had
been done, but it would·have been a slow, painful process.

I should work toward getting Papa's forgiveness, she
sometimes thought. Then I should insist that Garth go
with me once a week to visit them, and in time Papa would
accept Garth and Garth would come to respect Papa and
they could like each other.

But she never made the effort. Garth had been so uncomfortable at Papa's house, so out of place. Besides, Papa
didn't need Garth and Garth didn't need Papa. It was easier
this way. It was always easier to be a coward.

So when she visited Mama it was in the afternoons and
they did not speak of their husbands to each other. Mama
was always happy to see her and Mama was too innocent
to come at one with a poison dart or a piece of biting sarcasm. Mama said, "I'm glad to see you, darling." And she
meant it, and when she said, "Oo, what a pretty dress," she
meant that, too. But Brina and Aunt Gulda were often
there, and they were adept at the art of ambush.

"So how many rooms already in your house, Judith?"

"It's not a very big house really."

"One bedroom maybe?"

"Well, no. It's got—let me see—it's got—"

Brina said, "You know, Aunt Gulda, it's got four bedrooms."

Judith protested this. "I never said four bedrooms, Brina."

"No, three and an upstairs sun room. It could be four bedrooms, couldn't it, if your Papa and Mama came to visit a while and you had guests in the other rooms?"

Judith felt her face flame with anger against Brina. It was absurd that she should be angry at Brina. She, herself, was in the wrong. Brina fought for Mama, for Mama who wouldn't fight for herself.

Mama said, "Houses we gotta talk about? Are we in the real estate business that we must measure bathrooms and kitchens and dining rooms? Already I'm sick of houses. Tell me, Judith, did you know Kevi is getting fat. At last, after all these years, the boy is gaining a little weight. Isn't it funny? You remember how skinny he always was?"

Mama was wonderful. And so were Brina and Aunt Gulda when it came down to it. They didn't want anything for themselves. They wanted it for Mama, but they made visiting difficult and Judith got in the habit of going only once a month to see Mama.

Garth never mentioned Judith's people and Judith never mentioned them either. He had been generous, very generous. He had not said the things he might have said, and she was afraid to disturb the beautiful silence. It was best that things go along as they were.

Somehow I can take it, she thought. I can take those looks I get from Brina and Aunt Gulda. I can take the knowledge that Papa and Kevi are sick when they think of me. I can even stand knowing that Mama cries at night because instead of a daughter she now has a lady from Beverly Hills who drops in occasionally to see her. All this I can stand but I cannot stand Garth telling me that he does not want to know them.

She went alone to visit her mother, and Mama did not see Judith's house in Beverly Hills or any of the Marcaboths till Kenneth was born.

Judith brought him to the house on Silso Street when he was eight weeks old, and Mama cried at the sight of him. And Brina and Aunt Gulda cried, too, because Mama was crying and because Mama was afraid to touch a baby who was her grandchild but who belonged to a world she had never seen.

And when Judith put the child in Mama's arms, Mama forgot that his other grandmother was a princess, and she held him tight to her and she said, "Look, he likes me." That night it was Judith who cried herself to sleep.

After that she always took Kenneth with her when she visited Mama, and presently there was Lorna but Mama only saw Lorna once. For Garth broke his silence on the subject of Judith's family.

"I have to talk to you about something, Judith."

"Yes?" But she knew. She shivered when she answered him because she knew what was coming. She could tell by the way he was looking at her. It was the same old look she remembered from the days when he had found it necessary to criticize her clothes and her habits of speech. It was the same old thing. He even prefaced it all with remarks about what a good mind she had and how realistically she would accept things that would hurt the feelings of a less intelligent person.

"Honestly, honey, I hate to say this because I know I'm going to sound like a stuffed shirt, but Kenneth is getting to the age now where we have to start thinking of the impressions he's forming. It's easy to confuse a child, and when a child's confused he begins to feel insecure and unhappy. This creates a fertile ground for secret, inner thoughts that lead to—"

She spoke in a very low voice. She said, "Say it, Garth. I read my chapter on child psychology this morning. Say what you have to say."

He took her at her word. "It's about Silso Street. I don't want Kenneth going there any more."

She had known what was coming but it was a shock just the same. "Garth! Do you realize that Kenneth is part of that family of mine? He isn't all Marcaboth, you know."

"I know that. Good God, I'm conscious of the fact that I sound like a prize rat, but I think it's too confusing to a child who lives as our kids live to be plunged at intervals into an utterly strange way of life. He looks at a place such as your family lives in and he is told that these people are his. They're different from his father and mother—"

"They're not different from his mother."

"Yes, they are. Don't tell me you're like that Brina. I'd never have married you if you were."

"I'm exactly like Brina."

"The hell you are." He gave her a sudden, searching

glance, and she knew that all along he had known she was like Brina—Brina with a legal education. He looked away from her and began fumbling with his cigarette lighter. "When the children are older, when they understand some of the puzzling things about life, there's no reason why they shouldn't visit your people if they choose."

"That's awfully sporting of you, Garth."

He said, "We'll get nowhere if you want to take that attitude. Why don't you stop being sentimental and look at the matter sensibly? What do you suppose will go on in that child's mind when he's trying to understand why Silso Street is so different from Beverly Hills, when he's trying to figure out why one grandmother is so different from the other? Unless you help him, Judith, he's going to be a pretty mixed-up little boy."

"Nonsense. Plenty of kids have fathers who married beneath themselves. The kids pull out all right. Don't worry."

"Oh, I'm not going to worry, darling. I'm just going to ask you to keep things simple for Kenneth till he's old enough to have a clear explanation of this situation."

"You mean you're ordering me not to take him to Silso Street."

"It's not really an order, Judith. And it's not forever, you know. Some day we can explain and everything will be fine. But for the next few years he'll be gathering impressions and I don't want his little mind all muddled up."

She said nothing. She stood looking through the wall all the way to Silso Street. She could see herself sitting there with her mother trying to explain why she hadn't brought the children. She could see even further than that. She could see Mama trying to defend her against the others, finding reasons why Judith didn't bring the children any more.

Garth was talking again. He said, "When Kenneth can understand why one man is richer than another we'll tell him things about your people that will make him admire them."

"You mean you'll make something up?"

"No. We need only tell the truth. We'll tell how your people worked to educate you, how they were motivated by an earnest desire to give you advantages they'd never had. We'll tell how your father refused financial aid from me and how he was proud and self-sufficient and—"

"We could get out quite a pamphlet about them, couldn't we? Then we could hire a few salesmen to sell my family to my children. Good salesmen of course. It'd take a good salesman to sell them a pair of broken-down grandparents after they've been taught to accept Zeda Marcaboth as standard equipment."

"Any psychologist would tell you—"

She said, "I don't know what you're going to say but I'm not interested in what a psychologist would tell me. Neither are you. You're only interested in shielding your children from knowing that my parents are poor and uneducated."

"I tell you that when they get older and can understand—"

"Garth, for God's sake be honest with yourself and with me. Lie to anyone else you choose, but here between the two of us let there be truth. You never intend your children

to know my family. You shrink from the thought of my
mother speaking to them, expressing to them ignorant ideas
phrased ungrammatically and spoken in uncultured accents.
You hate my people, not as individuals of course, but as
symbols of a group that is distressing to you because, but
for the grace of God, there go the Marcaboths."

He said, "That doesn't even make sense. Let's talk about
this sometime when you are thinking clearly."

But they didn't talk about it again. There was no need to
reopen the subject. He knew that she would do as he had
asked. She knew it, too. There was no point in halfway
measures. It was stupid to wound your mother's heart just
enough to keep it aching. You might as well break it completely and at least have approval from your husband.

So she did not bring the children any more to the house
on Silso Street.

Brina said, "You think maybe they'll get smallpox here?"

Mama said, "So she'll bring the children next time. Today
she didn't bring them. She's committed a crime or something? Leave her alone, Brina."

But her visits grew even more infrequent because Judith
could hardly bear the look in Mama's eyes. Mama never
said anything that would indicate her hurt or yearning, but
Judith could not bear that look when Brina or Aunt Gulda
mentioned the children. And little by little she drew further away from Mama and she looked at her children and
she wondered if there really was a law of compensation and
the fear that there was made her tremble. And somewhere
she read the ancient story of a man who walked along a river

road with a huge basket in his hand and he met his son upon that road and he said to his son, "I have just carried my father to the river and drowned him for he was so old and frail that he was useless." And the son said, "Please do not lose the basket."

And Judith cut the ancient story out and put it in her drawer beneath a stack of sheer nylons. She did not know why she had to save the grim little tale. She only knew that she needed it to look at from time to time.

She never blamed Garth. None of it was Garth's fault. If she did not honor her parents, why should he? Judith had always been aware that the fault was hers. She had never been truly angry at Garth till now. She had never understood how low his opinion of her people was till today. It was obvious that he rated Ruby above them. Why, Ruby was Simon's wife! Despite any regrettable traits the girl might have she would be accepted by one and all because she was a Mrs. Marcaboth.

All right, I'm a Mrs. Marcaboth, too. What does it get me? A house? Clothes? An automobile? Could an intelligent person count these things as gain? No. She thought of her children. Yes. Now there was something. Her children. Her children who, if the law of compensation really existed, would one day walk away from her and leave her weeping.

The moment Solime reached home she began to change her clothes. Even in the midst of a California summer one did not attend a meeting of The Circle in a backless linen dress.

One wore stockings, a proper afternoon frock, and a hat. The absence of gloves was even frowned upon. The Circle made a point of retaining the old-fashioned niceties. It did not, in formal gathering, admit to the existence of uplift bras, strapless dresses, slacks, or plunging necklines. The motto of The Circle was "Reverence and Modesty." Members wore what they chose—but not to the meetings.

I could get away with anything, Solime thought, comfortably. Because I am Solime, my mother's daughter, I could wear a bathing suit to the meeting and there would be no comment. But she would not take advantage of her position. She would clothe herself discreetly in the little jacketed print. That, she thought, is the difference between Galals and riffraff. Galals don't take advantage of their position.

And as she showered she thought about riffraff. She thought about Ruby Marcaboth. Anything could happen to you in the matter of in-laws once you married into the Marcaboth family, anything at all. There was Enid of course. You didn't have to be ashamed of Enid but you couldn't be proud of her either. Enid contributed nothing to the business of living. She hadn't even borne a child. Enid was an idle, spineless woman without conviction or direction.

When I am her age, Solime thought, there will be something to show for my having lived. I can do anything my mother did and maybe more. Only—only—

Yes, there was that of course. Mother hadn't had the Marcaboths around her neck, weighing her down, embar-

rassing her. None of them are assets, God knows. And, un-
bidden, Hannah came to Solime's mind. No, no social asset,
Hannah. But Hannah was gone, Hannah, who up to the last
month she lived was still saying, "Sunday evening you
should all come for supper." Supper! Poor Hannah. She
hadn't learned much about how to be a social asset but Hannah was gone. And Solime knew that she was poorer for the
passing of Hannah who had been the ignorant sister-in-law.

Well, who didn't love her? she thought defiantly. Who
could help but love Hannah?

Solime drying her slim body on a fluffy, yellow towel
thought that some day Zeda Marcaboth, too, must die. And
I will cry and I will miss her, she thought. Two hours after
Zeda is dead it will seem to me that she was the most wonderful, most completely perfect person who ever lived.
Wouldn't it be great if I could feel that way about her
now?

Even after Zeda was gone there would still be enough
Marcaboths. There would be Judith for instance, Judith
who could somehow manage to stand at the perfume
counter of one of the country's most glamorous shops and
remind you of a woman squinting at the wares on a push-
cart, Judith, the intelligent Mrs. Marcaboth. How intelligent was she? She'd learned to be a lawyer. Couldn't anyone? The columns and columns in any classified directory
would certainly suggest that you learned to be a lawyer if
that was what you desired. Nothing difficult about it. You
gave a certain amount of time to it and you were a lawyer.
Solime thought about Judith's children, Kenneth and Lorna.

The names Judith had chosen for them! Soap opera names.

And there would always be Rome's sisters. No, there would never occur a shortage of Marcaboths. Zeda had buried five children but she had left herself a shrewd margin for mortality. There would always be a good supply of Marcaboths.

Solime was grateful that her mother couldn't read her mind. Mother believed that pride, far more necessarily than charity, begins at home. She had preached the gospel that the world respects only those who respect themselves. She would say that Solime could not think little of the Marcaboths without thinking little of herself. She would say that Solime could not betray them even in her thoughts without betraying Adin. These things Mother believed.

"I was a good daughter-in-law," Mother had said in other years. "Your father's mother was a difficult woman. No Chinese empress expected more submissiveness from her son's wife than your grandmother expected from me. I never crossed her. I never disappointed her, and the self-discipline I acquired in trying to please her has served me well all my life."

You drank little things like that in with your Coca-Cola when you were about fourteen sitting beside the pool with Mother in a reminiscent mood.

Sometimes nowadays Mother asked, "Are you happy, darling? Thoroughly happy?"

"Of course, Mother. Rome is perfect."

And Mother would be content with the answer though she knew very well that Rome was not perfect at all. If the truth were known, Mother probably detested Rome. Only with Mother it was the principle of the thing. A woman spoke well of her husband. To do otherwise was to degrade herself. And a woman did nothing that caused others to laugh at her husband and hold him in contempt. If she did, it was she who was contemptible.

So I will please Mother by not deceiving Rome except in small things like The Circle of course. And I will tell Mother every time she asks me that Rome is absolutely perfect.

He wasn't perfect. Nobody was.

But I always loved him. Even when I was just a little kid and he came to visit my brother. What big days those were, the days when he would notice I was there and say hello.

She had carried a snapshot of him away to boarding school with her. The girls said he was really dreamy and she didn't tell them that the snapshot had been stolen from her brother's memory album. She only told this painful truth to her roommate.

"He didn't give me the snapshot. He doesn't know about me. Oh, of course he knows my brother has a sister but—he's nineteen. Before I'm old enough to marry he'll have a wife."

Her roommate said, "You'll be old enough in another three years."

But three years was forever. And in the meantime anything could happen. Solime prayed that Rome Marcaboth would wait for her.

During the second year she thought he was beginning to

notice her a little. During the third year she was seventeen
and Jerome Marcaboth was going to war. In a lieutenant's
uniform, looking handsome beyond belief, he came to call
on the Galal family. Solime sat quietly by as he talked to
her brother and parents. Nothing she knew to say could
possibly interest him. She sat on a little carved chair and
worshiped him silently, but when he left he took her with
him.

"Just for a drive, Mrs. Galal. You don't mind, do you?
I'll have her home early."

After that he dated her steadily, and Solime knew that her
prayers had been answered. He had waited. She tried to tell
her mother something of what she felt in her heart, the wonderment, the gratitude. Her mother was so busy. There had
always been the charitable organizations and Mother's po-
litical interests to be served, but now with the war she was
extra busy—Red Cross, entertainment for service men, do-
nations, committees, all kinds of things. Solime came to the
confused little room that had once been the solarium and
was now Mother's office. She leaned across the desk that was
piled perilously high with mail and memoranda and checks
and file cards and laid her heart upon the miscellaneous as-
sortment, for her heart, she felt, was also something that
should be brought to Mother's attention.

"I prayed that I might have Rome," she said.

Her mother asked, "Really? Whatever on earth for?"

"Because I love him, Mother."

Mother said, "Oh, Solime! Darling, listen to me. You're
so young. You don't actually want Jerome Marcaboth."

"I told you I prayed for him, Mother."

"We should always be careful what we pray for. We might get it."

Solime was shocked. "That isn't a very—a very reverent thing to say."

"Maybe you're right but I'm not certain any sacred thing is involved here. After all, to whom would a girl pray if she wanted a Marcaboth?"

"Mother, if this is all going to be just funny to you I might as well leave. I came to talk to you about something that's very serious."

"Yes, dear."

"Are you ready to listen sympathetically?"

"Yes, dear."

"Mother, I love Jerome. I've loved him for ages. When I had braces on my teeth and used to tear around here in dungarees I loved Rome. Of course I don't know how he feels about me. Maybe he doesn't love me. I—I just thought I'd like to come to you and tell you how I feel about Rome so you'd know how things are with me."

Mother picked up a pencil and studied the manner in which it worked. Click. Black lead. Click. Red lead. She put the pencil down and fiddled for a moment with the snood that confined her heavy, black hair. They were wearing snoods that year. "Solime, I want to tell you something." She pursed her lips and half closed her eyes, and for a moment she was more ancient oracle than chairman of the hospital board. "You can marry Jerome Marcaboth any time you wish."

Solime felt the blood rushing to her cheeks. "He's spoken to Father?"

Mother shook her head. "Not yet. He will. Darling, you're a sensational bride for anyone and for Jerome Marcaboth— Well, I hope he knows how lucky he is." The eyes that were yellow like Solime's clouded. "Are you sure he's what you want?"

"I'm sure, Mother. Why shouldn't I want him?"

The pencil had grown fascinating again. Click. Black lead. Click. Red lead. Click. Click. Click.

"Solime, the Marcaboths are different than we are."

"In what way?"

"You know in what way. Don't force me into saying things that you will later hold against me."

"I won't hold anything against you, Mother. I just don't know what you mean."

Mother said, "You must know. Haven't you ever listened to his brother, Simon, talk? Haven't you ever seen his mother? Haven't you ever—?"

"Oh, that. I thought you were going to tell me something secret about them."

"It would be nice if it were secret. They're dreadful people, Solime. Dreadful."

Solime shook her head. "Rome isn't dreadful."

"You're in love."

"Of course I am. I told you I was. What Rome's family is like doesn't trouble me in the least."

"It will, sweetheart. It will."

"Never. The things that you value so highly, Mother, are nothing. They—"

"Don't tell me they're nothing. I won't stand for it, Miss. Two hundred years of importance is not nothing. An unbroken line of highly educated people for many centuries also is not nothing. We are not like the Marcaboths. In no way are we like the Marcaboths, and your being in love with Jerome is no reason for you to minimize the things that we are."

"No, Mother, no, but you mustn't overestimate those things."

"I do not overestimate them. I only want you to be fully conscious of what you are and of what the Marcaboths are."

"Mother, let's go back to the beginning. I love Rome."

Mother nodded. "Yes, dear. I suppose you do. There must never be anything between us except sympathy and affection so I'll say this: If you want Jerome Marcaboth your father and I won't interfere. But be sure you want him. Be sure you can be a good wife to him for I will never forgive you if you fail the man you marry."

"I won't fail him, Mother. And, thank you—thank you for—"

"Don't thank me. I'm doing the wrong thing and I know I am. I ought to lock you up till the fever abates."

Solime in her dressing room on June Street ran the comb through her hair once more and thought that it would have been a long wait behind the locked door. Not yet had the fever begun to abate.

She glanced at the clock. Well, luncheon would certainly

be over at Lisa Benrabnan's. However, she would be in
plenty of time for the discussion to follow. She hoped it
wouldn't last too long. Some day it might happen. Some day
Rome might get home early and be there on the doorstep
to meet her when she arrived.

"Where were you?"

"At the hairdresser's."

"No, you weren't. I called there."

That would be a day to remember all right. Or maybe
it would be one to forget as quickly as possible.

Miss Blount glanced into her employer's sitting room and
saw that Zeda Marcaboth had fallen asleep. She was happy
to see that the beautiful white wig was not askew. It was
anchored perfectly and Miss Blount was very grateful. The
wig caused her a great deal of distress. Neither she nor Zeda
had ever mentioned the wig to each other, and when it
slipped, during one of Zeda's naps, Miss Blount was always
in a quandary. To right it might be the unforgivable sin, but
if it raised itself up like an angry cat arching its back and
Zeda upon awakening discovered that Miss Blount had permitted her to sit napping there presenting this ridiculous
spectacle—well, Miss Blount never knew what to do.

Some day that wig will be my undoing, she thought,
gloomily.

She went back to the dining room and surveyed her
work. She thought of herself as the artistic type and, robbed
of all other means of self-expression, she enjoyed arranging

the table for festive occasions. It looked just wonderful, she thought. Of course when the orchids were piled in that triangular space and the candles were lighted it would be simply superb. She hoped Simon's wife would wear pale green. Miss Blount always hoped that everybody would wear pale green. It was a color she could never afford to buy. It had a theatrical look, she always thought, and of course in her position as a secretary-companion it just wouldn't do at all. She wondered if the new Mrs. Simon had ever seen gold dinner ware before. Miss Blount looked over her shoulder carefully and then dared to think that before marrying Mr. Simon, Mrs. Simon had probably never even seen sterling silver on a table.

My, my, it is gorgeous. Miss Blount thought that every time the table was set for a birthday or other holiday. It is just gorgeous. She wondered who would inherit the gold service when Zeda was gone. Mr. Simon as the eldest was of course the logical one to get it. Miss Blount was quite upset as she stood there in the dining room thinking of the new Mrs. Simon inheriting all this magnificence. Her nose twitched with annoyance and she tossed her head a few times just to show how she felt about the whole thing. Nothing soothed her until the thought came that the eldest daughter, the one who lived in New York, the one who was just a year younger than Mr. Simon, was the natural one to be given the gold service. Miss Blount felt better after that was settled. She took another good look at the table, patted the point de Venise cover, moved each crystal water glass a thousandth of an inch east of where it had been standing and whisked off to the kichen.

Margaret, the cook, looked at her without enthusiasm. "I'm getting along fine, Miss Blount," she said just before she was asked.

"Oh, I know. I know. But I get so excited on the birthdays."

Margaret nodded. "It's a good thing you're the only one who does."

"I don't think I'm the only one at all." She turned to the waitress who was shining up an hors d'oeuvre tray. "You get excited, don't you, Violet?"

"Only on Mr. Jerome's birthday. He's so good-looking."

Miss Blount said, "Yes. Well."

"It's certainly a good thing I don't get excited over anything," the butler remarked. He came in from the pantry to have his say. "You know what a crank she is about wines. With the chilling and the room-temperature lectures she gives I'm sure she's going to pop a thermometer down a wine bottle's throat some night. And then the cocktails. They're never dry enough or this enough or that enough. Tonight it's to be Martinis. I'll buy you each a pair of nylons if she says they're good."

Margaret snorted. "And who has the most responsibility, do you think? I'm the cook, don't forget. She's a nice lady and all that but today I almost died. Do you know what she says to me? She says, 'Margaret, you've heard people speak of dinners they've been to?' I says, 'Yes, Madame.' She says, 'Have you ever heard them speak of one particular dinner

and say of it that it was a very simple dinner but delicious?'
Now of course I brighten up like a Christmas tree having
visions of setting out a fine, easy something or other this hot
night. I say, 'Oh, yes, Madame. Often have I heard people
speak of simple but delicious dinners.' And she nods and
says, 'That's just the kind of dinner I don't want any part
of. Think up something very fancy.' I tell you I almost
died."

Violet and the butler shrieked with laughter. Miss Blount
was not amused. She was thinking of the table with its gold
service, of the orchids in the refrigerator, of Violet shining
the hors d'oeuvre tray. She was thinking of the extravagant
dinner that Margaret was cooking, of the wines being ex-
posed to room temperature or to ice. She was thinking of
the Martinis and the point de Venise table cover and the
thought and effort that had gone into all of this. And she
was thinking that Mrs. Simon did not know yet that she
was expected to dinner. Mrs. Simon did not know that her
mother-in-law knew it was her birthday. And Miss Blount
was thinking that if Mrs. Simon had wanted to come Mr.
Simon would have told his mother that this was his wife's
birthday. But he had not told her and that could only mean
one thing: Mrs. Simon did not want to come.

Miss Blount shivered and leaned against the wall. She felt
a little faint. Suppose Mrs. Simon didn't come?

"It's too hot for you in here," Margaret said. "You look
ready to pass out."

Miss Blount fled to the terrace and breathed deeply of the
sea air. Mrs. Simon didn't want to come. That was plain.

Mrs. Marcaboth wanted her to come. She would demand it if necessary. Miss Blount thought about Mrs. Marcaboth being forced to demand something. Miss Blount's imagination was staggered at such a possibility. And suppose Mrs. Marcaboth gave a definite, clear-cut order and it was disobeyed? Miss Blount gasped at the idea.

She thought about the new Mrs. Simon. Her name was Ruby. Miss Blount thought about Ruby. Mrs. Marcaboth would telephone Ruby soon and tell her to come for dinner. Ruby obviously didn't want to come. Mr. Simon was undoubtedly crazy about his new, young wife. What would he say if his mother demanded one thing and his wife another? Nothing like this had ever happened in the family before. It was, Miss Blount thought, going to be simply terrible. It was, she told herself, dramatically, going to be a test of strength.

Wolfe Marcaboth glanced at the clock on his desk. There was nothing to be done that couldn't be done as well tomorrow as today. He considered leaving the office. He could go to the club and have a swim and a rub-down. After that a nap. It was a pleasant thought. The food was wonderful at the club. He would have dinner there and then he would play bridge.

Simon had said to him, "Enjoy your poker game."

With Simon it would be poker. Wolfe preferred bridge. He had never believed there was any skill to poker. Poker players pretended that there was. As a matter of fact they insisted that there was, but Wolfe had long ago tossed poker aside as a game totally unsuited to anyone who demanded that his recreation include some sort of mental exercise.

That's what I'll do, he thought. I'll go to the club.

But he did not go at once. He remained at his desk tapping a silver paper cutter against his thumb nail. He was thinking about Simon. Where did duty end? Should he have gone with Simon and Ruby tonight? Should he have accepted the invitation? Wouldn't it be absurd for him to give up his bridge game just to please Ruby?

I don't know, Wolfe thought. I don't know.

It was seldom that Wolfe was in doubt. It was even more seldom that Wolfe questioned one of his own decisions.

The girl should of course go to my mother's house tonight, he thought. But that is beside the point. Ruby isn't even to be considered. Simon asked a favor, and whether it is for Ruby or not doesn't matter. Simon asked a favor.

And he knew that it wasn't enough that he had sent Enid with a present to Simon's wife. He knew that had been a device, something he had thought up so that he could say to himself: Enid went to see the girl. That's all that is necessary.

Simon had asked a favor, a simple favor when you came to think of it, a few hours out of life, a few hours of sitting with Ruby at Mocambo or Ciro's.

It couldn't have been too bad, he reflected.

He wondered why he had never considered the matter till now, why he had automatically refused without ever having given Simon's request a second thought. And he asked himself a question that he had never asked before, at what point in life had he and Simon begun to stand together merely as co-operating units in a family group instead of as two brothers who loved each other?

When I was a child I worshiped Simon, he thought. And he remembered that Simon at fourteen had been a man who went to work and who had brought home chocolate bars and packs of chewing gum to small brothers and sisters. Wolfe could recall how Simon had never disappointed them. There was always at least a few peanuts in his pockets and in the autumn there were bound to be chestnuts, no longer warm perhaps, but still welcome because they were surprises that Simon had brought.

I don't know, he thought again. I don't know what came between us. And he sat there thinking of Simon who in many ways was still the boy in the baggy, rain-spotted suit, Simon who had never made any real attempt to improve himself, Simon who expressed his ideas in vulgar ways, Simon who had married Ruby. He threw the silver paper cutter irritably across the desk. This at least I do know, he said to himself. I do know that such a man is less worthy than I to represent the family interests. What does it matter that he is older? He is uneducated and often crude. And he did not let his thoughts pause there. He forced them onward hoping they had not noticed his hurry or his fear, hoping they had not noticed that, independent of his will or desire, they had ferreted out the thing that had come between himself and Simon.

Sometimes here in the office during a quiet afternoon he

allowed his mind to wander far afield. He liked to think of himself as a realist. It is a horrible thing to contemplate, he would say to himself, but one must face facts. It is natural to suppose that I will outlive my mother and Simon, and if this should happen— Sometimes it would take an hour of dreaming to complete the reorganization of the business, the rearrangement of the family holdings, the replacement of lawyers who for years had talked, across Wolfe's head, to Simon. He always stopped dreaming at the place where it became evident that he had not only outlived his mother and Simon but also his sisters and even the two young brothers and stood alone, the last Marcaboth, save for a few infant nephews who would prove useful in carrying on the family name.

I'll go to the club, he thought again. It gave him pleasure to think of his club, to think how well liked he must be by the other members. He never drank to excess or in any other way behaved in an unmannerly fashion. His bridge game was excellent, and if he lost, his debts were paid immediately. He bought drinks at proper intervals and never refused to serve on committees. It was always a deep and very real delight to Wolfe to think how well liked he must be.

Perhaps I should have asked Enid if she wanted to go with Simon and Ruby. The thought was a surprise to him. Why should he have asked Enid? Simon was *his* brother. There was no reason why she should be consulted.

It occurred to him that it was quite some time since Enid had been to Mocambo or anywhere else for that matter. She would perhaps have voted for going with Simon. But no, he remembered now. She'd complained of a headache. Or was it an upset stomach? Something. He couldn't recall.

Well, in any case it wasn't serious. Enid would be all right again tomorrow. She always was. Marvelous creature. Marvelous resilience. No matter what happened to Enid, she was always well again in a twinkling. This time she had no choice in the matter. She had to be feeling in the pink by Thursday evening. Thirty-six for dinner, unless the Waldrons flew in from Honolulu, then they'd be forty counting the young Waldron and his bride. And Enid would be a calm and lovely hostess, graciously receiving the compliments that were always showered upon her. She would be amusing and beautiful as ever—well, not as ever. You couldn't completely cheat time. People didn't rave about Enid's looks as they once had. A pity. A terrible pity. Still, on Thursday night she would look more gorgeous than any other man's wife, more gorgeous than—

No, this was a dream like the one in which he stood honored and alone, the last of the Marcaboths. He would not be the last of the Marcaboths and never again would Enid be more gorgeous than any other man's wife.

But she is of higher birth than most men's wives. No passing of time can change that fact.

His mind returned to the old, old daydream, and he remembered how years ago, when the dream was new, he had fancied himself coming into complete and solitary control of the Marcaboth holdings and giving Enid's photograph to the press.

"No, please do not take my picture. She deserves the

credit for all I have achieved. Print her picture. She has been my inspiration. Enid Beasley Marcaboth, my wife. Yes, Caldwell Beasley's daughter."

That would have shown people something. That would have shown them. But he had not come into complete and solitary control of the Marcaboth holdings. Nobody had died. Nobody had trusted him enough to die.

I should have told Simon, he thought. I should have told Simon that I was sitting here every day imagining him dead. Wolfe smiled a little. I can see it now. He'd have knocked on wood, spit three times, and said, "Look, Kid, my part of the business you can have. Only stop imagining me dead." Poor superstitious Simon, ignorant Simon, Simon who was the first-born.

Why should Simon be head of the firm? Just because he was the oldest son? How stupid. How medieval.

And a moment ago I was playing with the idea of subjecting myself and my wife to an evening with him. I must have been crazy. I was going to do him a favor. After all the things he's done to me! When I think what I have put up with from the very beginning.

And when he looked back at the very beginning there was Simon again, Simon in an old suit that didn't quite fit him, Simon holding out chewing gum and peanuts to an expectant little child, chewing gum and peanuts that he had bought by stinting on his lunch.

Oh, Christ, Wolfe said. All right. All right.

He got up from his desk and walked into the corridor that connected his office with Simon's. Simon's secretary, at the sound of his footsteps, fluttered toward him from the reception room.

"Has Mr. Simon gone home?"

"No, sir. He has Mr. Iscanun with him."

"Oh, he has?" And the door was closed, closed as though Simon wished to prevent his brother from entering.

"Yes, but *you* can go in, Mr. Wolfe." She smiled at the idea of trying to keep Mr. Wolfe out.

"Why, thank you, Miss Cass. That's terribly decent of you. But really I don't think I want to get in the middle of one of those hysterical sessions."

The secretary looked as though she wished to say that the remark was uncalled for.

She hates me, Wolfe thought, suddenly. Simon's secretary hates me. Funny I never noticed it before.

"Is there something I can do, Mr. Wolfe?"

"No, just tell Mr. Simon that if he wants me—" His voice trailed off. Here was a problem. He had told Simon that he and Enid were going to be busy that evening. Now how could he say that he would be at the club? But how could he leave Simon without a number at which to contact him? He never did that. Suppose something happened and Simon needed him? Well, what the hell, Simon might as well know that he and Ruby had been insulted. He might as well take his slap in the face like a man.

"Tell him I'll be at my club."

"Yes, Mr. Wolfe."

Wolfe went back to his own office. But I was going to tell Simon that if he still wanted us, Enid and I would—

That had been before he had seen Simon's closed door and the way Simon's secretary hated him. So much for good intentions, he thought. People just don't appreciate them.

It was enough that Enid had called on Ruby and brought a present. He wished now that he had told Enid to simply telephone the girl and wish her a happy birthday.

Garth was polishing his glasses when his secretary came into the office. She said, "These calls came while you were busy."

He put his glasses on and looked at the list. "What did Mrs. Kenlund want?" he asked.

"Oh, she just said you weren't to forget tonight," she said.

He nodded. He was pleased. He had been concerned that the call had meant that the Kenlunds were forced to cancel the engagement. He wished that Magda had called Judith instead of calling him. This was just the sort of thing that always raised Judith's resentment against Magda Kenlund. It was foolish of course but Judith was very touchy.

"The Kenlunds," she had once said, "behave as though they had told you that you were welcome to bring a girl and that I just happened to be the girl you brought that night. Did you ever mention to them, Garth, that I'm your wife?"

The whole thing was ridiculous but he did wish that Magda had called his house and spoken to Judith. It was wrong of Magda not to handle things that way, but he certainly wasn't going to give up the Kenlunds' friendship just for a minor eccentricity of Magda's. He had damn near lost their friendship anyhow, he thought sulkily. Twice he had had solid, legitimate reasons for declining their invitations but twice there had been feeble excuses to cover Judith's flat refusals.

"You go alone, Garth. They only want to see you anyhow. They don't want me and I'll tell you straight out I get no pleasure in sitting there like a stuffed animal. They never address a remark to me. They never look at me."

"It's your imagination."

"Then I have the world's best, honey, because I imagine that Magda Kenlund forgot, last time I was there, to even ask me what I wanted to drink. If it hadn't been for the butler having better manners than Magda, everybody in the room would have had just what they wanted except me."

"An oversight, Judith."

"Certainly. I'm not flattering myself that she thinks enough of me to be pointedly rude. She simply doesn't know I'm there."

But he had caught Judith one day in a soft, forgiving mood and he had pinned her down to a date with the Kenlunds. Tonight. And Magda had called to check so everything was all right. It would have been only justice if Magda had made an apology and bowed out.

There had been a time when he had hoped that Magda and Judith would be friends. He knew now that was impossible. Judith had made it impossible by not trying to interest herself in the things that interested Magda. Magda liked gossip and smart clothes and luncheons at fashionable restaurants. Judith could have made the effort to like those things, too. For a girl of Judith's mentality it would be easy for her to pick up a working knowledge of Magda's small, bright world.

The way Magda Kenlund spent her time seemed very charming to Garth—very feminine and correct. He liked to think of ladies having their breakfast in bed, reading their mail there, and later languidly arising to bathe, dress, and go forth to luncheon with other ladies who had also breakfasted in bed. He liked to think of them trying on hats and frocks all afternoon and coming home to rest an hour before dressing for dinner. That was Magda's way. He smiled a little thinking that it was a gentle, civilized way, a trifle old-fashioned, but that only enhanced its appeal.

Judith, that woman of a new and vigorous day, bounded out of bed like a healthy, hungry boy. She was dressed in a trice and was off to oversee children and servants. All day long she was on the go, busy with uncharming business. She wanted to know about things in the PTA and in Shanghai. She did not write on delicate lavender stationery to challenge the bill from the service station. She would go there in person and stick her head under the hood of the car to see just what they had done that cost so much, and when she left she'd be off to settle a dispute between a shoemaker and his landlord or something equally feminine and appealing.

We have new servants today, he thought. Perhaps if Judith mentions that to Magda they will get off on a subject in which both of them have some interest. If Magda had children that would help or if Judith were more inclined to chatter about the private lives of prominent people.

He examined that thought carefully. If Judith had been inclined to chatter about the private lives of prominent people would he have found her company interesting or entertaining? Well, no, but—

That will do. Next witness, please.

Judith was basically just what he wanted, he decided. Basically. She was a good kid. Tonight she'd do some beefing of course about the Kenlunds but that was to be expected. She'd just have to put up with the Kenlunds for him the same way that for her he put up with— He tried to think of something or someone he tolerated for Judith's sake. There must be something.

His mind went back to the morning and it seemed to him that he'd been a little rough with Judith in the matter of going to Simon's house with a present for Ruby. He didn't recall what he had said or the tone in which he had said it but he had a definite memory of not having been pleasant to her. She was having a great day. Not only had he snapped at her but she'd had to call on Ruby. And tonight the Kenlunds. Poor Judith. Oh, well, he'd make it up to her some way.

Of course it could have been worse. If it hadn't been for the date with the Kenlunds he'd have dragged her out with Simon and Ruby tonight. He didn't like thinking about Simon's invitation. He felt that he should have accepted it. He told himself that if anybody but the Kenlunds had been involved he would have disappointed them. He remembered that Simon had sounded so eager and then so crushed.

The more he thought about Simon the more he regretted that he had turned him down. He thought of calling Judith and asking her what they should do. Only he was afraid that Judith wouldn't give him a fair shake. She'd decide against the Kenlunds without even hesitating a moment. She wouldn't see any reason at all for refusing Simon's invitation.

He'd have to say to her, "But we promised the Kenlunds three weeks ago that—"

And she'd say, "But it's Ruby's birthday. Surely Simon and Ruby must be considered before the Kenlunds."

Judith would think that way even if she didn't dislike the Kenlunds. Judith had a very strong family feeling. He didn't like to think about Judith's strong family feeling.

Suppose he got Magda on the phone right now and told her that it was Ruby's birthday? She wouldn't understand at all.

"You mean to say you can't come because your brother's wife is having a birthday?"

You couldn't expect people like Magda to understand the Marcaboths. You couldn't expect her to accept Ruby's birthday as a perfectly logical reason for breaking a long-standing engagement. And you couldn't explain it to her—not unless you also explained the Marcaboths. You would have to go back through the years and find for Magda the bright little bits and pieces of long-forgotten moments. You would have to search your memory and your heart to know why Ruby was both tremendously important and contemptibly insignificant. You would have to exert your subconscious and your imagination to explain the whims and traditions and deep-seated beliefs of the Marcaboths. And in the end, because Magda's ancestors had taken a fierce pride in being undemonstrative and unemotional, Magda would not understand. She would have learned nothing except that once again the Garth Marcaboths had turned down her invitation.

And never again would I hear from the Kenlunds, Garth thought, sadly.

He felt a quick rush of shame at his childishness. Suppose he never saw the Kenlunds again? What did it matter? They were no part of his life. They were people he saw perhaps three or four times a year. A man could certainly lose such a contact without grief, delightful though the contact was. What was the matter with him? Why were the Kenlunds so dear to him that he would let Simon down rather than risk the tenuous hold he had upon the Kenlund friendship? Why was it always so in human relationships? Why in hell do people who'd lie down and die for us always have to take second place to casual acquaintances? Why are we made so that I, for instance, will disappoint Simon but not the Kenlunds?

And he knew that it was because no matter what he did there would always be forgiveness from Simon. The Kenlunds would not overlook a slight hurt. Simon could be stabbed to the heart by his brother and still say, "Forget it, Kid."

That's the whole truth, Garth thought. We only hurt the people that we can get away with hurting.

That night, he thought, he would sit in the Kenlunds' elegant rumpus room with a drink in his hand. He would be alert and eager to drop a witty remark, to tell a good story and to laugh heartily at someone else's. He would be a splendid guest, courteous, conversational, and fairly sparkling with eagerness to please his hosts. This the Kenlunds would take in their stride. Their eyes would not gleam with pleasure at his performance. But Simon—Simon would appreciate his young brother's warmth and comradery. The Kenlunds didn't need it. Simon did. But Simon wasn't going to get it because Simon was only the brother to whom you turned when you were puzzled or troubled. Simon wasn't the Kenlunds.

They'd be sore if Judith and I didn't come tonight, Garth thought.

He couldn't bear the thought of the Kenlunds being sore. And, after all, Judith *had* brought a gift to Ruby.

Rome Marcaboth walked out on the little balcony that gave a view of the shop. He stood there gazing down at the salesmen and customers and wished that there was an excuse, as sometimes there was, for leaving his office to assist the salesmen. He had business waiting for him on his desk but he kept thinking about Simon. There had been that message from a salesman that Simon had come in to see him. Rome felt guilty about Simon. He knew he should call him and ask if he had wanted anything special. But he didn't like to call. He was afraid that he would awaken a false hope and thus disappoint Simon twice in one day.

We could have gone with him tonight, Rome thought. This other do isn't so important. I don't even like Canasta and Solime wouldn't have minded giving it up.

Only how could you reconcile yourself to spending an evening with Ruby? How could you act toward her as though you liked her? Rome knew that Ruby was a Marcaboth now and that as such he would have to accept her for himself and for Solime. But not on a moment's notice. It was inevitable that he would have to see Ruby again and that Solime would have to look upon the girl as a sister, but they needed time to prepare themselves.

He wondered if David Galal had seen Ruby. He wondered if David Galal had said to Simon, "How could you do this to my daughter? How could you give Solime Ruby for a sister?" If David had not said it then he must have thought it.

But Simon is my brother and Ruby is his wife. We should have gone with him tonight.

There would be other nights though. He shuddered at the thought that there would be other nights when he would be unable to avoid bringing Solime to Ruby. He thought about the time they had gone to Simon's to meet Ruby. Simon had just married her at Las Vegas and had brought her home. She'd received them wearing some kind of a hostess gown. She had been just a little drunk and the gown had kept slipping off her left breast and Simon had been very busy slipping it back where it belonged.

Simon, bless his soul, hadn't been the least bit embarrassed. Rome had loved him for the cool, matter-of-fact manner in which he had kept Ruby's clothes on her. It was wonderful because you knew that Simon had thought it all out before he had married Ruby. He had said to himself in his own way, in the way Simon would speak to himself: So all right, she's not a lady but I want her so I'll marry her.

Ruby had trotted out some gifts from Simon to show the girls. There was a tremendous emerald, a necklace, and a pair of earrings. There were some other things that Rome couldn't recall but he remembered one gift in particular—the coat. He laughed a little now at the memory of Ruby coming downstairs with the coat slung over her hostess gown.

"Look at this," she said to her sisters-in-law. "Know what it is?" She hadn't waited for an answer. "This," she had announced proudly, "is white mink. White mink, mind you, and I'm going to shoot the first son-of-a-gun who mistakes it for ermine."

Simon had sent for some coffee and after that Ruby had been more subdued. She had even been reduced to offering shy little smiles to anyone who happened to look her way. But it was too late. The Marcaboths had her number.

Even so we should have gone tonight, Rome thought. It would have made Simon happy.

He had no reason to suppose that Simon wasn't happy.

What he had really meant was that his acceptance of the invitation would have given Simon pleasure.

It would have been a good deal anyway. It would have settled our seeing Ruby again for a while.

There was no way of avoiding Ruby. She was Simon's wife. Little as he liked to force her upon Solime it had to be accepted as a patent fact that from time to time into their lives a little Ruby Marcaboth must fall. Simon shouldn't have gotten himself hooked. It was so hard on Solime.

She puts up with everything so uncomplainingly, he thought. He wondered if his mother loved Solime best of all her daughters-in-law. She ought to. Solime was certainly perfect in every detail. He thought how she had never protested spending all holidays with his mother, how she had resigned from The Circle because his sister was not welcome, how she respected and admired his older brothers.

Mama often speaks of how Hannah regarded her golden goblet almost as though it were a sacred symbol. Well, Solime does the same.

The thought of the golden goblets brought a new idea to mind. Maybe Ruby would establish a precedent. Maybe she'd be the first Marcaboth bride to receive her goblet by mail. What an embarrassment it must be to Simon that Ruby was not going to Mama's tonight.

Poor Simon. I should have gone with him to make him feel a little better. It always cheers him up to be with me.

Still there was no gainsaying the fact that Solime had made an engagement. Solime must be considered, too.

I'm not like Wolfe, Rome thought. To me wives are people. They have rights. I couldn't just cancel out Solime's plans as though she had no business arranging anything.

Still if he had asked her she would have gone with Simon and Ruby. Cheerfully she would have gone. She would have felt it a duty that must be discharged as though one enjoyed it. He shook his head in wonderment that anyone should be as thoroughly fine as Solime was and that he had had the luck to marry her.

She can't know how much I appreciate her. Funny how the time was so rarely right for a fellow to make a speech to his wife, telling her the way he felt about all the great things she did for him. Oh, sometimes the opportunity was there. Sometimes you said, "Gee, honey, that was swell." But the moments were infrequent, the moments when you could break out with a really big round of applause and not feel a little foolish. Perhaps there'd be a chance tonight to tell Solime how absolutely wonderful she was. A fellow ought to find a place for such talk occasionally. Maybe tonight would be just right.

No, he couldn't have asked Solime to change her plans so that they could go with Simon. What the hell, Simon could do his own entertaining for Ruby. Solime inconvenienced herself enough for the family. Even today she had bothered to run out and buy a present for Ruby and take it up to the girl. That was plenty. It was too much as a matter of fact. Or at least it would be too much if Ruby weren't Mrs. Simon Marcaboth, wife of the oldest brother.

Miss Blount was in the room. You didn't have to pay any attention to her. She was rather like a moth. You could slap her down or permit her to rustle aimlessly about just as you pleased. Zeda glanced at the clock. Four-thirty. Soon she would call Simon and in a matter-of-fact way she would tell him that he and Ruby were not to be late for dinner.

Though she would not be able to see his face it was possible to picture the way he would look. Many a time she had caused him to wear the same stunned, reproachful expression. He was fifty now, fifty with a streak of white in his hair and grandchildren in his will, but he had never learned that he couldn't fool his mother. Why was that? She liked to know reasons. Why had he never learned?

An answer so new and shocking came to her that it had to be examined. Was it possible that Simon was so thoroughly honest and aboveboard himself that he did not look for others to be devious? Could it be that because he set no traps himself he was in the habit of forgetting their existence? This was puzzling and interesting. She thought of Simon as a shrewd man. Perhaps he was a good man. Perhaps he had prospered not by skill but had actually received the fair rewards of the worthy. Could it be that what holy writings promised truly came to pass? Could it be that a man got rich because he was pure of heart? No, a man got rich because he was sharper than another man.

And Simon was sharper than other men. All right then. If he was sharper, why had he never learned that he couldn't fool his mother?

She remembered the night so long ago when she had gone to sit on the edge of Simon's bed, to tell the child that she had fought a losing battle, that his father was taking him out of school.

"Simon, we cannot fight him. I have tried. It is no use. He will not let you get an education."

"It don't matter, Mama. I don't care. Honest I don't."

He hadn't fooled her then. She had known that he was afraid of his father and of what awaited him out there in Marcaboth's dusty warehouse.

"You must obey him, Simon. You must try to please him."

"I will, Mama."

"It will be easier for you if you do not answer him back or make him mad."

"I will do my best, Mama." In the darkness he had reached for her hand.

"Poor Simon."

"No, Mama, I don't mind. Honest I don't. I'd never learn anything at school. I'm a dope. Honest I am, Mama. I'm a dope." He had wanted her to think that the small uncontrolled sound that blocked a word here and there was laughter. It wasn't laughter. Simon at fourteen, Simon at fifty could not fool his mother.

She remembered Simon going off to work that first morning. She had given him an apple to take with him. It amazed her to find that she could recall the feel, the look of that apple, satin smooth, bright scarlet with a bold band of gold.

"The apple will be nice, Simon, around ten o'clock maybe."

And so he had begun his career—a man, a man of fourteen going off to work with frightened eyes, Simon, Simon Marcaboth, the elegant Mr. Simon who had to have even his pajamas custom made. But on that faraway morning he had slipped the apple in his pocket and its scarlet brilliance had gleamed cheerfully through the threadbare material. Mr. Simon, the elegant.

Zeda laughed aloud remembering. Miss Blount glanced slantwise at her and Zeda thought: She thinks I'm crazy. With young people it's only today that counts. If you're not laughing at something that happened today then you're crazy.

Miss Blount said, "I came to wake you but I see you're awake."

"Yes, I'm awake." Zeda's eyes went to the clock. It was almost five. Almost five. Time to do the thing that she'd impatiently awaited all day. She reached for the telephone and dialed his private number.

"Simon, darling, tell Ruby happy birthday and please don't be late for dinner. I'm expecting you at seven-thirty sharp."

A SUDDEN cool breeze fluttered the curtains of Enid's room. She glanced at the clock in surprise. She had not guessed that it was late enough for the thermometer to begin its daily descent. But it was time. It was well after five. After five and the aspirin had not helped. The tooth still ached.

If I could only get my mind off it. I must think of something else. What else will I think of?

Of course there was always Wolfe. She could think about Wolfe. She could think that he didn't care that her tooth ached, that he didn't care that she was alone. He would go to his club tonight and he would play bridge and have a few discreet drinks and her toothache would be no concern of his.

If I were dying, she thought, it would be no concern of his.

Today it was only a toothache. She would not die from a toothache, but some day it would be something else, something from which she would die. Everybody dies. All the people on earth were waiting only to learn the name of the thing that would ultimately destroy them.

I don't know what I am going to die of, Enid thought, but I do know that as I lie in this room dying of whatever it is there will be no one to hold my hand, no one to understand what I'm feeling, no one to say the words that will bring me strength or peace. And what is the use of a marriage that can end like that?

She got off the chaise longue and walked over to the mirror and looked at herself. Come, come, my girl, she said. You're awfully damn sorry for yourself, aren't you? And she stood there studying the woman with the artfully bleached hair and after a time she said: Yes, I am. Yes, I'm awfully damn sorry for myself.

She thought that the aching tooth at least could have been helped had she seen the dentist today. But Ruby's birthday was important to the Marcaboths. You did the things that seemed important to the Marcaboths. You did these things because Zeda and Simon had never harmed you, because Garth and Jerome were nice enough kids. You did nothing because of Wolfe. Many a long day had

come and gone since Enid Marcaboth had done anything
for love of Wolfe. But you had to consider the family.
You had to consider the Marcaboth family because it was
so anxious to establish itself as something great and strong
and it was so pitiably vulnerable. You paid service to the
Marcaboth household gods. You had accepted your golden
goblet so you did not flinch when you saw that in return
for the goblet you must help build an indestructible temple
dedicated to the proposition that the unity of the Marcaboth family was important beyond all else in life.

And Enid stood there thinking of the other Mrs. Marcaboths. She thought of Zeda, the determined and clever, and
of good, conscientious Judith. She thought of Solime, so
lovely and perfect, and she remembered poor, dead Hannah whose soul had been a steadfast little light that had existed only to be of help to others. And then she was thinking of Ruby.

Styles in Mrs. Marcaboths have changed this season, she
said to herself. Ruby has a lover.

And she thought that she had never wanted a lover but
that there had been other things she had wanted.

I did not get them, she thought. I did not get them because I was not brave enough to get them. Always I was
afraid of angering Wolfe. Always I wanted to avoid a
scene.

She knew that there were people who boasted of do-
mestic concord. "Anything to keep peace," they said. And
they were proud of themselves and were often admired
and respected by their friends. But Enid did not admire or

respect them. She knew them for what they were because she was one of them—not strong, not selfless, just weak and timid, frightened of another's anger, quailing beneath sarcasm, weeping at an unkind word—cowards, not great-hearted peace-makers at all. They were only sniveling little worms who were afraid.

Only once was I brave, she thought. I defied my father. And if that was funny, then somebody else could laugh at it.

She thought that perhaps if her father had shouted at her she would not today be Mrs. Wolfe Marcaboth. But he had not shouted and so she had been brave.

And she thought that had she wanted a lover desperately she would not have had the courage to take one. But Ruby had the courage. Ruby was not afraid. She was not afraid of risks. Suppose Simon had walked in today instead of the sisters-in-law? It could happen and Ruby must know that it could.

Do I admire her for having a lover? Do I want her autograph?

Yes, maybe, for Ruby was not weak. She did not shrink from scenes. It did not matter that what Ruby wanted was shabby and cheap. It mattered only that Ruby was her own woman and would fight to remain so. Ruby wasn't a sniveling little worm. You would not wish your daughter—if you had one—to be exactly like Ruby Marcaboth, but you might pray that she would not find life endurable only when it resembled the peace and quiet of the grave.

And Enid thought that Ruby had broken her marriage

vows and therefore should be dismissed from the mind of
any decent woman.

All right. What do you mean by that? Do you mean
that you're a better woman than Ruby? Are you a better
woman because you never wanted a lover and would have
been too scared to take one if you had? Does that make
you a better woman? Who do you think would show more
guts if the chips were down? You or Ruby? What could
you face? What are you not afraid of?

Ghosts? Hold-up men? Thunder and lightning? Crazy
people? Fire? Flood? Plague? What wasn't she afraid of?
Everything. Anything.

God alone knew what Ruby had come through to reach
the place she occupied today. And now that she was there,
did she tremble at the thought of losing all that she possessed? Not Ruby. Simon could not conquer her with a
pink house and a regiment of white minks. She did as she
chose. She took risks. If she lost then she lost, but she
would not stay in the pink house simply because it was
safe and quiet. She was not afraid.

I guess I do want her autograph, Enid thought.

And she was not happy that she had brought herself to
a place in life where she could admire Ruby. She did not
like comparing herself to Ruby and finding that she liked
Ruby better.

But there is no reason why I should compare myself to
her. Good God, what's the matter with me? Earlier today
I saw Ruby for what she really is—a sharp little beast. She
sold herself to Simon. But literally.

That was a good point. Yes. Ruby wouldn't have married Simon had he been a poor man. She'd made a deal. Her youth and beauty for his money. Fine. She—Enid—had loved Wolfe. Ladies didn't sell themselves. She'd have married Wolfe had he been penniless. Ladies were entirely different than people like Ruby. And that was final. There was no reason on earth why she and Ruby should be expected to think or react in the same way.

Only there was one small question still to be answered. She had married Wolfe because she loved him, but it was true that she did not love him now. Then what was she doing here? She had not married Wolfe for his money. She had married him for love, but the love was gone. So what remained? What remained?

And she thought how she had never lived without servants or charge accounts or big automobiles and she thought that at her age it was certainly too late to start learning what that would be like.

Now, she said to herself, you're back to the same thing again. You're a coward.

And Enid was ashamed that she was a coward. She searched her mind for reasons that might explain why she was here in Wolfe Marcaboth's house, alone and lonely. And she could find no reason that did not hinge upon her cowardice.

Then suddenly it came to her, the thing for which she had been searching, a reason why she could not leave, a reason so sound and logical that she need never hear Wolfe's angry words or come to test her own fortitude. She could not go because the unity of the Marcaboths would be shattered if she left. If she remained then the Marcaboth temple would never be demolished, the shrine never discredited, the worshipers never silenced.

It was sound. It was logical but it wouldn't do. It wouldn't do unless you were searching consciously, realistically for a way to lie to yourself. Ruby knew nothing of family unity. She could not respect what she did not understand. From her the Marcaboths would learn something. They would learn that even with money there were some women who could not be held, quiet and submissive, at the hearthside. There were those from whom you could purchase anything and there were those like Ruby, wild and capricious, whose values and traditions changed from day to day.

There were still others who yearned for escape but lacked courage.

And presently because she was ashamed of her cowardice Enid Marcaboth dressed herself again in the shepherd's plaid skirt and the black blouse. She went to her closet and took down a black gabardine coat to wear against the cool of the summer evening.

She let herself out of the house and stepped into her car and drove away. She did not know the street or number of the house that she sought. She only knew that somewhere it was waiting for her. It had been waiting a long, long while. Ruby had been in kindergarten when the house had begun to wait for Enid. It had had to wait all these years, till Ruby grew up and had stood in the sunlight beside Simon Marcaboth's pool laughing at cowards.

And after a time on a street where dusty palm trees rattled in the small wind Enid saw a building with a vacancy sign upon it. She walked in and asked her questions.

"Seventy-five furnished. Bath, kitchenette, and a combination bed-living room."

"I'd like to see it, please."

"You would?" Sharp blue eyes running over the fit of the black gabardine coat, over the blaze of Enid's diamond. "You would really?"

They walked out into the patio again and crossed in front of a neglected little fountain and into a room that overlooked the street.

"Bed's in the wall. Bath there. Kitchenette behind the screen. For the money it's not bad."

Enid looked about her. She saw a room with a motheaten carpet and soiled wallpaper. She looked past the dirty curtains and out at the messy little fountain that had been expected to give tone to the patio. Upon the ceiling there was a wavy yellowish mark and behind the screen—there was what?

"Of course it needs a good cleaning. The stove needs a real good cleaning and the icebox, too, but that's no job at all, and look here at the closet space. For an apartment this size it's unusual."

Enid nodded. She wasn't afraid to wash curtains or stoves or iceboxes and she wasn't interested in closet space. She was looking at a chair, a chair that was neither new or

clean. It was just a big, cheerful slob of a chair that seemed
to be smiling all over its faded pattern. It was a big chair.
A woman could flop down in it and get as comfortable in
it and as fat as she chose. And it had arms. On one of them
you could hang a knitting bag. And you could sit there
and listen to the radio or read a book.

Enid opened her purse and handed the woman twenty
dollars. "I'll be back tomorrow with the rest."

"You will?"

"Yes."

"Wait till I give you a receipt."

She gave a new name to the woman, a name that had
just popped into her head. It would do. Davis. What was
wrong with being Mrs. Davis? Maybe Davis was a very
nice fellow.

She walked out of the patio and stood on the street.
Everything a person would need right at the corner, the
woman had said—stores, movies, everything. Enid walked
to the corner. Yes, everything was there, everything a person would need, everything she needed.

"Dr. Klushing. No Appointment Necessary. Open Evenings. Walk Right Up."

She stood there trembling. She? Enid, daughter of Caldwell Beasley, wife of Wolfe Marcaboth? She whose dentist
was privileged to fumble with the molars of the great and
celebrated? She felt the trembling in her knees and she
stood there beneath a skimpy palm tree and she knew this
was the pay-off. She either had the guts or she hadn't. She
either walked up those stairs or she didn't, and if she didn't

it was because there was nothing left of her worth saving.
And she knew that there were people who went to Dr.
Klushing and did not feel themselves degraded by his touch.
And she knew that it was not that they were less delicate
than she, less precious or worth while. It was only that
they were people and she knew that never in her life had
she been "people." She had only been Miss Beasley and
Mrs. Marcaboth and that was not even being alive.

And after a while the trembling stopped and she climbed
the stairs and met a man in a white coat who did not ask
how the Princess was nor try to relax her strained nerves
by talking trivialities over a cigarette. This man examined,
poked a bit, and said, "That'll have to come out."

"All right," she said. "How much will it cost?"

And she was crying. She was crying with sudden hysterical joy for the words had come naturally. They had
come from Mrs. Davis who lived in a little apartment with
a cat to keep her company, Mrs. Davis who only had three
thousand a year and couldn't be extravagant. Never before
had she asked such a question. How much will it cost? The
words were new to her but they tasted sweet in her mouth.
To Enid Marcaboth they tasted of freedom.

Judith remembered that the departed servants, during their
brief stay in her house, had used a certain amount of dishes
and kitchen utensils in their lunch preparations. She supposed they had cleaned up satisfactorily before leaving but
she thought it wise to check. Judith could not bear the

thought that something in her kitchen might be improperly washed.

She made a tour of inspection, examining saucepans and anything else they might have touched. Everything seemed in perfect order. She walked into the room behind the kitchen. It was neat. They had had no time to rumple its candlewick spread or disarrange the dotted swiss curtains. The ash tray had been forgotten however. There were two cigarette ends in it. She emptied them into the garbage disposal and wiped out the tray with a paper towel. Then Anne and Frederick were truly gone with no evidence to show that they had ever been in Judith's house.

Dinner would have to be considered now, she thought. She sat down at the enamel-topped table with a pad and pencil. She had ordered food for the servants and children. She had made no preparations for Garth and herself. They had expected to dine out this evening. Now they would dine at home and Garth didn't like chopped meat. He was expecting to go to the Kenlunds' for dinner. He wasn't going to be at all pleased to learn that there were no servants and that therefore he and Judith were going to have to stay home with the children.

But he could go to the Kenlunds' if he wanted. He didn't have to stay home.

God knows I don't want to go to the Kenlunds', Judith thought. It's a break for me to get out of it.

She laid her pencil down as an idea occurred to her. There had been so much quarreling and bickering about the Kenlunds that maybe Garth would think she had actually discharged the servants to avoid having dinner with these friends of his. Oh, no, he wouldn't think that. He wouldn't? Well, why wouldn't he? He was awfully damned touchy about his damned Kenlunds. Yes, but this was going too far. You just didn't discharge servants in order to— But how did you convince Garth of that? Especially if he was sore.

Judith picked up the pencil again. Oh, well, for dinner there'd be— So what did he have to get sore about? This hadn't been a particularly good day for her. If anybody was going to be sore it wasn't going to be Garth. Who had had to go prancing over to Simon's house with a present for Ruby? Garth?

Hell, no. I had to go. So where does he get off being so sore? If he doesn't want chopped meat let him go to his Kenlunds for dinner. Let him go anyhow.

Kenlunds! Ruby! A fine day she'd had, and Garth was sore!

She threw the pencil toward the tiled sideboard. I'm not right in my head, she thought. What's the matter with me today? He'll probably stay home and eat his chopped meat like a good little angel.

She glanced at the gleaming white clock above the sink. Half-past five. Were the Feltons going to bring the children home or was she supposed to pick them up?

If they're not here in another five minutes, she thought, I'll go get them.

Would he know it was chopped meat if it was baked into a lovely, tasty loaf? And what did it matter anyhow? Let

him go to the Kenlunds'. He was dying to go. Let him go.
Who was stopping him? Him and his fine friends and fine
family. She could tell him something that would surprise
him about what was going on in that family of his.

"Your sister-in-law, Ruby," she could say, "has a lover.
How do you like that? Simon's wife has a lover."

That would take his mind off the Kenlunds fast enough.
It would even take his mind off the chopped meat. But she
wouldn't tell him. He wouldn't thank her for the information. The Marcaboths liked to think of themselves in a special way. They liked to think that they walked in glory
before an admiring and respectful world. Well, Garth
would never learn from her that Ruby had a lover. Even
when he heard it from someone else she wouldn't say that
she had known all along.

When he heard it from someone else? Was it inevitable
that he should some day be informed that Simon's wife was
unfaithful? Judith considered the matter and decided that
it was inevitable. Ruby was not very smart, and like most
stupid people she thought no one smarter than herself. She
would be careless and impulsive. She would think that her
lies were clever and that everyone was fooled by them.
Her servants, her acquaintances, and friends of her lover
would talk about her, and eventually the word would come
to the Marcaboths. And they would know that Ruby had
a lover.

They won't be so proud then, Judith thought. And she
was surprised to find that there was no satisfaction in pic-
turing the Marcaboths humbled. There was only sadness in

229

the thought that a piece of glittering human junk like Ruby Marcaboth could wreck their dreams.

They had wanted to stand for all the virtues and graces. They had wanted more than it was possible for a family to achieve. A single human working alone may actually reach a kind of perfection, but an entire family group is a different thing. There will always be the son who marries a slut or the son who marries a girl from Silso Street.

But I tried, Judith thought. I tried not to shatter the dream. I sweated to give the Marcaboths what they wanted, a Judith molded to their tastes, to their needs, and it was all in vain.

And she thought how useless it was to wear the proper clothes and say the proper thing and be a proper Mrs. Marcaboth when all the time Ruby had a lover. Why should a woman break her mother's heart to please the Marcaboths when next month, next week, or maybe tomorrow Zeda and Simon and all the rest of them would know that they were building nothing?

I could buy a dress now, Judith thought, like the pink one I wore so long ago, the dress that made all the Marcaboths flinch at sight of it. It wouldn't matter now. We can relax. The Marcaboths need strain no more.

And Judith thought about the pink dress that her mother had bought for her.

I guess it was pretty awful, she said to herself, but it wasn't only my mother who was fooled. I liked the dress myself. It looked just fine to me. And if my taste is not the same as the Marcaboths, if I come from Silso Street, if

I've had no advantages, where is their right to complain? I, at least, will never be the subject of conversation in a cocktail bar.

And Judith got up and walked out of her kitchen. She did not stop to powder her face or to reset the line of her lipstick. She did not even pick up a coat. She simply walked out of her kitchen and got into her car.

In front of the Feltons' house she called to her children and they came running. Their knees were grass-stained and their hair uncombed. Kenneth had a tear in his T-shirt and there were fruit juice stains on the front of Lorna's dress. They jumped into the back of the car, and when Judith did not turn toward home Kenneth asked, "Where are we going, Mom?"

"Sit down," she said. "It's a long ride—all the way downtown."

"As far as Hollywood? Gee, there's a good picture playing in Hollywood."

"You're going further downtown than Hollywood, son."

"As far as Daddy's office?"

"Further than Daddy's office."

He sat down. He could think of nothing further away than Daddy's office. He was sobered by the sudden realization that the world then was not bounded by the Feltons' house and Daddy's office. The journey would be long and dangerous. "Sit down, Lorna," he said, irritably. "For gosh's sakes, sit down."

The trip was against traffic all the way. The city was coming home after a long, hot day's work. The city was moving toward Hollywood and Beverly Hills and West-wood and Santa Monica. It was moving toward dinner and whatever else the night might offer.

Lorna said that she was thirsty, and Judith promised that soon they would be where they were going.

"Where are we going, Mom?" Kenneth asked again.

"Silso Street," Judith said.

"What's Silso Street?"

It was a place you had tried to forget, a forbidden place, a place to which you were only free to return when you knew that Ruby had a lover. But to her son Judith said, "It's where my mother and father live."

"Gee, Mom, I didn't know you had a mother and father."

She said, "That is understandable." And she said it in a way that silenced the little boy.

When she stopped the car the children looked doubt-fully about them. Judith said, "Come on." And they went with her up the sagging steps. She tried the door and it was open. It was always open for Brina or Kevi or for Uncle Eli and Aunt Gulda. Judith walked through the dark hall with her children behind her.

"Mom," Kenneth whispered.

"It's all right, Kenneth. You'll see."

Brina was setting the table. She turned and looked at Judith with her bold, black eyes. "What's the matter?" she asked. "Is Beverly Hills on fire? Or does this look like a comfort station?"

"Brina, where's my mother?"

"She's across the street visiting. She'll be back. Hey, Papa. Hey, Kevi. Come see what we got here."

Kevi came from the kitchen with a bar of yellow soap in his hand. Papa, blinking his eyes, had obviously been awakened from his before-dinner nap. They did not speak to her. They just looked at her and at her children. Judith said nothing. She stood with Kenneth and Lorna at her side and she waited in silence for the judgment of her family, because she knew it was her place to be silent in the face of their righteous scorn.

"We could have been dead," Kevi said, "and she wouldn't have known or cared."

"Dead?" Papa shrugged. "Dead is the least."

Brina set the butter dish upon the table. "I thought she lost the address."

Lorna turned her face away from the dark, unfriendly eyes of these strangers. She wailed and Judith did not comfort her for the child was not only the daughter of Garth Marcaboth. She was of these people, too, and she must learn to take them as they were.

"We're scaring the children," Kevi said.

"It is natural. We are not Marcaboths and this is not Beverly Hills."

Judith still was silent. She was at fault and must take her punishment. Kevi turned back toward the kitchen. "I have to finish washing up," he said.

"And I my nap." Papa walked away.

Brina said, "But maybe her Mama will want to see her."

"Perhaps." Papa flung the word over his shoulder as he disappeared from view.

Kenneth looked entreatingly at Judith.

"No," she said to him. "We stay."

"How long, Mom?"

"We stay for dinner," Judith said.

Brina laughed. "If you're invited."

"I'll be invited. I came and I brought my children. I can do no more."

"But you could have done it sooner," Kevi said. He came back into the room, a towel in his hand, his hard face still dripping cold water. "You've almost killed your mother."

Judith nodded. "I am sorry for all I have done."

Brina said, "Every day of her life your mother has cried for the way you've treated her."

Judith looked down at the children. Kenneth was old enough to understand and he was listening intently. Lorna would know; the knowledge of what this scene meant would come to her in later years. They would know, Lorna and Kenneth, that their mother had not honored her parents. This, too, was part of her punishment.

Brina's eyes went to the children. She did not smile at them or they at her. Judith said, "The little girl is thirsty. May she have some water?"

Kevi uttered an oath. "Don't you know where the kitchen is?" he asked. "Brina's not your servant."

"I did not dare to use the kitchen freely," Judith explained. She knew that she would have been wrong no matter what course she had taken. To have moved ahead into the kitchen as though it were her own would have angered her brother as much as her request had done. She would have been wrong either way, and it was infinitely just that for her there should be no justice.

"Come, children," she said, taking a step toward the kitchen.

"Leave them here," Kevi said. "We won't hurt them."

She went out into the small, hot kitchen and drew a glass of water from the tap. Her children weren't given tap water to drink but here there were no large, gleaming bottles of sparkling spring water. And here they would drink what she had drunk as a child.

She gave the glass to Lorna. "Do you want a drink of water, Kenneth?"

"I asked him," Brina said. "Maybe he'd like a little milk."

Kevi glared at her. "Milk can be poison," he said. "On Silso Street it would surely sicken a Marcaboth."

"These children are only half Marcaboth," Judith said.

"They look like Marcaboths to me and so do you." He wheeled about suddenly. "I'm going home," he said to Brina.

"Your Mama's expecting us to stay here for supper," Brina said. "And—and here she comes now."

They were silent listening to Mama's heavy footsteps in the hall. Even the children turned expectantly toward the door, and Mama came in, puffing and sighing, and she looked at Judith and the children and she said, "How good is God!" And Judith went to her and was folded against her mother's broad, soft breast.

And Mama knew no bitter words. She only said, "How
the children have grown. So wonderful they are looking!
Come here, Kenneth, darling. Come here, little Lorna.
Come to Grandma, you sweet little lambs." And the children did not hesitate. They went to her for it was true that
they were only half Marcaboth. And Brina got three more
plates out of the cupboard and Kevi said, "Mama, that
boy's no baby. You can't take him on your lap." And after
a while Papa came out of the bedroom and he said, "So,
Kenneth, what do you learn in school?"

He was not ready to talk to Judith, but Judith was content. Papa was talking to her children and soon he would
talk to her. And when he did she would be at peace again.
It had been a long while, but as Mama had said, "How good
is God."

Solime glanced at her watch. The meeting had been in-
terminable. Every suggestion had been wrangled over.
Every motion had opened a new series of debates.

Lisa Benrabnan had convulsed the ladies by saying,
"When did Jacob Malik become a member of The Circle?"

They had not begun the discussion till Solime had arrived. Their politeness, she thought, was at times very inconvenient. Had they not waited for her the meeting might
have adjourned at a sensible time. Now who could tell
when there would be an end to it? What would she say to
Rome? Could she say she'd been shopping? From the way

things were going the stores might well be closed for two hours by the time she reached home.

She looked about her at the other forty-six members of The Circle. No, the other forty-five. Somebody—she couldn't remember just who—was in the hospital having her appendix out. Nobody, she thought enviously, seemed to have anything to consider except the Silver Star Ball. Everything was vigorously opposed or strongly recommended—decorations, orchestras, menus, prices of tickets. These things completely absorbed them. They sat on couches, chairs, and stools and on the floor and Solime observed with horror that they all looked willing and eager to stay till the last question had been thoroughly threshed out. Solime on a red satin chair close to Lisa Benrabnan suddenly wondered why she wasn't sitting on the floor. She had been the last to arrive. How had it happened that she had been given a chair? All older women naturally were given chairs, but Solime would not qualify on those grounds for many a year. Why had Baba greeted her and led her to this chair beside Lisa? Oh, well, it was undoubtedly because Baba was a darling and thought Solime would want to be next to Mother. It had nothing to do with Lisa at all.

Baba was sitting on the floor protesting hotly that nobody, just nobody, could offer only one name orchestra any more. There would have to be a rumba outfit beside the regular band, and that would have to be a good, well-paid aggregation, too.

237

"Don't you want us to make any profit for the Old People's Home, Baba?"

"That's just the point. There'll be more profit my way."

"I think she's right."

"I think one orchestra is enough. Listen, there's a law of diminishing returns, you know."

"What does that mean?"

"I don't know, but there just is."

Everybody laughed. Solime wished she could laugh as lightheartedly as the others. They were enjoying themselves. Their husbands knew where they were. Their husbands were happy to have them members of The Circle. Their husbands didn't have sisters who had no business aspiring to membership in exclusive clubs.

Lisa said, "Let's vote on the two orchestras."

They voted. The second orchestra was defeated. Mrs. Algazi, the oldest member of The Circle, sitting in a corner, her thick-lidded eyes closed, her sloping shoulders slightly hunched, murmured something. Everybody quieted down.

"Please, Mrs. Algazi, we didn't hear you," Lisa said.

"I said I'd pay for the second orchestra myself. The child's right. There should be two orchestras."

There was a round of applause for Mrs. Algazi.

"What else are we fighting about?" Mrs. Algazi asked.

"Decorations."

"I'll buy them."

"But should they be silver or floral?"

"They should be something you can decide on fast. I'm getting tired."

They decided on floral decorations—lots of them. Mrs. Algazi grunted as she drew another round of applause.

A great wave of generosity was sweeping over the members now. Why shouldn't they have the entire proceeds of the ball to hand over to the Home? Why should there be any bills to be paid when the ball was over? Surely in this group the members could finance the affair themselves. Solime cringed in the red satin chair. At least a hundred dollars would be expected of her. A hundred dollars was a very small amount and a hundred dollars was a very large amount. It was small when you spent it on something you could explain to your husband. It was large when you had no way of explaining.

I'd give five hundred, she thought, if it weren't for Rome. If I were single now I might give my whole year's allowance.

But because of Rome she must sit there in silence while pledges were coming from all parts of the room. Who was Jerome Marcaboth to do this to her? Who did he *think* he was? He was only a man with a dreadful mother and a set of perfectly disgusting brothers and sisters.

He ought to be glad I can belong to The Circle. If it wasn't for me there wouldn't be anybody to be proud of in the whole damn family.

She became aware of a silence that had fallen in the room. She looked toward Lisa Benrabnan. Lisa was about to speak.

"And now, my friends, we've settled the appropriations

and we've settled the details of the Silver Star Ball. And with that business concluded I say good-by to you."

"What?"

"Lisa!"

"Hush. Let her speak."

Lisa was weeping a little. "My husband has accepted a government appointment in Brazil and we are moving there next month."

Everybody was gazing at Lisa in shocked surprise, everybody but Mother and Mrs. Algazi and the mother of little Baba. These women had known, Solime realized.

"On your next president the committee has decided. It remains only for her to accept the trust. Her mother says she will not. The other two committeewomen say that she must. Now we shall see. Solime Marcaboth, will you succeed me as president of The Circle?"

Solime rose to her feet and looked about her at these women who were her sisters—charming women who had standards of deportment like her own. Yes, they were her sisters. She belonged among them, not among the Marcaboth women. Who were the Marcaboth women to her or she to them? Here in this room, perhaps within an arm's length of her, might sit one or more who had cast a black ball against Jerome's sister and she could not blame them for she felt no kinship with Jerome's sister—kinship was here with the women in this room.

And when it is in the newspaper that I am their president Jerome will be angry for he and his family have bragged to people that I resigned for the insult to his sister.

But I will tell him that he must manage somehow. This is important. This is really important.

She would be president of The Circle and thus take the place that once her mother had held. And she would move on as Mother had moved into other high offices which also would be her right for she was—as Mother had once told her—not like the Marcaboths at all but a person from a family of importance and standing. And her radiance would glow benevolently upon her husband, and she would take him with her and show him how to rise above the Marcaboths. And the husbands of The Circle members would see that all Marcaboths were not as Simon was, and finally Rome would be accepted, and little by little he would find less time for his brothers and in the end they would come to mean nothing to him at all.

Solime stood there looking at these women who were her true sisters. I tried, she thought. I tried to make sisters of the Marcaboth women but I could not. The females whom Zeda had borne could never be sisters to Solime Galal. The women Zeda's sons had married could not be sisters either—not Enid who contributed nothing to the business of living, not Judith from Silso Street, not Ruby who was only a talking animal, not Ruby who— Ruby! Solime had forgotten Ruby till now.

And suddenly she felt tears, hot and salty, streaming down her face, for in that moment Solime knew that the high place which Mother had attained would never be hers. For Solime there would be no wreaths, no trophies, no worship such as Mother had won. Solime had forgotten Ruby, but she was remembering her now. She was remembering that Ruby could quite easily appear one day in a gossip column or even in a divorce court. And she was remembering that you didn't live with barbarians and take their gifts and walk away laughing. You didn't weep beside the graves of their loved ones and bear their children and then pretend that you were not one of them. Which of the Marcaboths would fly from her if she were in trouble? Who among them would say, "She's Jerome's wife but she's nothing to me"? What man or woman of the tribe wanted an honor that shamed the others, that denied their indivisibility? What Marcaboth would stand on the sidelines and watch the others be destroyed? Oh, no, the barbarians had their standards. What are yours, Solime, my fine lady? What are yours? Will you stand with the Marcaboths even though scandal comes or will you identify yourself now and forever with those who want no share in the Marcaboths?

"I—I can't accept. I can't be president." Her tears were choking her but she plunged on. "As a matter of fact I came here today to—to resign."

She could see nothing clearly. She could hear the gasp from Baba and feel Mother's hand closing over hers. She wanted to shake that hand away. Wasn't it Mother who had brought her to this bitter moment? Wasn't it Mother who had instilled these cruel principles of loyalty? All right then. What did you do when your brother-in-law married a harlot? Did you stand with the family or did you act as though the sorrows of the tribe were not your concern at all?

"Resign, Solime?"

242

"Yes." In a very low voice.

Lisa Benrabnan could think of no words. Nothing like this had ever happened before.

Solime could see now. She could see that the members had been staring at her. They were turning away trying to look as though they had not been staring. Mother's hand was still on hers. There was a teardrop lying between the third and fourth knuckle. Mother's or her own? Solime did not know. She only knew that today she had cast her lot for all time with the barbarians. Mother certainly couldn't like it, and yet Mother's hand upon hers felt warm and strong. And when she met Mother's eyes it seemed to Solime that Mother was certainly a curious woman. She had chosen this moment of all others to look at her daughter with pride and satisfaction.

Simon brought his new Cadillac to a stop in the driveway and hurried toward his front door. He paused to pluck the evening paper out of the rosebushes remembering that the servants were off today. He fitted his key into the lock and stepped into the wide, dim foyer of his home. Ruby was sitting on the stairs. He was a little touched that she was there waiting for him.

"There's a big spider in the bedroom," she said.

"Oh."

She got up and began to climb the stairs. She was wearing a chiffon nightgown with a tremendously full skirt. On her feet there were odd-looking cloth-of-gold bedroom slippers and she seemed to have bathed in perfume.

"What's the idea?" he asked.

"Of what? Oh, your brothers' wives brought me some presents. I tried them on down at the pool and then when I went upstairs to change I couldn't get in the bedroom on account of the spider. Did you smell the perfume?"

"Not till I got to Sunset Boulevard."

"Solime gave it to me. It was so faint I couldn't tell I even had any on, so I kept putting on more and more and all of a sudden— Oh, by the way, Jim Clare dropped in today."

"Who's Jim Clare?"

"He's a fellow I know slightly. He dropped in to bring me a present. He bought me a stuffed dog as though I was a kid. The girls came while he was here. They couldn't stay for lunch so I asked Jim to stay. It was better than being alone but then he just gulped a sandwich and ran."

Simon thought: Wouldn't I be a fool to ask you how a fellow you know slightly remembers your birthday? Feeble-minded I'd have to be to ask how he had your address. And, sweetheart, don't make so many explanations. Between us there doesn't have to be any perfect understanding. It's better this way.

He followed her into the bedroom. It had been done over since Hannah's day—fruitwood furniture and walls covered in coral-colored satin. The telephone lived in a golden shell and the chandelier dripped long crystal tears.

Ruby climbed on the bed and pointed to the gilt swinging

doors that led to the dressing room and bath. "There," she said.

Simon and the spider looked at each other for a moment then each took a backward step.

"Whack him," Ruby said.

"Don't be a fool. You know it's bad luck to kill a spider."

"It's bad luck if one bites you, too."

"That's not a Black Widow."

"Then what are you stalling for? Put him out. Why don't you just grab him if he's an ordinary house spider?"

"Because this isn't an ordinary house," Simon said. He went over to the bureau and picked up an ash tray. "If he'd walk on this I could carry him out to the balcony—"

"Oh, for God's sake, just slug him and have done with it."

"That's bad luck, I tell you."

Simon and the spider considered each other for another moment then Simon said, "Get me a glass."

Ruby brought him one from the guest bathroom across the hall. Swiftly he surrounded the startled spider with the glass. It made a quick circled reconnoiter of its position then darted toward the bottom in search of escape. Simon had him now. He covered the top of the glass with his hand and rushed toward the balcony. "Open the door," he shouted to Ruby. "My hands are full."

She scampered ahead of him down the hall and threw the screen door wide open, then scampered away again from the liberated spider. Simon lingered a moment to be sure that his captive had not suffered any. He was content when he saw it hastening toward some new and less exciting adventure. It would have worried him if the spider had looked as though it had been injured. After you have hurt or killed a spider, you can expect anything to happen.

He went back to the bedroom. Ruby was sitting on the bed again. She had her legs curled up under her and she was fiddling with a lock of hair. He went over and kissed her.

"Happy birthday," he said. He sat down close to her and put his arms around her. "Pretty nightgown. Which one of them gave you that?"

"Enid. Let me alone."

He got up from the bed and walked away from her. It was always this way. Ruby was like the fellow who, on his wedding night, ran and hid in the closet when a knock came on the door. Ruby couldn't get used to being married either. She seemed to think that before giving in she still had to make a speech about not being that kind of a girl. He sighed heavily. He wanted her and he could have her but only after a lot of talk. He had hoped to skip the talk—just once. He had something else on his mind.

She said, "I've thought it all over, Simon, and I've decided."

He said, "Yeah? What did you decide? What did you think over?"

"About the trip. I've decided that I want to go to Canada."

"Oh."

"Well, you don't sound very enthusiastic. On the phone —the way you talked to me— Gee, I thought you couldn't stand it if I didn't want to go to Canada. Can we go tonight?"

She had been too fast for him. She had opened the subject before he had been quite ready. They were into it now and there was no way of going back. He took off his coat and threw it on the chaise longue. He reached into the gold box on the bureau for a cigarette. He went over to the satin slipper chair and settled himself carefully upon it. But after all that only a few seconds had been killed.

He said, "Ruby, I'll take you to Canada some other time if you really want to go. We can't go tonight."

"I want to go tonight. Why can't we go tonight? You said—"

"I know, baby, but something's come up and we can't go."

"What's come up?"

"Well," he paused, seeking the right words. He realized almost at once that there were no right words so he said the wrong ones. "My mother's found out that it's your birthday."

Ruby said, "So what?"

"We have to go to her house now that she knows."

"What the hell do you mean, we have to go to her house? Listen, nobody tells me what I have to do. I don't want to go there and I won't go. That's the damndest thing I ever heard in my life. We have to go to her house! Listen, Simon Marcaboth, you're over six years old. If we don't want to go, then—"

On and on. He stopped listening. She would feel better

when she had had her say. He sat on the slipper chair smoking his cigarette and wondering who had told his mother that it was Ruby's birthday. He wished he knew. It was convenient to know the people that a man could not trust.

When he became conscious of silence in the room he turned and looked at Ruby. She was glaring at him. Her cheeks were flaming and even her tousled hair looked angry. He forgot to speak, lost in contemplation of her extraordinary beauty.

"Aren't you going to say something?" she demanded.

"Yes," he said. "I'm going to say that we have to go to my mother's house for dinner tonight."

"I just got through telling you that—"

"I know, baby, I know. And it's good for you to get it off your chest. To me you can say anything. Go ahead, shout and scream and carry on, but between us we know that tonight we'll go to my mother's house for dinner."

She jumped off the bed. "I told you and I mean it. I'm not going—"

"Look, Ruby, my mother will be very nice to you."

Ruby said, "I don't see why I even have to know her."

"That doesn't make sense. A girl's gotta know her mother-in-law. Sooner or later you'll meet my mother. So why shouldn't it be tonight?"

"Because I'm not going to get myself chained down to spending all my birthdays and holidays with—"

He said, "Now it comes out, doesn't it, Ruby?"

She turned to him, a trace of alarm apparent in her eyes. But he was smiling a faintly amused smile at her.

"So it was an act, wasn't it, Ruby? You weren't in awe of Princess Zleki. You weren't nervous about meeting your mother-in-law."

"I—I—"

"Never mind, Ruby, it's all right. It's better now, much better. Now I know how to do business with you. I was in the dark before."

She glanced at him uncertainly from beneath her thick eyelashes. "Simon," she said, "I—"

"No, no, no, Ruby. Don't try to explain. For the first time I understand this thing."

She came closer to him and rubbed her cheek against his. "I was being nasty only because I was scared of your mother. I say anything when I'm worked up like that. I just can't go, honey. I'd faint, I think. Don't let's talk about it any more. Simon, kiss me."

He kissed her.

Later with her head on his shoulder she said to him, "And we can go to Canada tonight, can't we, darling?"

He said, "No, of course we can't. We're going to my mother's for dinner."

Ruby sat bolt upright on the bed and slapped him hard. "You son of a bitch."

He laughed. "You've been betrayed, baby. We have to go. It's a must. With my mother everything's a must."

"She's not my mother."

"You'll find that makes no difference." His eyes hardened. "Listen, we're in business now that I understand your true objections to the deal. So since we're in business I'll tell you that there's profit in going. She'll give you a present."

Ruby's eyes hardened, too. She said, "What will she give me?"

"First of course there'll be the golden goblet."

"You've told me about that. What else?"

"I don't know exactly, but she never gives unimportant presents. You'll get a piece of jewelry or—"

"I like jewelry," Ruby said. Her eyes went to the diamond bracelet that Simon had given her that morning. "I like jewelry very much."

He said, "Well, of course you won't get another diamond bracelet."

She looked at him coolly. "Why shouldn't I?"

"What?" He sat bolt upright, too, and stared at her.

"Why shouldn't I get another diamond bracelet?"

"Because my mother doesn't give presents *that* important."

"To hell with what your mother gives. Why shouldn't you give me another diamond bracelet?"

"I will next birthday maybe."

She shook her head. "I could be dead by then and I'd love two diamond bracelets before I die. In fact I'd like two diamond bracelets before tomorrow night."

"Don't hold your breath till you get them," he said.

She shrugged. "Okay, but you said we were in business. All right, we're in business. You're going to have one sweet hell of a time with your old lady if I don't go tonight, aren't you?"

"Well, she'd like it but—"

"Don't give me that. You're scared of her. I'm not scared of her. You know my secret now so I can speak freely. I'm not scared of her but you're terrified. You can't make me go, you know. I'll go only if it pleases me. And it'll please me only if I get another diamond bracelet."

He gazed at her disbelievingly. "Cripes, Ruby, do you think I'm made of money?"

"Yes," she said. "Do I get the bracelet?"

"You're crazy. Of course you don't get another bracelet."

She lay back on the pillow and closed her eyes. "That's that then," she said. "We don't go to your mother's tonight."

That had been a very smart move of his, telling her that they were in business—astute as hell. Why was it that a woman could walk through life throwing away a letter you'd saved for nineteen years or forgetting in which store she'd left your watch to be repaired but the minute there was an advantage for her, quick as a wink, her I.Q. became like Einstein's? One little mistake he'd made. He had told her that they were in business and all of a sudden she could see great possibilities.

He said, "Ruby."

"Hm."

"If I promise you another bracelet *and* a new ring for Christmas—"

She said, "I don't believe in Santa Claus."

"You should, you gold-digging little tramp."

She slapped him again. This time he didn't laugh. He

grabbed hold of her wrists and held them tightly. "Listen," he said, "don't do that. A joke's a joke, but I get mad, too. Take it easy." He released her wrists and she turned from him, her eyes sullen. He flicked her across the bottom. "Get up and start bathing and dressing," he said.

"Do I get the bracelet?"

"Yes, yes, yes. You get the bracelet."

She whirled around on the bed. "Do I really?"

"I told you that you do. Now get going."

She flung her arms about him and crowded him to the edge of the bed. "Oh, Simon, you are sweet. I really didn't think you'd let me have it. I'm so happy. I'm so—" She stopped and looked at him squarely. "You aren't fooling, are you? You will buy me the bracelet tomorrow, won't you?"

He pushed her over to her side of the bed. He said, "You'll get it. At my age I only betray a girl once a day."

She giggled.

"Go on," he said. "Get going."

She got up and walked toward the dressing room. He watched her gloomily till she had disappeared behind the swinging gilt doors. "Listen," he said to no one in particular, "there must be some mistake. I didn't even break one of its legs. It was perfectly healthy when I let it out of the glass."

Miss Blount made a final tour of inspection before retiring to her room for the evening. Mr. and Mrs. Simon should be arriving any minute, but there was time for one last look at everything. Miss Blount was quite certain that all was as it should be. She was not exactly checking. She was really looking the situation over for the sake of pure enjoyment alone. This would be a lovely evening. Things had all gone perfectly from start to finish. She had had a moment's doubt earlier in the day of course. She had wondered whether Mrs. Simon was actually coming. But, there, that had only added to the perfection of the day, had given it the spicy flavor of suspense. Of course Mrs. Simon was coming. And like all the other birthdays, this would be a grand success. Miss Blount was terribly happy. Everything was as it should be, and she was free for the evening, and in on her night table was a pound of chocolate peppermints and a new, very thick historical novel. Ruby's birthday, she thought, might well turn out to be the best of the lot.

She went to the dining room first to admire the table. It was beautiful beyond belief, she thought. Those little leopard-spotted orchids were simply divine, and heaped up in that extravagant, artfully careless way she had done them—well, they were just magnificent. She definitely had a way with flowers. Maybe she should have gone into that line of work, she thought regretfully. In a flash she saw what would have happened. A man who bought flowers regularly for a vain and pampered lady would, when his heart was broken, realize that the little florist girl who had been waiting on him was really all that he desired of love and of life. Ah, well. The gold tableware looked nice, too. Miss Blount had a sudden horrid thought. Maybe when you had a point de Venise cloth, gold tableware, fabulous china, and six dozen little orchids it wasn't difficult to make a table look beautiful. Nonsense. There's a knack to everything.

She left the dining room and went to see how Mrs. Marcaboth was coming along. Mrs. Marcaboth was coming along very well indeed. She was about ready to leave her room.

"I wanted you to zip me up," she said, "but I managed alone."

"I'm sorry, Mrs. Marcaboth."

"It doesn't matter."

"It does. I should be here when you need me."

"Well, I didn't commit suicide because you weren't. These things can happen. The truth is that when I really need someone to dress me, I'll lie down and die."

"Oh, Mrs. Marcaboth, you shouldn't talk like that."

Zeda made a clucking noise at her. "Such a serious little thing you are, Miss Blount. Now, how do I look?"

Miss Blount brought her attention to bear upon her employer. Since she had actually been invited to do so she took a good long look from wig to shoe tips. The wig looked wonderful. Just enough blue tint to make the white hair gleam effectively. Annette had arranged it well. Was it the regular wig? Or did Mrs. Marcaboth have a mess of them hidden away in cupboards and hat boxes all over her suite? The black velvet dress was lovely. Velvet on a summer's night? Maybe it was the thing this season. Miss Blount didn't know. Remarkable what shoulders and arms Mrs. Marcaboth had. A woman her age and they were still smooth and full and a compliment to her gown. She was wearing the diamond necklace of course and the two wide diamond cuffs that matched it, and the diamond earrings.

"Well," Zeda prompted, "such a big look you have to give me? Can't you say right off that I look gorgeous?"

"You do."

Zeda laughed. "Now you make up a lie for yourself. I gave you that one."

"No lies are necessary. You're lovely. You dazzled me. I thought to myself, 'She looks like a queen.' "

"Now, that was a good one. Come on, we'll see how the kitchen is making out."

They moved toward the kitchen, Miss Blount walking behind Mrs. Marcaboth, admiring the straight back and the easy, haughty tilt of the white-wigged head. Miss Blount had heard that long ago Mrs. Marcaboth had been a poor, hard-working woman, not just a typist or a file clerk or a salesgirl, but someone who scrubbed and—and did things like that.

I don't believe it, Miss Blount thought. She wished she had the courage to ask. She had a feeling that Mrs. Marcaboth would tell her whether or not the story was true.

In the kitchen there was calm. The generals had made their plans, had conferred on strategy and tactics. Nothing remained now but the battle itself. The servants said good evening and waited for Mrs. Marcaboth to speak.

She said, "Only a nuisance to you, my children's birthdays, eh?"

The butler said, "Not at all, Madame. A pleasure."

She stared at him. "Now how can that be true? What's a pleasure for you about all this?"

"We enjoy the excitement. We enjoy doing our best to please you."

She opened her mouth to speak but no words came. She drew her lips tightly together. Then she made a fresh start. "It wasn't a fair question. What were you to say? Could you say, 'Yes, this is a nuisance to us'? No, you couldn't say that. I put you on a spot. Excuse me."

"Would you care to sample the Martinis, Madame?"

"Are they ready?"

The butler, the cook, the waitress, and Miss Blount stood watching with eager interest as she took the cocktail. Miss Blount thought that Mrs. Marcaboth must indeed be in a splendid humor tonight. Otherwise she must certainly comment on the premature mixing of the cocktails.

Zeda sipped the Martini. "It's good," she said. "The best you ever made." She looked around, conscious that her approval had special significance tonight.

"Well," she demanded, "somebody tell me."

There was silence and Zeda looked hurt. Miss Blount couldn't bear the look in her eyes. It was true that a woman had no right to wear a million dollars' worth of diamonds and still expect to share a joke with her employees. No one should have everything, but Miss Blount could not endure that look in Zeda's eyes. Why should a million dollars' worth of diamonds stand between a woman and the people in her kitchen?

"He bet us nylons that the cocktail would be a failure,"

Miss Blount explained, deleting a few details that had led up to the wager. "He felt a little uncertain about his Martinis today. So now we get nylons."

Zeda laughed and everyone laughed with her. "I'll give you a chance to get even," she said to the butler. "You always pass cigars to Mr. Simon. A hundred times I've told you that it's only Mr. Wolfe who smokes them. Now, I'll bet you ten dollars that you'll forget tonight and pass cigars to Mr. Simon."

They laughed again, and while they were still laughing the bell rang. The butler composed his features and with customary dignity started for the door. Zeda moved regally toward the living room. Miss Blount took the back route to her own room. It was a wonderful omen, she thought. Mrs. Simon came to the house for the first time on a wave of laughter. Miss Blount didn't care *what* people said. There was something about an omen. There just was.

Dinner at the club had been the same rewarding experience that it always was. Wolfe thought that if there was one thing in life that never failed a man it was dinner at his club. Nowhere else was there the same quiet atmosphere, the pleasant sense of well-being, the knowledge that the food would be superb and the service elegant. Not a restaurant in the world could equal the excellence of a good club.

He seated himself in the reading room and picked up a magazine. It was slightly early. Men who had dined at home drifted toward the club for their bridge or chess a little later than this. There were a few games in progress, but they had started in the afternoon and the players had lost track of time. Wolfe smiled a little. Frank Hill had been called to the phone three times. Mrs. Hill was evidently getting very irritable about holding dinner. Some men, Wolfe thought, permitted themselves to be treated like naughty little boys. Was dinner at home so sacred a ceremony that a man had no right to miss it if he chose? Good God, why couldn't Frank Hill simply say, "I'm not coming this evening"? Amazing how civilized man, in his fanatical worship of home and fireside, had gotten himself enslaved. It had come to the place where those fine, home-cooked meals were eating the men. Life, liberty, and the pursuit of happiness were for many a husband definitely measured and limited by the hour in which dinner would be served in his home. The whole thing had become a monstrous and ridiculous ritual.

A title in the magazine caught Wolfe's attention and he began to read. For a half hour his interest was completely held and then the article ended. That had been just about right. A few more members would have arrived by this time and he would be able to get a game.

He took a turn about the card room. Three new foursomes had settled down. Frank Hill had gone but the game of which he had been part was continuing. They'd gotten Bert Fowler to join them. Wolfe thought it a pity that they hadn't noticed that he was available. Bert was an indifferent bridge player.

Two of the members were busy with double solitaire.

Wolfe went over to their table to assure them that it wouldn't be too difficult to get a fourth. They shook their heads. Not in the mood for bridge tonight. Going home early. Slight headache. Tough day tomorrow. Wolfe watched a hand played at one table and then at another and went back to his magazine. It was still a little early.

He turned the pages slowly, delighting in the bright advertisements and in the sight of his own well-kept hands. He was pleased with everything tonight—a good dinner in the past and a bridge game in the future. That was as close as a man could come to complete contentment. And, of course, he thought a man needed one more small thing to round out his happiness, the knowledge that he had chosen the shape of his evening for himself. It had not been forced upon him. Many of the poor fellows here tonight had no other place to go, no wives, no homes. He, Wolfe, had a wife and a home. Tonight he had chosen his club. Perhaps tomorrow night he would choose his home. It was such freedom that made a man feel thoroughly at peace.

Wolfe returned to the card room. A few more games had started but there was no opening. Well, it was still early. He walked about, pausing here and there to watch. An awful lot of bumbling was done, he thought. Very few of the members were really good players. Watching poor bridge was the same as watching anything else that was inferior and stupid. Pretty dreary, the whole business.

He returned to the reading room. This was going to turn out to be a dull evening. Some evenings did turn out that way. Beyond all reason, beyond all explanation, some evenings were just duds.

Maybe I'll go to the movies, he thought. There's a British one in town. British movies are always the best.

He made a few inquiries. Nobody wanted to go to the British movie. Such a bore going to a movie alone. He thought of Enid. That would be pretty inconvenient. He'd have to drive all the way out to Bel-Air to get her and then all the way back into town again. He'd tell her to get a cab. That made sense. He'd wait right here.

He went to a telephone and called her. The cook answered and said that Mrs. Marcaboth wasn't in. Wolfe had always thought the cook extraordinarily dim-witted.

"Let me speak to Katherine," he said.

Katherine came on the phone. "Yes, sir."

"What's this about Mrs. Marcaboth's being out?"

"Well, she is, sir."

"Where did she go?"

"I couldn't say, sir."

"What do you mean you couldn't say? Do you know or don't you?"

"I don't know, sir."

Wolfe slammed up the phone. Where had she gone? Where could she go? Not that it mattered of course. But she ought to leave word where she was going. Suppose he really needed her for something important? Suppose he was brought home ill or was in an accident? Fine thing when a man had no idea where his own wife was. Well, it was her loss. The reviews of the British movie had been wonderful.

He went back to the table and looked over the magazines. Nothing there now that he hadn't read. It was kind of too bad in a way that he hadn't agreed to go with Simon and Ruby. He really didn't feel much like playing bridge after all. Terribly inept players about tonight.

Maybe he'd call Simon, make Simon feel good. But there was no answer on Simon's phone.

He walked once more into the card room. Might as well let the fellows know he was available in case someone dropped out of a game.

Garth was not at all alarmed. He was merely curious and a little vexed. There was no reason to be alarmed. Women like Judith didn't take their children and jump off bridges with them or disappear into thin air. Judith was level-headed and certainly not neurotic. Wherever she was, she and the children were safe. But where was she? And where were the servants who had been hired and who had started to work that morning? Some kind of a minor mystery here. He hoped that wherever she was, she was prepared to find him not altogether in sympathy with whatever apology she made. He wasn't going to let her get away with saying, "Oh, I forgot about the Kenlunds."

He looked at the clock. Maybe he ought to call Magda and say they'd be a little late. Maybe he could start dressing. But what time would that save? Judith would still have to dress. He wondered about the children. If there were no servants then how could he and Judith go at all? Maybe Judith had made some kind of arrangements. Maybe she was out now bagging a baby sitter or doing something else terribly efficient. That was one blessing. Judith was no screwball. Well, he'd call Magda and say that they might be slightly delayed.

He turned toward the telephone and at that moment he heard Judith's car and the voices of the children. He hurried to the door and they came in, the three of them. The children, he noticed, looked as though their clothes had not been changed after playtime. Judith had a peculiar expression on her face. Well, he had no time to bother with that now.

"Where were you?" he asked. "What about the children with no servants? We have to dress. Did you do anything about—?"

Judith said, "Go on upstairs, children. Kenneth, you draw Lorna's bath and I'll be up soon."

"We didn't say hello to Daddy. Hello, Daddy."

"Hello, youngsters. Now you do as Mommy said. Run along. We're a little rushed."

The children ran along.

Judith smiled at him. "I'm not rushed. I can't go to the Kenlunds'. There's no one to stay with the children. You go. Come on, I'll lay out your things for you."

"Let's get somebody. I thought you were out doing that now."

"No," she said. "I've been down to Silso Street. I took the children to visit my family."

He said, "Judith, I expressly asked you—"

"I know, Garth." They were still standing in the hall, and she advanced toward the little rosewood table and laid her purse upon it. She turned and faced him then. "It was a bad thing you asked of me, Garth, a very bad thing. You didn't know how bad it was or you wouldn't have asked it."

"It was for the children, Judith."

She shook her head. "No, darling, it wasn't. That's what you thought. That's what you made yourself think. But all along, it wasn't for the children."

"Then who the hell was it for?" he demanded, angrily.

"It was for Garth. It was so that Garth could forget that he had married beneath himself, so that Garth would be saved from ever having to introduce fine friends to his wife's poor and ignorant relatives. It was so that Garth could feel lofty and superior and some day maybe forget that his own parents long ago would have lived on Silso Street had they come to California in their youth."

"You certainly think me a prize heel, don't you?"

"No, I love you, but you are not all fine and faultless. No one is." She spoke calmly, and he saw that she felt no guilt, no repentance for this thing she had done. There was a rested look upon her face and her eyes were bright with a secret, inner joy of which he was no part.

"Listen, Judith, you are an intelligent, realistic person, and that's why I can talk plainly to you. There's something I—"

She said, "Oh, darling, no. Not this time. It won't work.

I was so intelligent and realistic that I always let you have your way. This time it's different. This time try to be intelligent and realistic yourself while I talk plainly to you. You married me so you have in-laws on Silso Street. Your children have grandparents on Silso Street. And you, Garth Marcaboth, have a wife from Silso Street, and you can take her or leave her."

He studied her calm face. "I suppose you mean something pretty clever and drastic by that speech."

"Clever? No. Drastic? Yes. I've been living with you for ten years and all that time half of me has been sick-hearted. I am not going to put up with it any more, Garth."

"You mean you'd leave your children and—"

"Why should I leave my children?" she asked. "Somewhere in town there must be a good lawyer. As a matter of fact I should think that even a lousy lawyer could see my case has possibilities."

He stared at her. She wasn't fooling. If she'd only get mad, if she'd only lose her temper it would all end in nothing. But she wasn't getting mad. She wouldn't lose her temper. And, by God, he believed she really would leave him. He thought of the house without Judith and the children. He thought of life without them. That was a contradiction of terms. There would be no life without Judith and the children.

He said, "Well, now that they've been to Silso Street, it's pretty silly to argue about it, isn't it? They've been and that's that."

"I'm afraid that isn't that, Garth. There's more. My parents are coming here." He darted a swift glance at her. "They're coming here Saturday afternoon. Brina and Kevi are coming, too. And Uncle Eli and Aunt Gulda."

He said nothing. He thought of his house and he thought as a man thinks when invasion by savage hordes is inevitable and imminent.

She looked at him sadly. "Poor Garth. This is hard for you to take, isn't it? Do you think my family will bring a box lunch to your pool and leave banana skins scattered on the lawn?"

"I was not thinking that at all," he said. But it occurred to him that she had mentioned something which was certainly a lively possibility.

"There is only one thing for you to think, Garth. You must only think whether or not you love me. When you get the answer all else will come easy."

"Of course I love you. For God's sake, why do you think—?"

"Why do I think you married me with all my drawbacks? I think you did it because you loved me. I've always thought that, Garth. It's all that has sustained me at times, believe me. And since you do love me, don't let your rotten pride break us up, darling. This is *our* home, and my parents will come to it and be welcomed here, or it is *your* home and I am finished with it."

She meant it. Never had she meant anything more sincerely than she meant this. He listened to her cool and reasonable tone and he knew that his choices were few. He could keep Judith or he could lose her.

"Your parents will come," he said.

"And you will make them feel welcome?"

"I will try, Judith."

"That's all I ask. They have promised to try. Remember this is an ordeal for them, too. They are coming where they are not wanted because I begged them to come. Kevi and Papa have their pride, too, but for me they will try. And if you all try, Garth, after a while there will be no strain."

"I'll do my best," he said. And he thought of Kevi, the coarse, sullen-eyed man from Silso Street who, for his sister's sake, would make an effort to like Garth Marcaboth. Oh, no, there must be some way to talk this thing over.

But then Judith put her arms around him and kissed him. "Tonight I am completely happy," she said. "For the first time my heart is full of happiness."

And he knew that it was too late for talk. He held her tightly to him, thinking how dismal life would be without this woman who looked beautiful to no one except himself. In some undefinable way, to him she was both beautiful and remarkable. He loved her, and because he did, it was a fine feeling to know that she was happy and that he was part of her happiness.

"Garth."

"Yes."

"Would it be terrible if we asked the Feltons to keep the children overnight? We could bundle them down there in their pajamas and I could dress in ten minutes and we could go to the Kenlunds'."

He said, "You don't have to go to the Kenlunds', Judith."

She looked at him with her dark, shining eyes. "I wouldn't mind going, Garth. Honestly, tonight I wouldn't mind."

Solime walked into her bedroom just as Rome was beginning to feel a slight touch of real panic.

"Where were you?" he asked.

"At the hairdresser's."

"No, you weren't. I called there."

"Maybe I went to a new place today," she said.

She looked tired—tired and unhappy. She tossed her hat on the bureau and ran her hands wearily through her black hair.

"Where were you?" he asked again.

"I was at a meeting of The Circle."

Surprise caught him off balance. "You were? What for?"

She did not answer at once, and the delay gave him the opportunity to become as cold and dignified as he felt he should be under the circumstances. "Well, that's interesting news. You mean you've continued to be a member despite any statements you may have made to the contrary?"

"I resigned today."

"Splendid. However I must say it took you rather a long time to begin resenting their treatment of my sister."

"I don't resent their treatment of your sister and I don't feel like rehashing all that, if you don't mind."

267

He said, "It seems to me that the choice isn't up to you. Haven't you a little explaining to do?"

She did not answer. She walked over to the bed and flung herself upon it. She lay there staring up at the ceiling and he waited, feeling a little foolish. She was in the wrong but she would neither admit or deny. How could you argue under those conditions? An argument was certainly clearly indicated at this point, but she wasn't going about it properly. She just lay there looking thoughtful. There was one thing he could certainly do. He could walk out of the room. That gesture always had a certain amount of dignity.

He turned toward the door and she called him.

"Yes?" Very haughtily, very distantly.

"Please sit down, Rome. I have something to tell you."

"I'll stand if it's all the same to you."

"It's all the same to me but you might wish you had been sitting. The news isn't pleasant."

"What news?"

"Well— It's about your brother Simon and his wife. She has a lover."

"Ruby? How do you know? Who told you?"

"Nobody told me. I saw him."

"You mean he was up there at the house today?"

"Yes."

Rome lit a cigarette and took a turn about the room. He knew he had been outwitted. He could not continue to be angry at Solime when there was this more important matter to discuss.

"Are you sure?"

"Positive. On the last page it won't come out that he's her brother or anything like that. Ruby has a lover. Please accept that as a fact and then we can go on from there."

Rome nodded. "Yes. Of course someone will have to tell Simon."

"Tell Simon? Why, for God's sake?"

He gazed at her incredulously. "Did you think we'd keep it a secret from Simon? He has to know. He can't go on living with a—"

"Now wait a minute. Do you think Simon is under the impression that he married an angel?"

"No, but before marriage is one thing. After marriage is something else."

Solime sighed. "Listen, Rome, do you want a divorce in the family? Any fool can cause a divorce. I think it's better to make an effort to save the marriage."

"I don't see that I have a right to keep this a secret from Simon."

"You might ask yourself if you have a right to tell him. That involves even more responsibility than keeping quiet."

There was much in what she said but he didn't like to hear her say it. It implied things. It implied that Solime had always sorted out information, giving it only if the giving seemed wise to her. He had imagined her more simple, more straightforward.

"I think I should tell Simon," he said.

"Go ahead, Sir Galahad. Do as you please but I didn't

even want to tell you. I only did it because I had a plan and I couldn't work it out without telling you. You'd have thought I was crazy if—"

"What kind of a plan? What are you talking about?"

"Well—" She sat up and looked at him searchingly. He felt sure that she was weighing in her own mind whether or not he would have the intelligence to understand what she would say.

"Well?" he prompted.

"I thought this: I thought Simon's shame would be our shame. I thought the Marcaboths would be better off for dodging a scandal."

"I agree with you of course but—"

"There aren't any buts. Not if you really agree with me. Now, listen. It's all going to sound foolish to you, but that's only because you're a man. I have an idea that I could take Ruby in hand. Maybe she'd be a different person if she had interests and people to ask her to do things and—"

"Who's going to ask Ruby to do things?"

"In the beginning I am. I'm going to ask her to lunch and to go shopping and—and things like that. Then I'd get her into the Westland Club. That's a cinch to crack. Maybe she'd be fired with new goals, new ambitions. Who knows?"

He shook his head. "A girl like Ruby wouldn't go for that sort of thing."

"It's happened before. They'd make quite a fuss over Mrs. Simon Marcaboth in the Westland Club. With what she could donate they might even put her on a committee."

"I'd like a picture of that."

"You may get one. And then if Judith joined—"

"What would you want with Judith?"

"There'd be three Marcaboths then. Three."

He nodded as though he were following her train of thought. He wasn't. He understood that she, Judith, and Ruby would certainly add up to three Marcaboths. But what did that signify? Something evidently because her eyes were narrowed in thought.

"And if I got your mother in—"

"My mother? Good God, Solime, my mother wouldn't join a club."

"I think she would, Rome. I think if I went to her and talked very quietly and persuasively and told her how much the Westland Club would like a princess's name on their roster and—"

"Solime, you know perfectly well that my mother listens to nobody."

Solime stood up. "Don't be silly," she said. "Your mother is more intelligent than that. If I make good suggestions she'll take them. Come on. We have to dress. Mrs. Hillis will be at that Canasta thing tonight. She's a power with the Westlands."

He didn't feel like dressing just then. He didn't understand anything at all about women's clubs or whether or not it was possible to scratch a tramp and find a committee member. He wasn't sure that it was right to keep from Simon the information Solime had brought to him. He couldn't adjust himself to the idea that Solime at heart was and always had been an organizer, a planner. It would take a little time to examine all this welter of disturbing thoughts. He was thoroughly confused about a great many things. But of some things he was certain. He was certain that new, unpleasant elements had appeared in the solid little world that had belonged to the Marcaboths. Simon's wife had a lover. That was new and it was unpleasant. And there was something else that troubled him almost as much. It was the sure knowledge that his mother was going to be changed. By some mysterious woman's reasoning Solime had the power now to turn Zeda Marcaboth into a person who would say, "If you think so" and "At your convenience." He did not want his mother changed. He didn't want her to take suggestions. But she would take them. There were things men could not understand. Ruby had a lover, and for that reason Solime could go to Zeda and speak to her gently and sweetly, and, for all the gentleness and sweetness, when Solime left her Zeda would be less than she had been. And Solime could say, "I am only your daughter-in-law and of course you are wiser than I and always I will do as you think best." But because they were women, both Zeda and Solime would know that in the future it would be Zeda who did as Solime thought best.

And of another thing Rome was certain. He was certain that the head of the Marcaboth family would never be a man. Mama, God bless her, could not live forever, but long before she died Simon and Garth and even Wolfe would know that her passing would not free them.

Here in this room, at this moment, the future head of the House of Marcaboth was busy searching for a certain pink girdle. He could not help but wonder how in years to come Solime was going to look wearing a white wig.

RUBY had worn white satin. White satin always reminded Zeda of brides, but Ruby's gown wasn't like a bride's. It was very sophisticated and it seemed to have been designed with the main idea of showing that Ruby was tanned practically all the way to her navel. Well, she was a beautiful girl. It was no wonder that Simon had wanted her. Had he wanted to marry her? No. A man never wanted to marry a girl like Ruby. But sometimes it happened.

In the candlelight Zeda studied the face of her new daughter-in-law. You didn't actually have to study it. It was a simple face to read. This was a stupid girl, a girl without imagination or understanding but with rare beauty—if you were not one of those priggish people who insisted that beauty must have character. There was no character here, but there was perfect skin and perfect features. Mouth a little sulky, eyes too evasive, but these had never been flaws to turn a man away. She was, this Ruby, a woman who knew nothing and was good for nothing but sex. Well, wasn't that enough? No, not really. Zeda thought a woman should have some value standing up.

You could look at Ruby and think that she would have been a natural courtesan in a more romantic period of history, but that was too facile a thought. It did not take into account the things that had made Ruby what she was. She was the product of this age. She was what juke boxes and automobiles and movie magazines and hot dogs had made her. It was foolish to say, "Now, if she had lived in another century—" In another century she might have been another person. Not more admirable, not less shallow, just as cheap and flashy, but perhaps unaware that there was a large and profitable market for the thing she had to sell. News traveled more slowly in other centuries.

"As is always the case here, dinner was marvelous," Simon said.

"I'm glad you enjoyed it." Zeda turned to Ruby. "And you, my dear, did you—?"

"Oh, it was marvelous," Ruby said.

Yes, it had been a marvelous dinner, and Ruby had eaten well. Some day she would be as fat as a pig, gorgeous Ruby.

She was twenty today. Twenty. Zeda sighed thinking that she would not live to see Ruby fat as a pig. Such a pity.

Simon said, "I was leading up to something, Mama. In a very subtle way I would like to inquire if there could be maybe seconds on dessert."

Zeda did not ask if Ruby would also like a second helping. If she asked, the girl would decline, thinking no doubt that this would be extremely ladylike. If the dessert were set before her, she would eat it. Zeda had lived long enough to know that few quarrel with tangibilities.

"The table looked so lovely, too," Simon said.

"It sure did," Ruby echoed.

Zeda thought how odd and unpleasant it must be to be a girl like Ruby. Ruby hadn't dared comment on the splendor of the table until Simon led the way. Ruby had feared that perhaps such display was an ordinary occurrence in fine homes, and she did not want anyone to guess that her acquaintance with such homes was slight. How awful to be ashamed of having been poor. How awful to think you were kidding people.

The golden goblet had left Ruby cold. She did not grasp its significance nor did she guess its material value. Within her there was nothing that responded to the incredible perfection of the goblet's proportions and balance. It stood beside her wine glass, but she had given it only a moment's attention. She saw nothing and felt nothing. The golden goblet bored Ruby stiff.

She had been only a shade more interested in the pendant Zeda had given her. She had said, "Thank you," and at

Simon's suggestion she had taken off her pearls and hung the pendant on its slim platinum chain around her neck but she had not been impressed. It was a funny thing about people like Ruby. They never knew whether they liked anything or not. They couldn't be sure unless they could read the price tag.

Some day, my dear, Zeda thought, when you are a widow and have gone through all of Simon's money you will find that pendant mixed up in a drawer with souvenirs from Lake Tahoe and chewing gum wrappers and a few old pari-mutuel tickets on the wrong horse. And you will take that pendant out to hock it and you will be stunned at what you get for it.

When they had finished their second helping of dessert they would go out on the terrace for coffee. They would sit there in the sea breeze and they would talk in the idle desultory way that people talked after a large dinner. What would they talk about that would bring Ruby into the conversation?

We have no mutual friends or interests, Zeda thought. No mutual tastes. We both know a man named Simon and that is all. On Simon our paths have converged but we cannot talk about Simon. Even if he were not here we could not talk about him for she does not even know what he is like. He is only a man with a white streak in his hair and a lot of money in the bank. It would surprise her to know that there is any more than that to him.

And Zeda was disturbed at the way her thoughts ran. She was disliking Ruby. She was disliking her intensely and this was utterly unjustifiable. Ruby was trashy. Maybe she was even vicious, but certainly a girl would not choose to be as Ruby was. And how could a girl improve herself if she had not been born with wit enough to know that she needed improving? Ruby was beautiful and all her life she had been told that she was. How would it be possible for a girl in Ruby's intellectual bracket to know that she lacked charm and grace? Men had always desired her, and for Ruby that would be ample proof that she needed no conversational gambits. It was rather a shame, Zeda thought, that Ruby should be unaware of her possibilities. And it was a shame, too, that people—especially herself—didn't make the effort to be more lenient in cases like this. To dislike her is the same as disliking a beautiful dog. I like dogs and I never expect them to appreciate music or fine workmanship.

Yes, but it wouldn't work. It was a fine, civilized kind of thought but your son—your eldest son—had married this sulky-mouthed creature. And since she was your daughter-in-law you had to accept her as a human being. She must be judged by human standards if she was going to be a Mrs. Marcaboth. She couldn't have all the advantages. She couldn't sit at your table and also win a blue ribbon for best of breed.

Zeda looked back at Simon. He had married this girl. How long would it be before he was sorry? How long before Simon, the shrewd, the patient, the steadfast, would see Ruby as she really was? Would he be able to live with such a bitter knowledge?

And she thought of the Marcaboths as a family and she thought: He must not crumble till there is someone to take his place. For she and Simon had not believed in Wolfe or in Garth or even Jerome but had built their hopes upon Simon's training his son and later on Garth's son and even in time little Adin.

But perhaps he will not have the enthusiasm or the heart for training the children. He will ask of himself, "What for? What's it all about anyhow?" And he will say, "I am tired," and the warehouse will stand empty and everybody will each take a share of the money and that will be the end. There will just be lots of Marcaboths, no Marcaboth family.

All this would happen because Simon had married Ruby. Zeda looked at her daughter-in-law and she thought: She is neither good nor bad. She has not force enough to be actively either. She simply yields to impulse for she has neither principles or standards. And since she is not intentionally, not calculatingly evil then perhaps there is still a chance. No, this is a dream. There is no chance.

And Zeda sat a little straighter in her chair and wondered at her own easy acceptance of defeat. How did she know that there was no chance? Was she herself getting ready to ask, "What for? What's it all about anyhow?" Was she getting ready to say, "I'm tired"?

No, she thought, I am not tired. But I am realistic enough to know that because Ruby is in this family everything will somehow be different than it was. She is nothing. She is nobody. But she has the power to destroy us. Without being even mildly interested in us she can destroy us.

And it seemed infinitely sad that one could not go down fighting against a worthy, vengeful foe but must fall like a fly who is absent-mindedly swatted by a housewife who has other, more important things on her mind.

But I will not go down without fighting, Zeda thought. She will not destroy us without knowing that we were here.

And she thought that there was always something a person could do if that person was persistent and resourceful.

There is always something that can be done, she told herself. And she looked over at Simon and his wife. They had lighted cigarettes. It was time to move to the terrace.

"Shall we go outside?" she asked, brightly, giving Ruby a warm, loving smile. "And do not let me forget to show you sometime tonight the portraits of Enid and Judith and Solime. One must be done of you, too, my dear."

Simon was assisting her to rise from the table as she spoke. Ruby was pushing back her own chair, getting to her feet, looking up to return her mother-in-law's smile and flicking the ashes off her cigarette. A wave of faintness came over Zeda and she was forced to cling to the table for support. The world was reeling and there was a sudden, deathly, sickening sensation in the pit of her stomach, for Ruby had smiled sweetly, vacantly at her and, with no intention of insult or affront, had flicked her cigarette ashes into the golden goblet.

"Mama, what's the matter?"

She drew herself up straight and tall. "Nothing, Simon. Nothing. I am all right. It was just a slight dizziness. Truly it was nothing."

Simon was regarding her anxiously. "Mama, are you sure you're all right?"

"Oh, yes, perfectly. Only, please, excuse me now. I think I'll go to my room. Have your coffee on the terrace and don't worry, Simon, darling. I'll be fine. You will see."

She kissed him and turned to go. "Can Ruby go with you and help you a little maybe?"

"No, darling. Good night."

"Good night, Mama."

"Good night, Mrs. Marcaboth."

"Good night, Ruby. Happy birthday."

She knew that Simon was watching her as she walked away. She was glad that she could walk briskly. A sign of weakness now and he would not hesitate another moment. He would call the doctor. She did not feel like being bothered with a doctor. It would be a nuisance to have to manufacture symptoms just to amuse him. Certainly she wasn't going to tell him the truth. She wasn't going to tell him that she had made a mistake, that sometimes nothing could be done no matter how persistent and resourceful a person was.

I will lie down, she thought. Later I will undress. Right now I will lie down.

She stretched herself upon the bed and she thought that the golden goblet had simply been handy. Ruby had meant no offense. And she thought how bitter it was that Ruby

282

had meant no offense. She had only used the goblet as an ash tray because it was standing there and because Ruby needed a place to drop her ashes. No offense meant. But how beautiful, how promising, if one had a studied hatred to combat. No hatred here. Just indifference. Indifference and ignorance. These things you can't beat. These things, Zeda thought, you can't beat.

Ruby was in the family now. She was a Marcaboth, but the Marcaboths would never again be as they were. Things would happen now, things that had never happened before. You don't have a woman like Ruby around without things happening.

I do not know what things. I do not even know what kind of things. But we have Ruby now and so we are not as we were.

And Zeda lay silent and still and she thought that it was a mistake to build, for with the cornerstone you laid the certainty of future grief. If there was nothing built then nothing was demolished. There was no disappointment without there first having been hope, no destruction without creation. It was simple but nobody thought of it until it was too late. And she thought that as you planned a festival and hung the streamers of colored paper and the gaudy bunting and the bright balloons you were preparing for the day when with heavy heart you would walk through the deserted ballroom and remember when it had rung with laughter. You could do nothing in life without danger, without despair. You could not even buy a chair without one day weeping because he who had sat in it would sit there no more. Whatever you built or planned or bought, you were building and planning and buying a day of mourning. It was all there to see but no one ever saw it plainly. It was only seen blurred and distorted, through a rain of tears.

Her door opened and Simon came into the dark room.

"Are you all right, Mama?"

"Yes, darling."

"Are you sure, Mama, that you don't want the doctor?"

"Darling, I'm fine. Really I am. I was just thinking of ringing for some coffee."

"Then I guess you're all right." She could feel that he was smiling, that a load had been lifted from his heart.

"Did you have your coffee, Simon?"

"Yes, Mama. We are going home now unless there is something we can do for you."

"There really isn't a thing."

"I'll phone you in the morning."

"Yes, darling. I'll expect your call."

He went away and she lay there thinking that he had not asked, "Do you like Ruby?" Any one of her other sons would have asked the question. But not Simon. Simon thought as she thought. He was like her and so he understood her. He knew that there was no need for such a question. If you were forced to ask it then you had already been answered. This Simon knew.

And it came to her that perhaps she had not appreciated Simon enough. Always she had thought herself laughing alone at the absurdities of life. Always she had dreamed

that among the children who had died there might have
been one who would have laughed with her. But perhaps
all through the years Simon had been laughing with her.
And sometimes maybe it hadn't only been *with* her.

My favorite child, she thought. God help you now. God
help us all.

And she was immediately sorry that she had called upon
God, for He was a busy man and, considering the circumstances, it was foolish to annoy Him.

"Never mind," she whispered. "Forget I mentioned it.
Believe me, if there was anything that could be done, I'd
do it myself."

It was almost midnight. On June Street in the home of
the Jerome Marcaboths, in Beverly Hills where the Garth
Marcaboths lived, and in Bel-Air in the residence of the
Wolfe Marcaboths it was seventeen minutes of twelve.

Enid was awake. She could have taken a sleeping pill,
but she did not feel the need of it. Her thoughts were interesting company tonight and there was no longer any
pain. True there was the normal discomfort that follows
the extraction of a tooth, but the ache was gone.

Enid lay on her bed and thought of the future. I will
bleach my hair no longer, she thought. And I will grow fat
if I choose and it will not matter.

And she remembered that hours before Wolfe had come
home. She had heard him walk toward her closed door and
stand before it. She had remained quiet and he had gone to

his own room. She had thought his step had had about it
the sound of loneliness and sadness.

It was early for him to come home, she thought. I wonder why he came home so early.

And it occurred to her that she would never know, for
tomorrow they would not discuss inconsequential things.

Judith was also awake. She was thinking how differently
things had gone at the Kenlunds' this evening. You could
laugh at a banal joke if you were sure that your husband
adored you, that he wasn't wishing that he'd had the good
sense to have married any other woman in the room. You
could think Magda Kenlund a pampered little half-wit,
but you didn't hate Magda Kenlund if you looked at her
and wondered how she'd make out if she threatened to
leave her husband. You knew how you'd make out.

And Judith thought of Saturday when her family would
come to her house in Beverly Hills. She smiled a little
thinking that maybe they would toss a banana skin or two
around the pool. So what? This could be considered an
unimportant thing by a woman who loved her family and
by a man who loved the woman.

He does love me, Judith thought. I was always afraid to
put it to a test, I guess. But I know now that I'm on solid
ground. For the first time I am absolutely sure.

She wondered why she had never dared till now. She
was beginning to grow very sleepy. She could not think
clearly. For the life of her she couldn't remember what

had caused her to make up her mind just today. It would come to her tomorrow, she thought. She would remember tomorrow.

Solime watched the patterns in moonlight that drifted across the wall. A branch moving slightly in the breeze created a new design, a new picture in silver.

"We could have silver trees grouped about," Baba had said. "Maybe with stars on them. You know, to carry out the theme."

Solime closed her eyes against the tears, her mind against the foolish pain that the memory had brought her. She thought about the Westland Club. She thought about Mrs. Hillis who had been a hatcheck girl before her marriage. A pleasant woman, Mrs. Hillis, and especially designed for the needs of the moment. She couldn't be snooty about Ruby—at least not about Ruby's background. Of course if Ruby didn't behave herself then Mrs. Hillis had every right to turn thumbs down on her. Mrs. Hillis was a thoroughly respectable woman.

And suppose Ruby didn't behave herself? Suppose she didn't want to be a clubwoman? Suppose she didn't enjoy going to luncheons and on shopping trips with her good little sister-in-law, Solime? Then what?

Then at least, Solime thought, we stand together, we Marcaboths. We present a solid front, and we lie and deny and protect her to the end. Or perhaps together in a solid front we repudiate her. It makes no difference as long as the

Marcaboths stand together and I am standing with them. As long as I stand with them there will be people to say, "The Galals' daughter is on their side so it must be all right."

Ruby would be given every chance. The Marcaboth women would move in on the Westland Club in force and make it their own private property, their strength, their fortress. Judith would be smart about such things after a little coaching.

And we will stand together, Solime thought. Forever and ever I will stand with the Marcaboths.

She went back to watching the silver patterns on the wall. Up near the ceiling there was a new design that actually did look like a spray of silver stars. In time, she thought, the pain would grow less and some day she wouldn't feel it at all.

Ruby Marcaboth in the house north of Sunset Boulevard wasn't awake. Having nothing at all to think about, Ruby had gone quietly to sleep.